Don't miss these other exciting titl

Vickie McKe

The Pelican Pointe Series
PROMISE COVE
HIDDEN MOON BAY
DANCING TIDES
LIGHTHOUSE REEF
STARLIGHT DUNES
LAST CHANCE HARBOR
SEA GLASS COTTAGE
LAVENDER BEACH
SANDCASTLES UNDER THE CHRISTMAS MOON
BENEATH WINTER SAND
KEEPING CAPE SUMMER (2018)

The Evil Secrets Trilogy
JUST EVIL Book One
DEEPER EVIL Book Two
ENDING EVIL Book Three
EVIL SECRETS TRILOGY BOXED SET

The Skye Cree Novels
THE BONES OF OTHERS
THE BONES WILL TELL
THE BOX OF BONES
HIS GARDEN OF BONES
TRUTH IN THE BONES
SEA OF BONES (2018)

The Indigo Brothers Trilogy
INDIGO FIRE
INDIGO HEAT
INDIGO JUSTICE
INDIGO BROTHERS TRILOGY BOXED SET

Coyote Wells Mysteries
MYSTIC FALLS
SHADOW CANYON
SPIRIT LAKE (2018)

Shadow Canyon

by

VICKIE McKEEHAN

Castletown Publishing

Copyright © 2018 Vickie McKeehan

Shadow Canyon
A Coyote Wells Mystery

Published by Castletown Publishing
Copyright © 2018 Vickie McKeehan
All rights reserved.

Shadow Canyon
A Coyote Wells Mystery
Copyright © 2018 Vickie McKeehan

All rights reserved. No part of this book may be reproduced, scanned, or distributed in any printed or electronic format without written permission. Please do not participate in or encourage piracy of copyrighted materials in violation of the author's rights. Purchase only authorized editions.

This book is a work of fiction. Names, characters, incidents, locales, some landmarks, and dialogue are drawn from the author's imagination and are not to be construed as real. Any resemblance to actual events or persons, living or dead, businesses or companies, is entirely coincidental.

Castletown Publishing

ISBN-10: 1985861941
ISBN-13: 978-1985861947

Published by
Castletown Publishing
Printed in the USA
Titles Available at Amazon

Cover art by Vanessa Mendozzi

You can visit the author at:
www.vickiemckeehan.com
www.facebook.com/VickieMcKeehan
http://vickiemckeehan.wordpress.com/
www.twitter.com/VickieMcKeehan

"May the stars carry your darkness away.
May the flowers fill your heart with beauty.
May hope forever wipe away your tears.
And above all, may silence make you strong."

CHIEF DAN GEORGE

Shadow Canyon

by

VICKIE McKEEHAN

1

During the Sun Bringer Festival, Coyote Wells burst at the seams with tourists. Crowds jammed the streets, often overwhelming the five-man police force. Visitors came from as far away as Colorado, Montana, and Idaho to compete in the local marathon or to participate in the steeplechase held by the Longhorn family every year.

The park around Lighthouse Landing turned into a midway with carnival rides and games set up for the kids.

Out-of-towners brought their RVs and their money. They posed along Water Street for pictures with the natives dressed in beaded regalia, wearing their tall headdresses adorned with bright feathers and decorated buckskin. The local tribes didn't disappoint. Yuki performed alongside Penutian and Hokan as families strolled through the shops buying trinkets and souvenirs to take back home. They browsed through the line of vendors selling Indian jewelry, original handwoven baskets and blankets, and pottery made by artisans from the reservation.

Some came for the beach and all it offered. Sunbathers in their barely-there bikinis sported skimpy thongs and slathered themselves with enough suntan oil to keep their skins slick and brown. Others drank beer and played beach volleyball, while still more never left their thin piece of towel as they soaked up the rays.

Since the celebration always coincided with the summer solstice, it brought out its share of kooky New Age types looking for a Stonehenge vibe. If they were seeking knowledge from a Merlin, they'd have to settle for a shaman or getting advice from a slew of out-of-town fortune tellers who'd paid their fee to set up shop in a tent with a crystal ball.

Everywhere she went, Gemma Channing cringed at how the Sun Bringer Festival had changed from what she remembered as a kid. She'd seen her share of floats and parades and innocent enough enterprises through the years. But this time, the three-day event seemed to bring out a cheesy element. The fortune tellers were just a hint of what had gone wrong with the celebration originally meant to honor the town's founding father, Sun Raven Coyote, and those who'd followed him off the reservation to start a new life.

Once upon a time, the powwow had started out as a family favorite. Gemma wasn't sure she could say that about it now. But she was too busy at the moment to do anything about it.

Every day the Coyote Chocolate Company had seen long lines out the door. Demand was so great, she had trouble keeping up with inventory. She glanced over at her only employee, Lianne Whittaker, who'd worked her butt off for three straight days waiting on people, cleaning up, hauling trash out to the dumpster, all chores that allowed Gemma to focus on making chocolate. Hiring Lianne had been the smartest move she'd made to date. Without her help, Gemma would've been swamped and overwhelmed.

She hadn't seen Lando since early that morning when they'd started their day by grabbing a quick muffin and a cup of coffee. But with so many people in town, they were both stressed and stretched way too thin---Lando keeping the hordes in line, keeping the peace, even making a few arrests, and Gemma attempting to satisfy everyone's sweet tooth.

As if reading her mind, Lianne spoke up. "You'll never believe what I saw when I took my break this afternoon, walking down to Lighthouse Landing for some fresh air. Lando broke up a fight over at Babe's, pulled both men out of the joint and cuffed them right there on the sidewalk."

Gemma blew at a stray lock of toffee-colored hair that had fallen out of its band and into her amber eyes. Swiping it back with her forearm, she continued to wipe down the stainless-steel counter to a shine. "It happens even at restaurants where long wait times can make people crazy and cause tempers to reach a boiling point. Lando says fights break out all the time these days during the lunch and dinner rush during the festival. I remember a much calmer crowd when I was younger. Lando says it's not like that anymore."

"Over food?"

"Over anything. Even though business has been great, I'll be glad when tonight gets here and people start heading back to wherever they came from." Gemma made a face. "That sounded sort of rude. But I can't help it if I want things back the way they were. And I want Lando to have a little peace and quiet for longer than five minutes."

"Not rude," Lianne clarified. "It's perfectly reasonable to want things…calmer around here. Maybe not so many people crammed into the heart of town. Although have you noticed the uptick in our online orders? Wow."

"You bet I have. A welcome sight. It's not unusual now for us to get twenty orders in one day, and even more page visits that might turn into customers in the future. I keep track of the web traffic. And the orders are coming in from all over. I packed up one shipment this morning going to Boston. I'm not even sure how they found the website, but I'm glad they did."

"The reviews are coming in kinda slow, though," Lianne pointed out.

"Yeah, I know. So far, we only have eight, all five stars. But overall customers seem not to bother unless they're complaining about something."

"Luckily we haven't had anybody complaining, except that one."

Gemma lifted a shoulder. "Not a verified purchase. Did you notice that? I suspect it's someone local who just wants to run down the product and the store. After all, we ship same day and the chocolate is first-rate. What's to complain about?"

"I have some idea on that. Not to point fingers or anything, but do you remember telling me to steer clear of Mallory Rawlins?"

Gemma frowned. "Sure. That woman's as crazy as a bag of hungry rats and doesn't care who she zeroes in on. Why? You didn't mess up and go near her, did you?"

Lianne looked remorseful. "Not on purpose. I bumped into her at the post office when I went in to buy stamps. She cornered me after I left the window. She really doesn't like you, not one bit. She spent twenty minutes telling me what a mistake I was making working for you. I tried to make excuses and bolt, but she followed me to my car.

Everything that came out of her mouth is the reason I think Mallory is the one who left that one-star negative review."

Gemma rolled her eyes in disgust. "Probably. She's petty enough to do stuff like that just to make sure the shop doesn't succeed."

"She all but admitted it, daring you to do something about it."

"That woman is such a bitch. It's a wonder Rance McIntire didn't make her one of his victims."

"Yuck. The idea that Mallory slept with a serial killer is so…off-putting. That's something you don't do every day."

Gemma chuckled. "More like repulsive. Even for Mallory that's a new low." She glanced up at the clock and then out the plate-glass window looking at the foot traffic on Water Street. "Thirty more minutes and we close the door. Th,e street vendors are already packing up. I'm ready to get off my feet. I know you are, too. I must be a glutton for punishment or maybe it's greed. This is the only time of the year Gram broke her own rules and opened up on the weekends. I followed her lead and it really paid off. I can see why she picked this weekend to keep the doors open. I might be able to make a profit for the first time since taking over."

From behind the counter, Lianne grinned. "Look at you. You aren't the failure Mallory said you'd be."

Gemma hooted with laughter. "She'd love nothing better than if I failed. I don't want to talk about Mallory anymore, though. I'm getting jazzed about the fireworks over the water tonight. Do me a favor, though. Remind me tomorrow morning to make Duff Northcutt a batch of chocolate covered cherries. He always comes in on Mondays. I'd hate to disappoint him."

"Why don't you just write it on the calendar?"

"Good idea." Gemma went over to the chalkboard where she'd written each kind of candy scheduled for the upcoming week and added Duff's favorite. "There. Now there's no excuse if I forget. Do you and Luke have plans for tonight?"

"He's been running himself ragged at the clinic. That's why we're staying in, watching the fireworks, ordering Chinese takeout from the Happy Wok, and binge-watching *Stranger Things*. How about you and Lando?"

"I'm stopping by the house and grabbing Rufus, then heading over to Lando's place at the beach---perfect spot to take in the show. I'm hoping he'll stop at the Grill when he's ready to go home and pick us up something to eat. I'd cook but I don't want to see a kitchen again until tomorrow morning when I come back here. I don't even want to smell buttercream or chocolate for at least twenty-four hours."

"Same with me."

Their last two customers of the day turned out to be two teenage girls from Crescent City who ordered an entire box of dark chocolate bonbons filled with strawberry crème filling. Gemma watched them giggle out the door, talking about boys and nibbling on a swirl as they headed for the beach. "Leia and I used to act like that when we were that age. Who was your bestie?"

"Collette. As sisters we were always so close we did everything together. We hardly ever fought."

"How is it living in her house?"

"Strange. But it's like she's there, you know. It's helped to have friends like you and Leia to get me through her death. And meeting Luke has been a godsend. He's so wonderful to me. Don't tell Lando but I think his brother might be *the* one."

"Luke's a sweetheart."

"And Lando?"

"Lando is the love of my life, but he's harder to fit into that sweetheart mold. The cop side of him is just too hard-edged."

"But you love him anyway."

"Oh, yeah. He's my best friend."

The women watched the clock tick down and at a few minutes before five, Gemma turned the lock and flipped the CLOSED sign around. "That's it. We're out of here," she announced. "See you tomorrow. Enjoy your evening. And stay off your feet."

Lianne grabbed her purse and headed for the back door. "You too."

Gemma followed Lianne out into the alleyway. While Lianne jumped in her little Volkswagen bug and took off, Gemma rounded the corner on foot, heading for home.

She could tell the tourists had loaded up their cars, done with their three-day adventure, by the way the street parking had opened up. Vehicles had cleared out, no longer lined up bumper to bumper on the side streets and parked haphazardly next to the curb. They'd left behind a string of trash and debris, bottles and cans, and all types of litter lining the pavement.

Clean-up on Monday would no doubt be a bitch, Gemma decided as she approached Peralta Circle.

The property she'd inherited had started out as the town's administrative offices. But at some point in the 1950s the building had fallen so far into disrepair that the town moved its government offices two blocks over to Water Street for safety reasons, where they remained today. The structure had survived several earthquakes that left a foundation dotted with cracks that needed fixing.

By the time her grandparents snapped it up for a song, it had been rezoned and was badly in need of remodeling. Over a span of ten years, Marissa and Jean-Luc had put a ton of work into the project, adding on a series of rooms bit by bit to the main building to make it large enough for the family they hoped to have.

The combination of carpentry from a series of different contractors and from the work Jean-Luc had done himself made for an interesting blend of Pueblo and Spanish Colonial architecture not seen in any other part of town. The structure's terra cotta roof and rounded archways was often the reason people mistook the building for an old mission rather than the place where Gemma now lived. Tourists often pulled up to the driveway expecting a tour of sorts only to find a sign that read: Private residence. No trespassing.

Gemma understood the draw and the curiosity. Her "hacienda" included grounds that might be seen in a fanciful European setting, like the courtyard, and the fountain out front, with at least a half-acre of gardens on the side and around back.

She'd seen to it herself to improve her horticultural skills, determined to turn her brown thumb into a growing machine that could get lavender to thrive within the same general ground space as rosemary, and lilies and monkeyflower to flourish in the same raised bed.

Instead of simply hiring a gardener, she'd read every book in her grandmother's personal library on soil and plant care, determining when to water and when to let the soil dry out.

Not only that, but she was still reading through all the journals her grandmother had left her hidden in the cairn, the one built in memory of her grandfather. The journals were almost a how-to guide on getting through life in Coyote Wells, a fascinating look back at the 70s and 80s from Marissa's point of view and unusual way of thinking.

Gemma let herself in the front door only to have Rufus, her chocolate lab, slide on the tile floors scampering to greet her.

She brushed a hand over the dog's muzzle and brought him in for a hug. "You're full of energy and ready to get outside, I bet. We're having us a sleepover tonight at Lando's place. How does that sound? Feed you first and take a few treats with us. And don't worry, I'll even pack Mr. Sock Monkey. Wouldn't want you to have to sleep without him."

The dog woofed in delight.

"Gotta pack a bag even for an overnighter," Gemma mumbled to herself as she let the dog out the back door. She glanced briefly at the doggie door, an expense she now regretted, and looked fondly at the hound who refused to use it. "Waste of money installing that thing, huh? Wish you could've clued me in before I wrote the check."

Again, the dog yipped on his way to pure enjoyment at smelling fresh air. He sniffed at every rock and leaf as if he'd never seen them before today. After initially going from one bush to another, he raced out into the garden and bounded toward the nearest patch of grass, eager to roll on the lawn.

"I wish that's all it took to make me happy," Gemma grunted as she headed into the bedroom to throw a change of clothes---and the Victoria's Secret teddy she'd bought just for this occasion---into a little travel bag.

Snatching up her toothbrush, she thought about taking the car and driving to Lando's beach house, but decided it was too much trouble to navigate what was left of the festival traffic. "Better to walk and give Rufus plenty of exercise so the jaunt will run some energy out of him."

Her cell phone trilled with a text message from Lando.

Will be wrapping things up in about an hour. I'll pick up a couple of Leia's stir-fry dinners and meet you at the house.

Sounds good. Are you exhausted?

Not for what I have planned.

She sent him a smiley face back. *Good to know the teddy I bought won't go to waste.*

What color?

Black.

Maybe I'll let Payce wrap things up and see you in about thirty.

She sent him another smiley face. *Be careful.* And got the same response she always got when she used those two words.

I'm always careful.

Sometimes she worried about his cockiness on the job. She supposed all law enforcement types had to show an over-confidence in their work. But sometimes she thought Lando's brash demeanor included too much swollen ego. Not that he was careless in the way he handled himself. A testament to that was the takedown of Rance McIntire and his cohort, Smitty Bernal. After all, Lando had gotten the savvy mob-type to flip on the entire organization, bringing down the head honcho, Marshall Montalvo. A feat that had not gone unnoticed by the entire county. Even the sheriff had tried to recruit him. But Lando had turned down the job offer, opting to stay put in Coyote Wells.

It was a decision that had Gemma breaking out into a happy dance.

She and Rufus reached Lando's beach bungalow around six. She shoved the key Lando had given her into the lock and entered a narrow vestibule with a table for keeping track of keys, loose change, and wallets.

She realized now this was the perfect place to unwind after the stress of the last three days, the perfect place to forget about facing a massive clean-up task beginning Monday morning, and dealing with the aftermath of a festival that always brought too many hijinks from the teenagers and too much vandalism from people who just liked to make trouble. Tonight, they could shelve any thoughts about that and simply relax.

Looking around the living room reminded her why Lando loved this place. He was steps away from the soothing sound of the sea, the sugary sand, and the enormous breadth of a blue horizon that seemed to stretch on and on.

Warm beachy colors greeted her as soon as she headed toward the bedroom to put her stuff away. Soft peach-painted walls accented a room with leather furniture and cherry woods. The open dining room snapped to cooler, watery blues that reminded Gemma of an Easter dress she'd worn for Sunday service as a kid.

In the kitchen, a bank of windows bathed the room in radiant hues of soft yellow and mint green. The entire house brought to mind those summery, buttery days of June that ended in spectacular sunsets dipping across the golden sky as twilight gave way to nightfall.

She stepped out on the front porch and understood why he didn't want to give this place up. The view alone was worth the real estate.

And when she spotted his police cruiser pulling up in the driveway, her face broke out in a wide grin.

The love of her life stood six-two, a tall drink of water with soulful coffee-colored eyes and a mischievous grin. He held up a bag of food from his family's restaurant, Captain Jack's Grill. "No stir-fry on Sunday nights but Leia assures me the pot roast is tender and the potatoes and carrots cooked to perfection."

"I'm pretty much starving so I'd eat anything in that bag, good or bad. Were you as busy as you were the first day?"

Lando swiped a hand through his hair. "The first day was nothing compared to today. Fights broke out up and down Water Street over stupid stuff, people were drunk and disorderly at the beach, and I don't know how many calls we took about disturbing the peace. And then I had to stop Silas Macon's boy from spray-painting graffiti on the side of the bank building. He's ten years old. Maybe next year I should think about taking on another patrol officer."

"Maybe you should make a point this fall when the school year starts up again to visit that boy's fifth-grade class, wearing your uniform, and explain the downside to graffiti. Explain that if he wants to paint something he should begin with something like a mural. Maybe start with that ugly, empty warehouse near the wharf, paint the entire side in his favorite color. That would spruce up that whole block."

"You're a nut, you know that?"

"So I've been told. I'm thinking about taking music lessons, maybe the piano."

"Really? Why?"

"If I'm standing on stage singing with your group…"

"Our group," Lando corrected. "Fortitude is glad to have you part of the band."

"Okay, our group, then I should know more than I do about music. All of you play an instrument. I know the lyrics, I can sing, but I don't think that's enough."

"You're really getting into this." He spotted the token dangling from a chain around her neck. "What's that?"

"This? Don't you recognize a medicine bag? It's a gift from Paloma. She handed this to me before the festival started. I wear it along with my turquoise necklace. These make me feel…like I belong to something greater than myself. My new grandmother has been very generous with her time, explaining so much about my native heritage. But you know what's odd? The minute the conversation seems to reach a point where she has more to add about my father, she changes the subject, like it's too painful to go on. I haven't pushed her for details. I wish I could've gotten to know him, even briefly. I wish he hadn't died in that car accident."

"Do you really think Michael would've left his wife to marry your mother?"

"No. No, I don't. But I think I could have eventually been part of his life had he lived. At least I like to think so. Did you ever have time to dig out the photos of his car accident like I asked?"

"Not yet. But I will. I haven't had time to sit at my desk for three days."

She held onto the medicine bag, a small pouch made from deerskin and decorated with tiny ornamental beads. "Well, I'm Hokan now, or at least half." She noted the look of disapproval on his face. "I remember a time when we were kids when you carried a medicine bag around wherever you went. It meant something to you back then."

"A young, naïve kid doesn't know any better than to carry a talisman around for luck. It gives you a false sense of confidence. It leaves you unprepared when the rug is likely to be pulled out from under you by someone you know, quickly, without any feeling."

Gemma flinched, believing he was referring to their short-lived marriage and the hurt he'd felt after she left. "If I had a part in changing the way you feel about that, I'm sorry."

"You didn't. Or not much. It's my cop mentality now. I'm harder to convince about most everything, more so than putting faith in a bunch of power stones or totems."

"Yukians are skeptics. And stubborn."

Lando cocked a brow. "You've known you were Hokan for what, a month, less than that? Try embracing it for a longer period of time than that. Try relying on your new medicine bag for power. It doesn't afford you good luck any more than that turquoise stone you wear around your neck."

"How can you say that? I found Sandy Montalvo's remains, didn't I?"

"Not criticizing the way you did that or solved your grandmother's murder, or Collette's, or Marnie's. But thinking your necklace is a source of all-seeing power is…"

She poked him in the ribs. "Be careful how you describe that."

Lando chuckled. "Maybe I won't. The way it turned out made me go back and take a second look at all my old unsolved cases."

"Really? Why? I didn't do it by myself. I had help. And you're the one who got Bernal to confess. Without that…"

"Yeah, but you're the one who uncovered the critical pieces of evidence. I give you credit for all of it coming together like it did. You're the one who was able to ID McIntire and Bernal in the first place and put them at the scene of the dump site. Which brings me to what I'm getting at. I still have five very thin folders sitting in a dingy little file cabinet mocking me and gathering dust. Each one is left over from the days when Caulfield reigned supreme and didn't solve any of those cases."

"But what could I do?"

"Look over the case files. There aren't that many things in there that lead to a suspect. Just a thinly-veiled police report and an autopsy done by the county. One is still a Jane Doe."

"Never identified? That's so sad. Are you still thinking about charging Caulfield with obstruction in Mrs. Montalvo's murder?"

Lando shook his head. "I ran it by the district attorney. Caulfield bragged that the DA wouldn't touch it. Turns out, Caulfield was right. The prosecutor said no. Pisses me off."

"But if you could find another case that Caulfield mishandled and maybe colluded on for money, you'd have a stronger case to take to the prosecutor. That would change things."

Lando smiled. "Exactly." He shifted in his chair and opened the drawer of the hutch behind him and pulled out a ring box frayed at the edges.

"Oh, my God. Is that what I think it is?"

Lando held out the silver ring with a moonstone setting. "When you left, you took this off. I found it on the kitchen counter. I don't even know why I kept it. I was cleaning out my closet the other day looking for my extra service weapon and came across it in the bottom of one of the cartons. I don't see any reason after all these years you shouldn't have it back."

She threw her arms around his neck. "I thought my wedding ring was lost forever. I thought you'd probably have thrown it away by now."

"Oh, I thought about it. I guess I kept hoping one day you'd come back."

She held out her left hand for him to slip it on her ring finger. "You found this stone in Shadow Canyon when we were thirteen. Remember that? You gave it to me while we were sitting on a rock, scarfing down bologna and cheese sandwiches. We were on a rock hunt. Remember all those scavenger hunts we took out there? You told me it was too girly for you to keep in your medicine bag. When I got home that night, Gram looked at it and told me it was from mother moon, a sign of feminine power and healing."

She took his head in both hands, forcing him to gaze into her eyes. "Gram said it also stood for love, strong and enduring. That's why the day you asked me to marry you, I ran home to get this and told you I wanted this for my wedding ring."

Lando nodded, a little embarrassed at the reminder of how sentimental he'd been back then. "I took it to the jeweler in town and he helped me pick out a band that would be worthy of it."

"Solid silver." She looked down at her hand and sighed. "I can't believe you kept it all these years. Thank you." She kissed him lightly on the lips and wasn't surprised when he deepened the kiss.

Lando backed her up toward the hallway. Heat merged with urgency. "We can eat later, nuke the food in the microwave."

"I'm all for that."

They fell asleep after they made love and woke at nine to the boom of fireworks. Rufus reacted to the noise with a whine and a whimper and scooted under the bed.

"I don't want to miss the fireworks," Gemma muttered as she lunged for her clothes.

Lando grabbed for her hand and missed. "I'd better stay here with Rufus. You should stay, too."

Laughing, she tried to pull him out of bed. "Come on, get up. It'll be like it was when we were kids, dangling our feet off the pier, looking up in the sky and guessing which color will pop up next."

"But…it feels…so…good…not moving from this spot."

"All right, I'll watch by myself." She pulled on her shorts and her top and headed for the front porch. Leaning against the railing, she gaped in awe when the bursts of light blasted the night sky and then floated down, scattering over the water like giant fireflies. Like kisses that exploded in passion, the moment was far too brief. Like a waterfall that cascaded in streams of scarlet, silver, or sapphire, the lightshow evaporated. Like an array of fast-moving shooting stars.

Lando wrapped his arms around her from behind and whispered in her ear, "Gotcha."

She leaned her body against his. "I know you're tired, but I was so looking forward to this."

Lando nipped her neck. "I know. I forgot how much you get a kick out of it."

"I think it's magical. Remember our trip to Disneyland, senior year? The light parade, the music, the buildup, followed by the spectacular fireworks show? I felt like a little girl again."

"I prefer you all grown up."

"So I noticed. I suppose it is silly for a grown woman to get such a thrill out of something so…childish. Want a beer? We should eat."

"Eat and go back to bed."

They enjoyed the food, and soon after enjoyed each other again before falling asleep, exhausted.

Gemma heard whining and sat straight up in bed. The nice dream she'd been having faded---people who took her seriously as a psychic were asking her to solve murders. The FBI, those gray-suited agents who like to make fun, were begging for her help.

Instead of going back to sleep, she heard a female voice in her head. Unwilling to ignore the shaman's words, echoing like a loop, she was forced to listen to Kamena. One of three mystical shamans who would supposedly enter her life and set her on a quest of knowledge and power, Kamena, the giver of visions, had been the first to confirm she had the gift of sight. *You must seek and gather potent medicine, the more medicine you gather, the more powerful your gift and ability will become.*

Gemma gripped the pendant she wore around her neck, the one made from the turquoise stone she'd found in the waters at Mystic Falls, and glanced down at the wedding ring on her left hand. Zeroing in on her ring finger, the moonstone glowed in the dark. Lando had found the strange-looking rock in Shadow Canyon during one of their teenage misadventures. Now she wondered if this could be the gift from Aponivi, the holder of truth, the shaman who appeared as a powerful dervish often seen winging his way between canyon walls.

She was about to grab her phone and make herself a note to set up another meeting with Callie Lightfeather when she heard the whining again.

Rufus.

Snuggled under the covers, reluctant to move, she tried to ignore that pitiful sound, but it was no use. After the third whimper she couldn't take it any longer and tossed back the comforter.

She looked over at Lando, who'd always been a sound sleeper, and noticed he hadn't so much as moved at the noise.

Eyeing the dog, dancing in place by the door, clenching his favorite toy between his teeth, Gemma tugged on her shorts and pulled on the first thing she could reach---one of Lando's sweatshirts.

Scowling at the dog, she whispered, "Come on, before you have an accident in here and I have to clean it up. But make it quick. I'd like to get back to my dream. You know, the one where I'm an internationally famous, hugely successful psychic in demand all over the world, hired to solve their toughest cases. Even Interpol needs me."

With Mr. Monkey gripped between his teeth, Rufus looked skeptical.

Gemma clipped his leash to his collar and led the way outside, trotting toward the beach at a fast pace.

A full moon had taken center stage over the water. It emerged from behind a cluster of ivory clouds and hung suspended over the earth like a gigantic frosted-white Christmas ornament.

Okay, maybe taking the dog out for a moonlit stroll wasn't so bad after all. Getting up from a sound sleep to trek outside had its perks. The moon looked so close to the earth that she could all but reach up and run her fingers over the craters.

In bare feet, her toes sank into the sand on the narrow slip of land designated as the dog park. Trying not to step in poop, she followed the little paw prints Rufus left in the powdery grains of dirt and watched as he picked out the nearest tree, a twisted birch no more than a bush.

The wind picked up, causing the feathery leaves to dance in the breeze.

Rufus began to bark.

"Shhhh," Gemma said, cautioning him to be quiet. "We're not trying to wake the neighbors." But when he kept pulling on his leash to change direction, she knew something was up. "Why are you making such a fuss? Just do your business and let's hurry back."

She tugged on his leash again and realized the pooch had now focused on something where the dunes were thickest. Maybe Rufus had picked up the scent of another dog. But there was no canine or anyone else in sight. By now it was two-thirty in the morning and they had the entire beach to themselves. But no matter how hard she pulled on his leash, Rufus wouldn't budge or shut up. She slackened her grip. The dog took advantage and pulled her to the far edge of the water, near a channel known for its dangerous riptides.

Gemma stopped in her tracks.

The body of a woman was stretched out on the sand, lying on her back. Nude, her skin seemed translucent in the moonlight.

Gemma jogged toward the dog in a rush, grabbing him by the collar right before Rufus reached the body.

She sucked in a breath as she recognized that platinum blond hair. No one else in town had that same distinctive shade of silvery tresses.

Frozen in shock, it took her several minutes before she could move, but move she finally did. She half-dragged, half-carried Rufus back to the dog park before breaking into a run to get back to the house.

The minute she crossed the threshold, she called out for Lando. Running to the bed, she shook him hard to get him fully awake. It all gushed out in one nervous breath. "There's a dead body on the beach. It's Mallory Rawlins. She's dead."

Lando sat up, rubbing the sleep out of his eyes. "What? Who? Are you sure?"

"Yes, I'm sure. I had to take Rufus out for a pee break. We ended up on the beach. That stretch of sand where the tide comes in the strongest is where she's…where she ended up. She's all the way dead. And she's not wearing any clothes."

"Jesus." Lando grabbed his jeans and stretched on a T-shirt over his head. He sat back down on the bed to tie his tennis shoes. "You didn't touch anything, did you?"

"Of course not."

"Did Rufus?"

"No."

"Stay here."

"No way. I have to show you where she is."

"Right. Like I won't be able to find a dead body by myself near the channel. Okay. Come on. The dog stays, though." He opened the nightstand drawer and pulled out a flashlight, then grabbed his service weapon, a powerful Colt Commander.

They jogged back to where Mallory's body rested in the basin, a small inlet between two competing riptides. Gemma stood back several feet while Lando charged ahead, studying the corpse.

He saw right away that Mallory's pretty face was purple and swollen, proof she'd been in a fight.

Without moving from her spot, Gemma pointed downward. "There are bruises on the front of her neck and throat. I don't think she drowned."

"She didn't. Here, hold the flashlight."

"That means I have to get closer, doesn't it?"

Lando rolled his eyes and squatted down next to the body to take pictures with his phone. Adding several critical shots to the camera roll, he tried to turn the body over and look underneath. He saw nothing but sand. "Who the hell took her clothes?"

"Get a picture of her hands," Gemma suggested. "Her usual manicured, pristine fingernails are all broken off like she's been in a fight."

"Yeah. A fight for her life that she lost," Lando murmured. He stood up and punched in the number for Payce's house. "I need you at my house pronto, the strand along the beach. And don't use dispatch. If you have to call me back for any reason, call me directly on my cell."

"What's up?" Payce asked.

"Dead body. It's Mallory Rawlins."

"Oh, my God. Louise is gonna be devastated."

"Yeah. That's why you need to get out here and bring the good camera we use for crime scenes. I'll need you to secure the scene and wait for the coroner to show up while I go wake up Louise. Not that he'll get here before I get back. But I can't leave Gemma out here to guard the body."

"Jeez, Chief. What's Gemma doing there?"

"She found the body."

"I'll throw my clothes on and be there in fifteen minutes. I don't envy you none, Chief. Louise will be…pissed."

"Don't say anything to anyone, Payce. Not yet. Not until we do the notifications by the book."

"Got it, Chief."

Lando ended the call and stared at Gemma. "You know there's bound to be talk since you found the body."

"I already thought of that. But I didn't wake up in the middle of the night to take my dog for a walk and bump into Mallory and decide to take her down on the beach."

"I know that," Lando snapped. "But I can't stop people from talking. Everyone in town knows you two didn't get along."

"Yeah. Well, save your breath. You'll need it to convince Louise. Because it won't matter to her. She'll use this as a rallying cry against the shop."

The thought of informing his surly dispatcher about her only daughter's death had Lando rubbing his forehead, already beginning to pound from a nasty headache. "Count on Louise to raise holy hell and interfere with this investigation every step of the way."

"Okay, so you'll step up your game because I don't see you letting that happen, not if you set her straight right up front."

"I'll do what I can, but don't be surprised by mid-morning if she has half the town pitted against the other."

Gemma noticed Lando punching in another number on speed dial. "Who are you calling now?"

"Luke. He's my go-to guy who'll be able to give me a heads up about how long she's been dead. So far, he's two for two."

Gemma rested her hands on her hips and stared over at Mallory's body. "Another murder so soon after the others. This town's changing, Lando, and not in a good way."

2

As Lando expected, Louise Rawlins, the woman who'd worked as police dispatcher for more than twenty-five years, took the news hard. She cried for ten minutes or so and then recovered enough to start pointing fingers at Mallory's enemies. First on that list was no surprise. "Your ex-wife hated my daughter. Gemma should be your number one suspect."

"Sorry to disappoint you, Louise, but Gemma was with me all night."

"Isn't that convenient? If that's true, then how do you explain her finding the body?"

"She took her dog out to pee around two-thirty. From what I saw, Mallory had been dead at least four hours. I'm certain the medical examiner will back me up on that."

Louise bit her lip. "You're certain Gemma didn't do this to my baby girl?"

Holly Dowell appeared at the bottom of the stairs, wearing her robe, tears in her eyes. "*Our* baby girl," Holly corrected.

Landon knew the history between the two sisters. Holly had been Mallory's birth mother. At the time an eighteen-year-old girl who had big dreams of becoming an actress. Louise had showed up in Los Angeles to take care of Holly after the birth but ended up bringing the baby back to Coyote Wells to raise as her own.

Lando wasn't about to stir up whatever animosity existed so he put all that history aside for now. "I'm positive Gemma isn't the one who killed your daughter. Mallory put up a fight. And that's all the information you're getting. From this point going forward, you're on paid leave."

"You're suspending me? You can't do that."

"I just did. You aren't suspended; you're on paid leave. Huge difference." Lando pointed a finger at his dispatcher. "I don't want you anywhere near this investigation. And I don't want you going around town pointing fingers at people. Do we understand each other?"

Louise narrowed her eyes. "You can't stop me from…"

That's as far as Lando let her get. "I will stop you from running your mouth and interfering in *my* investigation. You do that, and you'll end up looking for another job. Plus, I'll arrest you for obstructing justice. I'm sympathetic to your emotional state right about now, but I won't put up with innuendos and harassment. You'll let me do this investigation by the book or I'll find out the reason why. Are we clear?"

Louise patted her face with a tissue and nodded. "You'll at least keep me informed."

"I will not. I'll share what I can, but I won't jeopardize this investigation in any way. It should take the coroner a few days to finish his findings. You'll be given the high points. But anything I need to keep from the public will also be kept from you."

"That's not fair."

"I'm truly sorry for your loss. I am. But I have a job to do. If finding Mallory's killer means I won't be able to pass along everything I learn to you, then so be it. Look, I have to get back. If there's anything you need, you let any of us at the department know."

"I need to know who killed Mallory," Louise shouted as her boss turned to go.

At the door, Lando stopped and turned back. "Why don't you make me a list of everyone who had a falling out with Mallory in, say, the last thirty days? Had she been dating anyone new?"

Holly cleared her throat. "She'd started a relationship with Billy Gafford about two weeks ago. He owns a cabin out on Lone Coyote Highway."

"I know the place. Okay, thanks, I'll start with the boyfriend."

By the time Lando arrived back at the beach, it was almost daylight. The sun peeked over the mountains to the east. He found his senior patrol officer, Payce Davis, and Jimmy Fox, having a difficult time shielding Mallory's body from onlookers.

"Louise and Holly must've started making phone calls the minute I left," Lando grumbled.

"Did you get anything out of Louise?" Jimmy wondered.

"You mean besides a hard time? Were you aware Mallory had started dating Billy Gafford?"

Jimmy and Payce traded looks. Payce bobbed his head. "Go ahead. You tell him."

Lando squinted into the sun. "Tell me what."

Jimmy looked none too pleased. "Dale had a date with Mallory last week."

"Well, damn," Lando groused. "I don't suppose there's another Dale Hooper who's *not* on the force."

"Sorry, Chief," Jimmy began. "Dale said Mallory kept asking him out…several times before he said yes."

"He couldn't have said no? This just keeps getting more awful by the hour. One of my cops involved with the victim. Louise already blaming Gemma. This is gonna get messy real fast. What else do I need to know? Either of you guys go near Mallory?"

Payce looked horror-stricken. "Not me. My wife would have my head. It's a small town, though," he pointed out. "I mean it's not like single people have a lot of options."

"Not helping," Lando grunted with an eye toward several of Louise's friends he'd spotted, inching their way closer to where the body still waited for the coroner. "I'm putting a stop to this. Now."

Lando herded the nosy busybodies onto the far end of the beach. Some had even brought their pets as an excuse to walk their dogs.

"You can't be here," Lando began. "Turn around now and go home. Fix breakfast, have a second cup of coffee, whatever, but don't plan on camping out near this crime scene again with the intent to report back to Louise."

The sheepish look fifty-five-year-old Claude Mayweather gave the chief of police meant he didn't like getting caught without succeeding at recon. "We just wanted to see for ourselves, Chief, see what was what. But your boys over there are blocking us from seeing anything."

"That's the point, Claude. Now move along before I arrest you for refusing to leave a crime scene. This place is off limits until the medical examiner shows up, maybe longer."

Claude picked up the chihuahua he called Peanut and raised his chin. "Louise is one of our oldest and dearest friends. What are we supposed to tell her?"

"Tell her the truth. Tell her I ran all of you off the minute I spotted you hanging around here. And if I see you back any time today lurking near this spot, you'll be spending the night in a cell. Is that clear enough for you?"

"We're going," Janet Delgado grumbled, tugging on the leash of her black and white terrier. "Anybody ever tell you how mean you've gotten lately, Lando Bonner?"

"You have no idea how mean I can get, Mrs. Delgado. But keep standing where you are, and you'll easily find out."

"I'm telling your mother. Lydia will hear about this," Janet promised as she shuffled off down the winding pathway. "Come on, Claude. Let's go. Chief Bonner has no intention of letting us see what happened to Mallory."

Claude gave Lando the evil eye as he lumbered past the police chief. "You're up for reelection next spring."

"Don't remind me," Lando huffed under his breath while he exchanged looks with Payce and Jimmy. "See what's already happening? Sometimes I hate this job."

"No you don't," Jimmy asserted. "You love being in charge."

"And you're a lot better at it than Caulfield ever was," Payce added. "My wife thinks so, too."

"Yeah, but it's times like these I wonder what the hell is going on with our town and the people in it. You guys make sure they don't come back to gawk. I'm heading in the house to get us some coffee. I don't want anyone getting a look at Mallory like that."

"You got it, Chief."

Inside Lando's kitchen, Gemma and Luke were still trying to recover from the shock. She stared at the doctor from the other side of the table. Even though she'd had coffee---she'd started a second pot---the caffeine didn't help much. Finding Mallory dead would stay with her for some time.

"So you think she died between ten and eleven o'clock last night."

"That's my best guess, yeah. What I can't figure out is how she got dumped on the beach without any clothes on."

"And practically right in front of Lando's house," Gemma added. "He's taking that pretty hard."

"Because it might've been on purpose."

"You mean like sending a message?"

Luke patted her hand to keep her from getting worked up. "It's probably just a coincidence."

"Lando doesn't believe in coincidences."

"I know. Before he headed to Louise's house, I've never seen him so mad. I had to threaten to drive just to calm him down enough to deliver the news."

Gemma rested her fist under her chin. "Louise will be taking to the streets to find the killer."

Luke, whose face looked just like his brother's minus the dimple in the chin, shook his head. "Uh-uh. Lando will never stand for that. He'll kick her off the force if she even tries to conduct her own investigation."

"We'll see about that. I'd better load up a Thermos and take the fresh pot of coffee over to the guys. I know Lando jumped out of bed without so much as a shot of caffeine."

"Right now, he's running on pure adrenaline."

"I'll throw together an egg sandwich for him, too," Gemma said, getting up to dig in the refrigerator. "Want one?"

"Nah. I need to be getting home so I can take a shower and then head off to work. Nothing like the smell of a dead body to put off patients, not to mention Lianne."

"How's that going anyway? With Lianne?"

"She's amazing. We have a lot in common, which is hard to find these days."

The front door opened, and she heard Lando stomping the sand off his shoes before tracking the dirt onto the hardwood floor.

"Hey, I was just getting ready to make you breakfast and bring you some coffee."

"Not sure I can hold down food. But my head is aching for caffeine."

Gemma took hold of his shoulders and pushed him into a chair. "How did Louise take it?"

"Like you'd expect. She's a hard-nosed woman, always has been. Did you know Mallory was going out with Billy Gafford? And last week she had a date with Dale."

Gemma frowned into her coffee. "Dale? Those two have nothing in common. But it's odd that whenever we have trouble around here, like say the last month or so, Gafford's name keeps popping up."

Luke rubbed the stubble on his chin. "Maybe it's because he hasn't been in town that long and doesn't like other people. Gafford is about as antisocial as they come."

"Which has my cop instincts working overtime," Lando noted. "Why does a guy like that pick little ol' Coyote Wells to settle down in the first place? With so many other coastal communities out there, why here?"

"We do offer a beautiful, quiet, scenic place to live," Gemma proffered. "But to a guy like Gafford, he seems to prefer his solitude."

"Yeah, but that doesn't make sense," Luke said. "If he feels that strongly about keeping to himself, then why date a local in the first place? Gafford would have to know that the town would get wind of him going out with her. Word would spread eventually."

Gemma wasn't so sure. "Not if the two of them were really careful. Maybe they really clicked with one another."

"Has anybody ever really clicked with Mallory?" Lando wondered aloud. "Think about it. In all the years we've known her she's not exactly the type to stay with one man."

Luke stood up to leave. "There's a first time for everything. Maybe Mallory fell hard for Gafford and he didn't want…complications. It happens all the time."

Gemma nodded and sipped her coffee. "I could see that. Gafford likes his space. Mallory pushes him to make a commitment he didn't want. She was moving too fast. Not everyone gets on the same page as fast as you and Lianne did."

Luke grinned. "Yeah. It just…when it feels right, it's like everything lining up for once. Look, I gotta get out of here and get to work. Let me know if you guys need anything else."

Gemma sighed. "This isn't exactly the way I wanted to start out the week. Mallory and I certainly didn't like each other, but I can't believe she's dead, ending up like that…in such a violent way."

"As soon as the coroner arrives, I'll have to check inside Mallory's house, interview my own patrol officer, and then go track down Gafford."

"Why talk to Dale?"

Lando took a slug of coffee. "Because I was informed earlier that he went out with Mallory on a date last week."

"That certainly puts the kibosh on the theory that Mallory was serious about Gafford."

"Mallory has never been serious about anyone that I know of, that was my point."

"No argument there. One date hardly amounts to homicide, though. Dale just isn't the killer type."

"I've been doing this a long time. You'd be surprised how easy it is for the average person to lose control enough to murder someone."

Gemma pursed her lips. "I still say it's not in Dale to do that, even to someone like Mallory. My money's on Gafford. Do you know where he works? All I know is he's a construction worker. That's what he told me anyway."

"You talked to Gafford? When did you two cross paths? Did he come into the shop?"

She'd walked right into that one. "Okay. Here's the deal. When I was looking into Gram's murder back in May, I went out to visit Duff Northcutt. You remember Duff, right? He owns that spread near the bend in the road. You know, lives in a house that looks like a barn."

"I know the one. But that still doesn't tell me what Duff has to do with Billy Gafford."

"Duff told me that Billy bullied him several times after moving into his cabin. Billy's standoffish, yes, but not afraid to get into a neighbor's face when he's threatened. You might get Duff to tell you why exactly. Duff wouldn't tell me. Maybe it's a prideful guy thing. Anyway, all I know is Gafford threatened him."

"Threatened him over what? How serious was it?"

"That's just it, I don't know. But that's why Duff keeps his shotgun nearby, just in case."

"Okay. I'll stop by Duff's and get the lowdown on what's going on. Maybe I can make a case against Gafford through Duff."

"Do you really think Gafford could've killed Mallory?"

"He's a good place to start. You don't plan on admitting you stuck your nose into my investigation, do you?"

"I was trying to help, remember? Besides, I'm curious as to what crazy Mallory was doing out there on the beach. Ever since I found her...like that...I've been trying to get a handle on her kind of crazy."

"Her kind of crazy? What does that even mean? Why?"

"Isn't it obvious? Mallory picked fights with people, stirred up all kinds of chaos that wasn't even relevant most of the time. If we don't try to figure out how crazy thinks, then how do we solve this thing? What's the point? Before you warn me not to butt in...it won't do any good. We both know who Louise will blame." She ran a soft hand across his rough cheek. "You've been up for several hours already. You look exhausted. I'm worried about you."

He pulled her closer and nuzzled her neck. "You've been up that long. This sure isn't the way I wanted our morning to start out."

The rap on the door broke the moment.

Lando let out a loud sigh. "That's probably Payce. Let's hope he's here to tell me the medical examiner is outside."

"I need to get going anyway," Gemma offered. "Candy to make. If you go see Duff, stop by the shop and take him a box of his favorites for me, will you?" She brushed a kiss across his lips. "Keep me updated, okay?"

"Will do. Sorry about breakfast. I'll make it up to you over dinner tonight."

"I'm holding you to that, Chief. Come on, Rufus. Let's pack up and head home."

3

At the shop, Gemma got started on Duff's chocolate covered cherries. She had two dozen sitting on a tray before Lianne walked in the door.

"My God, you must've gotten here at the crack of dawn," Lianne began, shoving her purse under the counter. She popped a chocolate drop into her mouth. "Luke told me everything he knew. I can't believe Mallory's gone."

"Did he mention that Louise thinks I did it?"

Lianne's mouth opened but no sound came out. A full thirty seconds went by before she was able to get her voice to work. "He left that part out. Why would Louise think that?"

"Like mother, like daughter. Mallory and I have been at each other's throats since first grade. Ask anyone. She was a bully her whole life and Louise, even now, isn't much different."

"No one's gonna believe you got up in the middle of the night to walk Rufus and murdered Mallory on the beach and took her clothes."

Gemma smiled. "Let's hope not. Louise has a lot of friends here, though."

"So do you," Lianne insisted.

"No, I have a small but very loyal circle. Louise, on the other hand, has an army, one she's cultivated over the past three decades."

Leia swept into the shop full of news. "Not even nine o'clock and we're in the middle of a town divided. Mom says Louise has been burning up the phone lines with accusations…about you."

Gemma looked at Lianne. "Told you so. Although I thought she'd wait until the body got to the morgue."

"We have to counter these attacks," Lianne directed. "We should make our own calls."

Leia shook her head. "Won't do any good. Lando has to find out who the real killer is, otherwise Louise will make Gemma's life miserable."

"Then what do we do, sit here and take it? Wait for her to say enough bad things that the business implodes?" an indignant Lianne asked. "That's not me."

"Or me," Leia concluded. "But…"

"No buts," Gemma said. "If Louise wants to run her mouth, none of us can stop her. I didn't hurt Mallory. If people want to believe Louise instead of me, there's not a thing I can do to change their minds."

"You just let them come up to me and accuse you of murder to my face," Lianne stated.

Gemma patted her friend on the shoulder before turning back to the chocolate. "Who needs an army when I have friends like you guys."

Lando took Payce with him on his second stop of the morning---Mallory's house at 722 Sands Point. The little two-bedroom shotgun-style bungalow had started out in 1920 as a Sears Roebuck kit house. After getting the keys from Louise, Lando found the inside tidy as a model home.

"Cute," Payce commented. "What are we looking for exactly?"

"Anything that tells us why she was killed."

"Her bed hasn't even been slept in," Payce pointed out. "And the bathroom looks like it's been recently cleaned."

"Kitchen is immaculate, not even a dirty plate in the sink. Was she spending a lot of time away from here recently?"

"Sure looks like it. Did you talk to Dale yet?"

"I spent thirty minutes' face time with him and he swears he only went out with her that one time."

"Do you believe him?"

"I've known Dale since we were running around on the playground together. I don't see him strangling a woman. Although we all know, at times, Mallory could test the patience of a priest."

"So what do we do now?"

"Use that camera to capture as many details as you can in each room. And remember there's no such thing as too many photos at a crime scene. You do that while I start the background check on Billy Gafford."

The in-depth report gave him the address of where Billy worked. But before meeting with Gafford, he took a drive out to see what Duff Northcutt had to say about his prime suspect.

Duff was a crusty old soul, who lived on Social Security, and rarely, if ever, made trouble for anyone. But he did have a feisty side that showed people they'd be better off not to mess with him.

Sure enough, as soon as Lando stepped out of the cruiser, Duff greeted him carrying the shotgun.

"No need for that," Lando shouted. He held up the bag of chocolate. "Gemma sent me out here with goodies, your favorite, so I wouldn't show up empty-handed."

"Why didn't you say so? Come on in. I'll put on a pot of fresh coffee. That Gemma, Marissa would be proud of her, don't you think?"

Lando followed Duff inside the cluttered house. "I'm sure Marissa would be. Look, does Billy Gafford still bother you?"

"Not in a while because he hasn't been around much. But make no mistake, that's one mean hombre. Got a temper to go with his bad attitude. That's why I don't intend to let some wet-behind-the-ears asshole bully me."

"Why does he try to bully you, Duff?"

"Maybe because I ran off his dog. Gafford's got one of those pit bulls that he's trained to be a guard dog. That little monster killed two of my chickens, even caught him in the act once. So I fired up in the air to run him off. Next day Billy comes storming down here cussin' me out something fierce and claiming that if I ever fire another shot at his dog again, he'll kill me. I asked him why he let his dog run loose like that. He just looked at me and said he'd let his dog do whatever he wanted."

"Why didn't you call it in, Duff?"

Duff looked insulted and wiped his mouth. "'Cause I don't have no phone. Besides, I can take care of myself just fine. I don't need nobody worrying about me. Marissa used to, but that was different. She came out here to pay me a social call, to visit, have a cup of coffee without trying to dig information out of me. Why do you want to know about Gafford anyways?"

"You don't live in town but I'm sure word will eventually spread. Gafford was dating Mallory Rawlins of late. She was found dead this morning on the beach."

Duff slid his frame into the nearest chair. "Well, I'll be damned. You know Gemma thought Gafford had something to do with those other two women that disappeared. I'll tell you the same thing I told her. Gafford's got the rage and the temper for it."

"What else do you know about him?"

"Gafford works construction out of town. I don't know what he did with that dog he had, but I haven't seen hide nor hair of that critter for weeks. Which is fine by me because that dog's mean, like his owner."

Lando spent another half hour drinking some of the strongest coffee he'd ever had in his life before getting up to leave. "Anything I should know about Gafford before I interview him?"

"He'll probably be armed. He doesn't go anywhere without his guns."

"Okay. Good to know."

Just as Lando started to slide into his cruiser, he spotted an old beat-up vehicle at the edge of Duff's property sitting in weeds up to its windows. It was so rusted out, he could barely make out the faint writing on the side. "Is that what I think it is?"

"Yep. A 1957 Chevy panel truck. Used to be owned by Jean-Luc Sarrazin, his major source of transportation he used in his carpentry jobs."

Lando began walking in that direction with Duff trailing after him. "The paint's almost faded out but you can still see the advertising on the side."

"Jean-Luc did the paint job hisself to advertise The Coyote Chocolate Company. He swore up and down that it caused business to pick up after he drove that thing all over the county."

"I want to buy it. For Gemma. Does she know it's sitting here?"

"Not that I know of. She was out here but I think her head was going in fifty different directions that day. Come to think of it, it was coming on dark when she left out of here heading for Gafford's place." Duff caught the disapproval on Lando's face. "Hey, don't look at me like that. I did my best to talk her out of it. But that's one stubborn gal you got there."

Lando huffed out a breath. "No gal. She's a headstrong female who thinks she's Nancy Drew."

Duff chuckled. "Sounds like your problem, not mine."

"And then some. How much do you want for it?"

"That thing ain't run since Marissa parked it there after Jean-Luc died. Said it held too many memories for her to stare at every single day sitting in her driveway. She brought it out here because she couldn't look at it. I didn't pay nothing for it and she didn't ask. So I reckon I can let it go for the same."

"You sure? It's bound to be worth something."

"You take it. Fix it up for Gemma. Makes me feel good knowing I can return the favor for all the chocolates I eat. She won't take money for 'em, you know."

"She likes doing things like that."

"Like her grandmother, that one."

Still eyeing the hunk of junk, Lando scrubbed a hand over his jaw. "First thing is getting it towed out of here. I could send Dale Hooper over later today with his dad's tow truck, see if he can pull it out of the weeds."

"That'll work. You really gonna fix this thing up?"

"I'll give it my best shot."

Lando had to go all the way to Crescent City to track down Billy Gafford, only to learn that Billy had been assigned as a runner to go pick up supplies at the local lumber yard. Undeterred, he followed him there and sat in his squad car for an hour waiting until he spotted Billy coming out of the store, pushing one of those massive carts heading for his blue pickup.

Lando got out, strolled up to the man, who by this time had begun to unload lumber into the bed of his truck. At six-six, Billy looked like he'd have no trouble handling the massive five by five redwood beams by himself, or carrying the heavy posts from point A to point B.

"You Billy Gafford?" Lando asked.

"Who wants to know?"

Lando flashed his badge. "Chief of police. Coyote Wells. I need to ask you a few questions."

"What for?"

"Were you dating Mallory Rawlins?"

Billy snorted a laugh. "Dating? We went out a couple of times, shared a meal once or twice, slept together afterward. I wouldn't exactly call it dating. Hooking up? Yeah. Why?"

Lando sucked in a breath. "Because she's dead."

"What?" Billy almost dropped the heavy length of beam on his foot.

"I'm sorry, but her body was found this morning on the beach. I need to ask you where you were last night."

Billy's brash attitude fell away. "You think I did it? No way. I was here all day Sunday. Ask anybody on the crew. They'll tell you I slept in until ten-thirty or so and ate breakfast with a couple of my buddies. Then I did laundry, which had piled up. Took me most of the afternoon. Sunday night I was here playing cards with the rest of the guys I bunk with."

"Seriously? That's your story?"

"It's the truth. During the week we stay at the Luna Court Motel. None of us are from Crescent City. The boss was the low bidder on this job and brought in his own crew from all over. Instead of getting up at four o'clock and making the drive from Coyote Wells five days a week like I'd have to do if I drove here from my cabin, I sleep at the motel for the duration of the job like most of the other guys do. You can ask anybody. I played poker last night from seven-thirty to midnight, lost twenty bucks. Then I went to bed."

"You have to know I'll verify everything you just told me, right? You know better than to lie to law enforcement, right?"

"I don't care, check it out. I'm telling the truth."

"So when was the last time you saw Mallory?"

Billy's face tightened. "Okay, here's the thing. I drove back to Coyote Wells Thursday night to check on my cabin. I texted Mallory that I was coming. We agreed to meet up there…for…to spend some time together. She picked up some fried chicken from one of the restaurants in town and we had sex Thursday night. I left around midnight. That's the last time I saw her. I swear it."

"You were back at work on Friday morning right on schedule? And yet, you want me to believe you didn't see Mallory over the weekend?"

"Look, Thursday night I discovered Coyote Wells was a madhouse. People everywhere. I didn't go back Saturday or Sunday because I…I didn't want to see Mallory or put up with the traffic. Mallory could be a bit…overwhelming at times. I tried to break it off, several times, but she didn't seem to understand that I needed a break. She wouldn't listen."

"Except for Thursday night when you weren't trying to break up with her."

"Hey, I just wanted to keep it casual, hook up when I was free. You know how it is. I'm a normal guy. I thought if she was in the mood to hook up, I'd take advantage of it. What man wouldn't? But Mallory, she wanted more, always more."

"So it works out for you now that she's dead? You wanted to break up and now your problem just rectified itself."

"I didn't kill her. I wasn't in Coyote Wells the entire weekend. I'm telling you, I was right here. I never left Crescent City after I made it back in time to start my shift Friday morning."

"Okay. I'll check out everything you've claimed. But if I find you've lied to me, about anything, I'll be back."

Billy's face went white at the threat. "Can I ask you something? How did she…uh…die?"

Lando looked into Billy's eyes. It was at that moment Lando knew Billy hadn't killed Mallory. "Someone beat her, and then strangled her."

"She suffered?"

"She did."

"She didn't deserve that."

"No, she didn't." Lando turned to go and then angled back. "What happened to your dog, the pit bull?"

"My dog?" Billy looked puzzled. "I let him wander through the woods too much I reckon. One night before I started this job he didn't come back. I haven't seen him since. That was about four weeks ago."

"Did you look for him?"

"Of course. I even went and grilled that old man who lives down the road from me, the one who got mad when Spike ate a couple of his chickens. I suspect he did something to my dog."

"Don't threaten anybody, Gafford. Okay? And don't go anywhere. Stay close where I can get in touch with you. In other words, don't decide to fly off to Jamaica at the last minute. I may have some more questions for you about Mallory. Routine stuff because you might hold the key to all this."

"Me?" Billy nervously swallowed hard. "Okay. Sure. But I don't have any vacation days coming to me to take off...anywhere. Uh, Chief? Thanks for letting me know...about Mallory. No one else bothered to call me."

"You bet."

On the drive back to Coyote Wells, Lando pondered Gafford's reaction to the news and his demeanor. The man seemed genuinely upset, but then most sociopaths could pull off acting normal when the situation warranted it. Even though Gafford's alibi had checked out, it didn't mean squat if the guys were simply covering for him. Which is why for now, he put Gafford on the back burner.

He took a side trip to the county morgue and pulled into the lot. Dr. Jeff Tuttle wasn't pleased to see him.

"Are you kidding me? I've had this body less than four hours and already you're bugging me. Get out of here."

"Bugging you is the highlight of my day," Lando sniped back. "Didn't you know that? I need to know if she was sexually assaulted."

"My assistant did a rape kit. But you'll have to give me longer than a few hours for results. Now get out of here and let me earn my pay."

"When do you think you'll have the full report?"

"Twenty-four hours for my opinion. Longer for the full lab report. Now go far, far away and bug someone else."

4

By that afternoon, the news about Mallory had traveled like wildfire, spreading to every corner, giving people a reason to gab.

Gab they did at Captain Jack's Grill. Mallory's death was the topic of discussion all through lunch. While that wasn't a surprise, everyone's reaction was.

Standing behind the grill, Leia Bonner couldn't believe how hard everyone seemed to be taking the news. Even the kidnapping and murders of Collette Whittaker and Marnie Hightower hadn't left this many people in shock. Not even the death of Marissa Sarrazin had caused such a buzz. And Marissa had been a defenseless elderly woman who'd been viciously attacked in her own garage.

As the eatery cleared out and people went back to work, Leia found herself getting angry over their response. What had been so special about Mallory Rawlins, a self-described bad girl with a penchant for deceit and lying and finding her way into trouble?

For as long as Leia could remember, Mallory Rawlins had been at odds with somebody---teachers, principals, and later, the law. Arrested for shoplifting at fourteen had only been the beginning but certainly not the end of Mallory's fondness for breaking rules. By using her position and considerable influence, Louise had always managed to yank her spoiled brat of a daughter back from the brink of spending time in prison. Whatever infraction Mallory committed---and the list was long---she always seemed to bypass doing jail time.

Mallory's death made Leia wonder what mess the woman had gotten mixed up in this time. Whatever it was had gotten her killed.

And the town seemed shocked? How was that possible?

Leia looked up to see Zebediah Longhorn, the tribal police chief on the Rez, stroll through the front door. Her main squeeze looked wrung out and worried.

"Want coffee?" she asked.

Zeb slid onto a stool at the counter, scrubbed both hands down his face. "I could use about a gallon."

"What's this? You're usually calm, cool, and collected. What's wrong?"

Zeb glanced around the room to make sure no one was listening. He didn't start talking until Leia appeared with the coffee in hand. Leaning closer, he shifted in his seat. "That's a loaded question. I've been hearing bits and pieces all morning about Mallory's death. Along with a lot of accusations regarding Gemma. None of it good or flattering."

"I know. I saw Gemma this morning before I opened up. She was taking Louise's allegations in stride. It's flat out ridiculous to think Gemma could kill anyone. But you want to hear what really pisses me off? I've been here all morning listening to customers act like the queen died or something. I didn't realize before today that Mallory was so popular or had such a following. They act like she was a saint or something. And we both know better."

"Yeah. Louise and her PR group are hitting the streets hard and heavy against Gemma. And get this. People around town are saying Lando is covering for her."

"Maybe we should get everyone together tonight and figure out a way to fight Louise on her own terms. She needs to know Louise's agenda will only get worse."

"Tonight's fine. But I have a better idea. Why don't we plan on spending an entire day out at the stables? Maybe this Sunday. We could ride horses into Shadow Canyon, like we used to do when we were kids."

"How's that a better idea?"

"We get Gemma's mind off all this and show her she has support in her corner."

Leia lifted a shoulder. "Sure. I guess it couldn't hurt. We haven't done that since we were sixteen."

"Okay then. We'll bring it up tonight at dinner and see what happens."

That evening, Gemma hosted supper at her house because Rufus seemed to be acting strange since finding Mallory's body that morning.

Gemma stood at the counter chopping cloves of garlic, then mincing them into tinier pieces. She dropped the little chunks into the simmering spaghetti sauce. "Look at those sad brown eyes. He hasn't been himself all day. He even whined when I started out the door this morning for work so obviously I couldn't leave him here by himself tonight."

Leia ruffled the dog's thin coat of fur. "He does look…peaked. He usually has a lot more energy."

"That's just it. He's been lethargic all day," Lianne added. "Ever since Gemma brought him in, all he seems to want to do is curl up in the corner of the shop. What do you think, Luke? Is he sick?"

Luke sent her a sidelong glance. "Doctor of people here. But I'd say he's depressed." Luke took hold of the pooch's muzzle, noticed it was wet. He checked the dog's eyes. "I'd say he's been crying."

Gemma left the stove to see for herself. "He's always been a sensitive little thing. Seeing Mallory like that…it was his first dead person. So of course he'd be upset and depressed."

Zeb walked over to the counter, picked up a chip and stuck it into the dip. "No one forgets their first DB. Am I right?"

Lando bobbed his head. "I had hoped that we wouldn't have to discuss this tonight. But hey, I also know it won't go away."

"Not any time soon," Luke said. "If what I'm hearing is any indication, Louise is determined to win over everyone to her way of thinking." Sensing they needed a change of topic for now, he sniffed the air. "That sauce is getting to me. When do we eat? I'm starving."

"I'll just give the pasta a quick stir," Lianne offered. "If that's okay with you, Gemma. You should stay with Rufus."

Gemma ran her hands around the dog's collar and felt Rufus shake a little bit. "Thanks. My mind's not really on the meal, is it? Sorry. I think I'll make an appointment for him tomorrow to go to the vet just to make sure nothing else is in play."

Lando got comfortable next to her on the floor. Sitting cross-legged, he held the dog's head in his lap. "Rufus is just sad is all. He'll be okay."

Luke snuck him a bite-sized treat out of the big doggie jar sitting outside the pantry. "He's gonna be fine."

"Pasta's ready," Lianne announced. "Luke, will you finish setting the table?"

Luke got up to get the plates but handed them off to Lando. "Do your part. Any word from the coroner? Did I get the time of death right?"

Lando took the plates and did as he was told. "I don't how you manage to do it, but yeah, you were right. Whoever killed Mallory did it sometime between ten and eleven o'clock. And it's Tuttle's opinion for now that she wasn't sexually assaulted."

"Then why didn't she have a stitch of clothes on?" Leia asked. "Did the killer not yet get around to it?"

"Maybe the killer was interrupted and ran off. Maybe he heard someone coming," Gemma suggested as she got to her feet. "Not me. The time of death pretty much lets me off the hook. Lando and I watched the fireworks at nine. That lasted about thirty minutes and then we ate the pot roast he brought home, and by ten o'clock we crawled back into bed. If you know what I mean."

Zeb traded looks with Leia. "You want to tell them?"

"Not really." Leia glanced at each face and then zeroed in on Gemma. "Louise is working overtime to make sure you look guilty. She's gone out of her way to tell everyone Lando's covering for you. And…rumor has it you put some kind of spell on Mallory and then killed her."

Gemma winced. "And people believe this crap? A spell? Really? I would have to be a witch to do that. Right about now I wish I could conjure up a cauldron and throw Louise into it. Hard to believe folks used to like me here."

"What about the carnival workers?" Lianne pointed out. "They were packing their stuff up between nine and midnight. Luke and I saw them after the crowds thinned out. By the time the fireworks kicked in the crowd had pretty much gone."

Zeb stuck a fork in his pasta. "I saw them breaking down the tents and hitting the road shortly after midnight. Lianne could be right. Maybe one of them killed Mallory before leaving."

"I'd already thought of that," Lando admitted. "I have a list of all the workers, plus the vendors. Payce and Jimmy spent the better part of the day tracking them all down. According to the carnival owner, everyone knows the drill after a festival ends. They immediately start breaking down the rides and gathering up their equipment in preparation to move on. It's like a well-organized machine. He says everyone was where they were supposed to be and ready to pull out by midnight. It doesn't mean one guy didn't stray from his assigned duties. It just means the carnival workers are down on the list."

"For now," Zeb added in between bites. "The thing is we don't let these allegations against Gemma take hold. Lando shouldn't be put in a position where he has to defend his…Gemma."

"I just found the body. I wish Rufus and I had never been out there. Look at my dog. He won't eat. He's depressed. He's…can't you see this has made him sick." She studied the table and realized something was wrong. "I forgot to set out the salad."

Gemma tried to act like everything would be okay by going to the fridge and taking out the Caesar salad she'd thrown together that afternoon, but her knees wanted to buckle. "Lianne and I figured Louise would try to turn the entire town against me. I just thought it would take longer than a day. I should've known better. I can't believe the same people who knew me as a kid are so easily fooled by Louise's claims. Why is that? Because now they treat me like an outsider. Me. For Pete's sake, I was born here, went to school here…lived here nineteen years."

She brought the bowl of salad over to the table, let out a huge sigh. "It's a shame, too. The shop was just starting to turn the corner as far as seeing a profit."

Lando walked up behind her and put his arms around her shoulders. "It's nothing we didn't expect and can't handle. We'll beat her at her own game. You'll see."

Leia gritted her teeth. "That's right. If you think the people in this room are going to stand by and let Louise win over public opinion, you don't know us very well."

"Damn straight," Lianne chimed in. "Louise doesn't get to dictate public opinion, especially when it's so damaging to your reputation and your career. It's not right."

Gemma looked around at her friends. "What would I do without you guys? Before you answer that, it means we all have to find out what happened to Mallory."

Lando and Zeb exchanged cop looks that spoke volumes. But it was Lando who cleared his throat. "You know how I feel about you interfering in an investigation. And this is a tricky one. I won't even bring up how you went around my back and talked to Gafford about

Marissa. Yeah. Duff confirmed it for me. That giant of a man could've had a screw loose and you confronted him on your own with no idea what you might be walking into without backup. Gafford is a wild card. I want you to steer clear of Mallory's homicide."

"Sounds to me like you have no problem bringing it up," Gemma countered as she plopped into a chair and gave Lando a death stare. "Since you just brought it up in front of everyone in the room, what exactly am I supposed to do? Sit idly by while Louise ruins me by spreading a bunch of lies she knows will hurt my business? This morning I thought I could just ride it out. But that won't work with Louise. She's a bully just like her daughter. I won't be bullied into losing the business Gram worked her ass off to keep going. I'm not going down without a fight."

Exasperated, Lando took a seat next to her. "Here's an idea. How about you let me do the fighting for you? By finding the killer my way."

Zeb cut his eyes to Lando in sympathy before going forward with his idea. "I had a thought that I wanted to run by you guys. I have several horses that need exercise. Some of their owners pay for boarding but don't seem that interested in coming out to ride them. Anyway, I was hoping this Sunday you could help me out with that. We could all go horseback riding up in Shadow Canyon. It'd be a good time to get away from all this crazy talk concerning Gemma."

"And I'd get to take Rudy for a ride," Lianne piped up. "I'm in."

"If she's in, then so am I," Luke added, dishing a pile of greens onto his plate. "We used to take horses up there all the time, especially during the spring. We'd cram picnic stuff into the saddlebags and stay out there all day."

Gemma looked at Lando. "I think it'd be a great way to spend the day. But you look like someone just punched you in the stomach. What's wrong?"

"Dale going out with Mallory. I can't get past it."

"You aren't letting him anywhere near the investigation, are you?" Zeb asked.

Lando sent him a cool stare. "I'm not a rookie at this. I warned him about keeping his distance from anything that had to do with Mallory."

"So what's bothering you then?" Gemma wanted to know.

"Dale doesn't have an alibi for Sunday night."

Gemma's eyes widened. "Oh, come on, you can't possibly think Dale killed her."

"I don't know what to think. When I talked to him I got the feeling he was holding something back. He downright denied having anything to do with it though."

"What a mess," Gemma said, glancing over at her dog. "Would you really fight for me?"

"What kind of a question is that? You know I would." Lando looked around the faces at the table. "Everyone here would. Louise won't win this war of words. Just promise me you'll stay out of Louise's line of fire. Don't antagonize the situation. Let me handle it."

"Okay, but if she comes after me, I won't just stand there and take it."

5

While Lando became consumed by the investigation, Gemma had to get her dog some help. Rufus was more than tired. He was listless and sleeping all the time.

The town veterinarian was Cheyenne Song, a woman with a bubbly personality to go with eight years of experience looking after an array of animals. Large or small, domestic or wild, Cheyenne treated them all the same---with tender, loving care and a gentle hand.

Raised in Great Falls, Montana, as part of the Little Shell Tribe of Chippewa Indians, she'd arrived in California as a sixteen-year-old prodigy to attend college at UC Davis. Because she adored animals, vet school had been a piece of cake. Thanks to her grades she'd been offered internships at a variety of top clinics, but settled on Coyote Wells because her father, a full-blooded Chippewa, was best friends with Dane Barstow, the vet here. Three years into her residency, Dane passed away after a hard-fought battle with lung cancer.

Cheyenne decided to stay on and keep the practice running. Grateful animal lovers rejoiced.

With a crop of coffee-brown hair that hung down her back in a long, layered cut, she could wrestle with a stubborn mastiff or a temperamental stray. It didn't matter. She could contain a feral cat without breaking a sweat. Cheyenne had a way with animals and everyone within a hundred miles knew it.

Her eyes were a piercing shade of green that sent out a confident vibe. She loved her job and proved it every day because she was the best at what she did and because everyone who worked for her gave off that same professional, confident demeanor.

Dr. Song's staff included a receptionist named Ebbie Lucas, who'd been with Dane Barstow from the beginning. Ebbie ran the office like a well-oiled machine, taking care of billing and all the things Dr. Song found boring. Ebbie had hired a competent tech nurse named Corkie Davenport, a newcomer to town with big-city experience from Oakland.

Ebbie had Gemma fill out a series of paperwork that the receptionist double-checked in detail, reading every answer to every question before getting a stamp of approval. "I see you haven't been in before. You're both from San Francisco and this is Rufus's first visit to see Dr. Song."

"It is. But I hear Dr. Song is the best vet around for fifty miles."

"More like a hundred," Ebbie boasted. "Dr. Song insists on not turning away new patients even though she's swamped. Some days she doesn't get out of here until eight o'clock at night."

"That's dedication," Gemma volunteered.

"We're all devoted to animals here," Ebbie added. "Take a seat. Corkie will be out in a jiffy to take you back."

After a fifteen-minute wait, a bubbly Corkie came to get them, instructing Gemma to guide Rufus onto an oversized weight scale in the hallway.

Gemma watched as her pooch sat obediently in place.

"Such a good dog," Corkie remarked. "And he's weighing in at seventy-seven pounds. Does that sound about right prior to moving here?"

"Maybe down three pounds or so, but then he hasn't been eating."

Corkie made the notation in the dog's chart. "He's in exam room five. Has he been having any other problems we should know about?"

"Not really. Not until recently." Gemma decided to hold back the dead body info for the doctor as she guided Rufus up a few steps onto the exam table. The goal was to make him feel more comfortable and less anxious, so she stroked his back and neck. "There you go, boy. It'll be okay. You'll see. It's just a checkup to make sure everything's okay. You aren't due for any shots so stop shaking."

Which prompted a smile from the tech. "I can always tell a true dog lover. We like to see concerned owners and you certainly fit that category. The doctor will be with you soon so just relax. Both of you."

"Easy for her to say," Gemma whispered. "Don't worry. We're in this together, pal."

After thirty minutes, Dr. Song came in with a wide smile on her face. Either she hadn't heard the rumors that Gemma was a card-carrying, spell-casting witch, or she didn't believe such nonsense because Dr. Song was downright friendly. Pulling up a stool, the doctor sat down and immediately went into a soothing routine using her voice to calm the frightened dog. "Hello there, Rufus. You should know I love labs. You're the best, aren't you? What seems to be your problem today?"

"You must be a dog whisperer. Look at that. He stopped shaking."

Dr. Song gave Rufus a hug. "Animals take to me."

"I can see that. You have such a calming aura about you. It doesn't hurt that you're absolutely gorgeous."

"Why thank you. What a nice thing to say when I've just come out of surgery."

"I like you," Gemma announced and went into how Rufus found the dead body. "He hasn't been the same since."

"That would be frightening for anyone. But tell me, have there been any other changes besides his eating habits? I see you haven't been in town for that long, just a few months. Do you think he's fully made the adjustment to his new surroundings?"

Gemma told her about the doggie door. "For some reason Rufus just doesn't like it. But other than that, he was fine until…you know, the beach and the body."

"Okay. Is he still playing with his same toys? Is he pooping the same? Doing the same routine things he's always done?"

Gemma leaned against the table, wrapping her arms around Rufus. "It all changed that morning."

"Hmm." Dr. Song felt the dog's throat and neck, checking for lumpy things. She shined a light in his eyes, looked in his ears. "This dog seems to be in perfect health. We'll take a specimen anyway to detect any parasites that he might've picked up. But I have to say, I really don't see any medical issues. He's even up to date on all his shots. You're a very responsible dog owner."

"I try. He takes vitamins. I buy him a top-of-the-line dog food. Like I said, he was fine until the…incident."

"Well, if he's still playing with his toys…"

Gemma's jaw dropped open as if she'd just thought of something. "Wait a minute. Oh. My. Now that I think about it, I haven't seen his sock monkey since Sunday night or rather Monday morning. That's his favorite. I mean Daffy is his backup, but he doesn't go anywhere without Mr. Monkey. The last time he had it was when I took him out to pee that morning." She chewed her lip. "I wonder…could he be missing that enough to completely shut down?"

Dr. Song smiled. "Could be. If Mr. Monkey is that important to him, it'd be like missing a part of him. But if you like, I'll look him over, draw some blood, and make sure he's got nothing else going on. I'd say he's out of sorts for a reason."

Gemma grimaced. "You're gonna draw blood? Is that absolutely necessary? Because I sort of promised him this visit would be needle-free. How about we do this? Could you hold off on all those tests until I locate the sock monkey? I mean, I'd hate for him to go through all that if he's just missing his favorite toy."

Dr. Song grinned again. "Sure. You call the office if he doesn't get any better. I'm here most days until eight."

"Absolutely."

Once they reached Gemma's Volvo, she headed straight to the beach, driving through town over the twenty-five-mile-per-hour speed limit. She parked across the street from Lando's house and got out, letting Rufus dash out of the car and down to the water's edge on his own. But Gemma stayed close behind. "I know you had it during the first part of our walk. But then when you spotted Mallory, you must've dropped it when you started barking. The spot's down here. Come on."

Rufus dashed off to the left, heading back around the bend where they'd found Mallory. Sure enough, the dog began to bark.

She spotted a light blue, fat piece of fabric lying between two sand dunes. Gemma watched as Rufus wasted no time snatching up a dirty and soggy sock monkey.

She winced at the condition of it---smelly and dirtier than ever. "It's amazing that I'm even considering letting you drag that thing into my car. Just know this, as soon as we get home it gets tossed into the washer. Don't look at me like that, sport. That thing smells like dead sardines."

A wave crashed on the rocks behind her. When she whirled at the sound, she caught an image---a brief snapshot in time---of Mallory fighting for her life, fighting with someone not very tall. As fuzzy and undefined as the image was, it caused her heart to race.

"What are you doing out here?" Lando asked, making Gemma jump.

She pivoted around to see him standing on a sandbank. "You scared me. We're here to retrieve Mr. Monkey."

Lando looked over and spied Rufus, his jaws locked around what seemed to be a bluish-gray, puffy sock. "So that disgusting object is Mr. Monkey?"

"In the flesh, so to speak. Uh, did you cross Gafford off your suspect list?"

"Not yet. I'm still checking his alibi but so far what he told me is on point."

Gemma didn't see any other way to work up to what she had to say so she blurted it out. "Mallory was arguing with someone that night, but it wasn't Billy Gafford."

Lando's brow crinkled like an old man's. "How do you know that?"

"I...uh...got a vision...just now. It didn't last long, no more than ten seconds."

Lando sighed and rubbed the back of his neck as if a pain refused to go away. He stood there staring out at the waves for several long minutes in silence. Finally he turned back to Gemma. "Don't take this the wrong way, but Sunday night the fog rolled in before we went to bed. It was clear during the first part of the fireworks. That's why they cut the show short. The fog began to roll in around nine forty-five. I checked with the weather service."

"And your point would be...what exactly?"

"I'm not saying you didn't see...someone...in your vision. I just wonder how you managed to see two people fighting when it was so foggy, so soupy that it was difficult to see the end of the pier."

Not surprised that he'd question her about it, she spun around to face him. "Still a skeptic, huh? Okay. Fine. The person I saw was much shorter than Gafford with a much different build, much slimmer with slightly longer hair...but still a short cut that came to the chin area." She stopped and frowned in thought. "And he might've been wearing some kind of pants other than jeans, khakis maybe."

That part of the description sounded legit. "Did you see anything else?"

She bit her lip. "No, not yet, but I intend to keep trying just like I did before when things were fuzzy."

He rocked back on his heels. "I'm not a skeptic, Gemma. It's just that…by nature, I'm a detailed person who notices the little things."

"Like what time the fog rolled in? I get that you have to ask because maybe the summer fog rolled in around the time she died. All I know is by two a.m., the marine layer had lifted. Unusual for this time of year? Maybe. I know for a fact it was breezy out and clear. I know because I could see the full moon so close it looked like I could reach up and touch it. Check that with the weather service and the Coast Guard."

"Look, I wasn't trying to make you mad. I think you should…keep at it…the vision. Your seeing McIntire and Bernal bury Collette broke the case wide open. If I've learned anything it's that you have a knack. If there's anything I can do to help you *see* more, let me know."

Her face broke out into a wide grin that transformed her mood. She threw her arms around his neck. "I'll do that. What do you have planned for this afternoon?"

"Not much. I'm helping Zeb out with a problem over on the Rez."

"It's good to see you two bonding after spending so many years competing with each other."

Lando found that amusing. "Is that what we're doing? Bonding? Since it seems he and Leia are really serious about each other---as in heading to the altar one day---the last thing I want to be is a problem."

"According to Leia, it seems his parents have made a complete U-turn from the dark side like they'd hoped. Apparently, the Longhorn family wants to support their son's decision. Imagine that. With a mother like mine, that's either a freaking miracle or a Hallmark card."

"We could've used some of that."

"Tell me about it. Is Fortitude still on the bill for Saturday night at the Duck & Rum?"

"Sure. Why? You aren't backing out, are you?"

"Nope. But I'd like to add a few songs from this Canadian singing duo I have on my iPhone. There's one song in particular I'd like you to hear. We could rehearse at my house tonight."

"Is that a euphemism for fool around?"

She linked an arm through his. "It could be, *if* you play your cards right. Tell me something. Why did you never teach me to play guitar? As much as you were around my house, you never once tried to teach me."

Lando looked taken aback. "Probably because you never showed the slightest interest. Besides, that wasn't our thing---you liked to sing, and I accompanied you on guitar."

"Yes, but I've rethought those piano lessons. I want you to help me pick out a guitar."

"You don't need to do this, Gemma."

"I want to, unless you think I have no talent for it."

He pressed a kiss to her lips. "Gemma, you're a natural. Are you asking me to be your teacher?"

"I could ask Jimmy or Bosco, but what would be the point. You're better than they are."

"Now you're just flattering me."

"Is it working?"

He grinned. "Doesn't it always?"

"So when is my first lesson?"

He blew out a sigh. "All right. Before heading to your place tonight, I'll stop and grab my guitar."

Glad to have her dog back in high spirits, she headed back to the shop. With a happy dog in tow, Gemma figured she should return the favor. The staff at Dr. Song's office deserved a huge box of chocolates. That way, they'd all know how much Gemma appreciated their work with animals.

Like a whirlwind, she entered through the front door practically walking on air.

Lianne was behind the counter helping Suzanne Swinton pick out candies to put on her husband's birthday cake.

Suzanne chatted with Lianne like she'd known her for years. "I thought what I'd do is put the candle down in each piece of chocolate. Buddy has such a sweet tooth now that he's given up drinking. Who knew he'd do that to save our marriage. I sure didn't. I thought for sure we were a lost cause."

"That's great news, Suzanne, congratulations," Gemma offered as she started picking out an assorted array of chocolates and lining them up in a bright red carton for Dr. Song. "Be sure to wish Buddy a happy birthday from Coyote Chocolate."

"Oh, I will. And don't worry. Buddy and I don't believe a single word that comes out of Louise's mouth. Not since her daughter tried to make a move on my Buddy when we were taking a break."

"She didn't?" Gemma said, looking shocked.

"I'm telling you that hussy moved on him the same afternoon we split up. Can you believe that? Let me tell you everybody knows that woman was an S-L-U-T. Big time. Anybody says different, they're lying through their teeth. And I'm not spreading a single rumor that isn't God's honest truth, am I right? Everybody in town knows that woman would sleep with anything wearing pants."

"Suzanne's not wrong," Lianne chimed in with a grin. "Deep down people know what Mallory was like."

Ecstatic to know she was getting through, Suzanne went on, "You know that old saying, you can't make a silk purse out of a sow's ear?"

"What does that even mean anyway?" Gemma asked.

Lianne nodded. "I've always wondered about that, too."

"I'll tell you what it means. You can't ever expect anything good to come from a naturally evil thang like Mallory Rawlins. Mallory fit that saying to a tee."

"No argument there," Gemma said as she finished packing up Dr. Song's care package. "I gotta run an errand. You tell Buddy I'm throwing in an extra half-dozen, milk chocolate bonbons covered in almonds especially for him."

"You're the best, Gemma," Suzanne gushed. "Do you have plans tonight? Because if you don't, Buddy and I would love to have you both come to his blowout party."

"Oh, that's so sweet, Suzanne, but Lando's coming over tonight for supper and I've already committed to the menu."

"Too bad," Suzanne said, quickly shifting her focus to Lianne. "What about you?"

"Uh, same thing. I'm fixing dinner for my guy."

"Well, maybe another time then. Let's make a point to get together before summer's over for a barbecue."

A barbecue, thought Gemma as she dashed out the door. She didn't really have the menu planned for tonight. She felt bad about lying to Suzanne, but she didn't care to spend an evening listening to the couple's bickering, which even during a reconciliation could get ugly. That said, she wished the Swintons well.

Gemma swung open the door to Dr. Song's clinic, and spotted Ebbie sitting behind her computer on the telephone.

Ebbie looked up, surprised to see Gemma back so soon. Once Ebbie ended her phone call, she frowned. "What's wrong with Rufus?"

"Not a thing. He found his sock monkey, and all is right with the world again. Here. These are for all of you. Just my way of saying thanks for being so great with Rufus." Gemma set the bright red and gold box on the counter and opened the lid. "Chocolates make a great pick-me-up in the afternoon. They also go great with a cup of strong espresso in the morning. Enjoy."

"Well, isn't that sweet of you," Ebbie cooed, turning from all business to a woman delighted about receiving a gift. Getting to her feet to retrieve the box, she took out a truffle. "What's this one?"

"I think that's Aztec Delight, a little on the spicy side, but not fiery enough to worry about."

After one sample, Ebbie's eyes closed, letting the flavor sink in. "Oh my, that's good. I mean really good. I needed this to get through the afternoon."

Corkie came up behind Ebbie and reached over to get a chocolate coconut cream for herself. One bite and her lips curved. "Delicious. What about that one?" she asked pointing to another.

"Nougat filling with caramel and sea salt."

Corkie picked it up, bit into the soft shell. "Oh, that's wonderful, creamy. You make these all the time?"

"Every day," Gemma said, her face breaking into a proud grin at their reaction. For once, sheer pride in her work ran through her veins from head to toe. "Don't forget to save some for Dr. Song."

"She'd better hurry up and get out here otherwise there won't be any left," Corkie warned. "Trust me, these will be gone before we go home. Better if I go take the box back. Want to wait?"

"No, I've got to get back to the shop. You guys enjoy. And don't be strangers. Stop by the store any time."

"Thanks. We will," Corkie promised.

6

Gemma got home from work in time to throw together one of her favorite summertime meals---her grandmother's pasta salad. Gram always served it with grilled corn on the cob and veggies. Tonight, she planned to roll out the barbecue grill and try her hand at cooking outdoors.

She'd surprise Lando with a picnic in the backyard under the stars. What better way to begin guitar lessons than having a light meal and spending a summer evening outside.

Skewering veggies to a stick was her specialty. She alternated cremini mushrooms, slices of cut red pepper, green and yellow zucchini, and purple onion chunks until she had one complete kabob. After repeating the process three more times, she started on the marinade, a simple olive oil base with a healthy dose of fresh lemon juice and minced garlic tossed in for texture, topped off by sprinkling sea salt and ground black pepper into the mix.

At five o'clock she rolled the grill around to the back patio and texted Lando. *Got an ETA yet?*

She waited for a response, but when nothing came back a feeling of dread washed over her. She tried to tell herself this was what it was like being married to a cop, a cop who was always out there putting his life on the line every single day without fail.

But by five-thirty that stalwart notion began to fade. She tried to fight off the sinking feeling in the pit of her stomach that something was wrong. It wasn't like Lando to ignore her texts.

When the doorbell rang, relief spread through her entire body but that only lasted until she answered the door.

Zeb stood on the cobbled brick pavement, his brown eyes trying to hide the reason he was there.

"What's wrong? Where's Lando?"

Zeb reminded himself that bad news was like ripping off a Band-Aid, better if done all at once. "There was a shooting. He's okay. But he wanted me to come and get you."

"If he's okay, why isn't he here? Why didn't he call himself?"

"Luke's with him at the hospital."

"Hospital? Is he in surgery?"

"Not yet. But they might be taking him in shortly to get the bullet out of his shoulder."

Gemma felt like someone punched her in the gut. "Bullet? Let me grab Rufus, then plan to get me there as fast as you can."

"That's the idea. You should know that it's my fault, Gemma. I'm the reason he got shot."

"Oh, Zeb. I'm sure that's not true."

She hurriedly grabbed Rufus, encouraging him to hop into the back seat of Zeb's squad car. Once she'd settled into the passenger seat, Zeb zoomed off in the direction of the hospital.

"Why do you think it's your fault?"

"Because I asked him to go with me to serve a protection order on Ben Akin, a guy who's been dodging me for a week. His wife was getting antsy that we weren't doing anything to get the restraining order in his hands, so I asked Lando to be my backup so that if Akin ran out the back door, we'd have his apartment covered."

"And this Akin had a gun?"

"A little twenty-two pistol that wasn't listed in the complaint. Akin high-tailed it out the back door just as I thought he'd do, but when he spotted Lando, he already had that pistol out and fired. Got Lando in the shoulder. I reached the backyard as soon as I could, but Lando had already hit the dirt. I'm not sure how he did it, but he managed to get to that Colt Commander he carries and stopped Akin cold."

"Lando shot Akin?"

"Yeah. The good news is Akin won't be beating anybody else up or trying to kill them with a gun, least of all his wife any time soon."

Zeb pulled up to the emergency room entrance and turned in his seat to stare at Gemma. "I'm sorry. I really am."

She squeezed his hand. "We'll talk about this later. Right now, I need to go see about Lando. But I'll say this here real fast. Stop blaming yourself, okay? Just stop it. It wasn't your fault or anyone else's except Akin's. Now, if you're staying in the car with Rufus, make sure he behaves himself. That goes for both of you."

With that, Gemma opened the car door and made a beeline through the double doors. At the receptionist desk, she called out so everyone nearby could hear her. "I'm looking for police chief Lando Bonner, gunshot wound."

"Are you family?" a stout nurse asked.

"Yes." She held up her left hand with the moonstone ring on it, hoping the nurse would take that as enough evidence to let her through.

For half a second, the nurse looked skeptical, but finally bobbed her head toward a curtain at the far end of the hallway. "His mother and sister are with him."

Gemma pulled back the curtain and spotted Lydia dabbing her eyes and a concerned Leia standing in the corner, arms folded across her chest.

Her focus turned to a gray-faced Lando lying in a sea of hospital white sheets.

"How is he?" she asked Luke. But he was leaning over his brother, a stethoscope attached to his ears, listening to a heartbeat or checking vitals. Either way, it didn't look good. Waiting for an answer seemed like an eternity until Luke glanced over at Gemma.

"The gang's all here now," Luke said in sing-song fashion. He straightened his back. "He's gonna be fine. It's just a scratch."

Gemma shook her head and reached out for Lando's hand. "Zeb said surgery. They wouldn't be doing surgery for just a scratch."

"Yeah? Well Zeb didn't go to medical school, now did he?" Luke quipped. He winked at his brother. "Tell her you're fine."

Lando squeezed Gemma's fingers. "Zeb overreacted. Luke's right. The bullet just grazed my shoulder. Akin was a lousy shot. I'll be out of here by tonight."

"No surgery?" Gemma finally let out the tight breath she'd been holding, her lungs finally able to work. She pressed her lips to his, then whispered in his ear, "You'd better be. I had tonight all planned out. Looks like now we'll have to go easy."

"Define easy."

"Uh-uh. I think your blood pressure might skyrocket and then they'd have a reason to hold you longer. Face it, for the rest of the evening you're gonna be all mine, Chief."

With her bravado at a premium, she wanted the truth and turned to Luke for answers. "What gives? I see the bandage on his left shoulder. It isn't exactly a Band-Aid, so will they really let him go home tonight after getting shot?"

Luke flashed his pearly whites at his brother. "I told you she wouldn't fall apart. Chief Bonner is getting released as soon as he signs his paperwork. He wouldn't let a little thing like a bullet nicking his arm keep him chained to a hospital bed, not when he can go home to his girl." He pivoted to Gemma. "I trust you to keep him from doing anything strenuous."

"Party pooper," Gemma good-naturedly muttered. "I'll do my best. But not before I kill Zeb for scaring me half to death."

"Get in line," Leia grumbled. "Zeb had Mom and me thinking the worst. We locked up the restaurant and ran out of there like the place was on fire. We had to push old man Cathcart out the door. I don't think he believed us. He's probably still there in the parking lot waiting for the fire department to show up."

Zeb stood in the doorway with a hangdog look on his face. "I'm sorry. I wasn't sure how bad it was. I was just trying to let everyone know and get them here."

Immediately contrite, Leia pulled him through the doorway. "It's okay. You did the right thing. It's not your fault Mom drove like she was in a race at Daytona to get here."

"I only ran two stop signs," Lydia fired back. "Any mother would've done the same thing."

An hour later, after Luke had given her a packet of bandages and instructions on how to treat the wound at home, Gemma wheeled Lando to the curb to where Zeb waited in his cruiser.

Gemma leaned down near Lando's ear and asked, "Decision time, big guy. Your place or mine? What's it gonna be?"

"I thought you said you had the evening planned out."

"I did. But I understand if you'd be more comfortable at your own place…"

"I'm comfortable wherever you are."

Zeb drove them back to Gemma's place, still apologizing.

Sitting in the passenger seat, Lando rubbed his temple. "Give it a rest, Zeb. I'm serious. How many times have we backed each other up now? Getting shot is one of the everyday risks that go with the job. We both know the dangers."

"Yeah, but Leia read me the riot act and told me never again to ask."

"Do you do everything Leia says?" Lando challenged. "I'll set her straight on that score. We're each other's backup, now and forever. Enough already. It could've just as easily gone the other way and you know it."

"But I asked you to cover the back."

"You did and Akin could just as easily have charged past you. I think he was on some kind of PCP or maybe angel dust. Something. Did you get a look at his crazy eyes?"

"Not while he was alive. Maybe he wanted you to do what you did. You know, death by cop. He wasn't happy about his wife filing for divorce."

Lando scowled into the sun. "All I know is we both have very inexperienced staff to count on in a crunch, a force that doesn't exactly bring to mind confidence. That's why we look after each other in situations we know might turn serious."

"Now see," Gemma began from the back seat. "That right there makes me feel better knowing you're looking after each other. Personally, I'm not even sure Jimmy, Dale, or Payce could have handled an Akin."

"See?" Lando said. "I don't want to hear any more apologies, Zeb. Got it?"

"I guess," Zeb muttered. "I'm just grateful you're able to sit here and lecture me."

"I'll do more than that if you bring it up again. I'll kick your ass first chance I get," Lando countered.

"You and what army?" Zeb fired back.

"Boys, could we just focus for ten seconds here? Want to stay for dinner?" Gemma asked Zeb. "I have plenty."

"No, but thanks. You two make a night of it. I have to go write up my report on Akin."

Lando opened the car door, ready to bolt to get away from the situation. "You need me to fill in the blanks, give me a call."

Gemma settled Lando in the backyard and started the grill. She put the corn on first, letting it simmer in aluminum foil filled with melted butter. Then she put on the kabobs, searing them on each side enough to still crunch.

"That smells good."

"You're okay with all veggies? I wasn't sure."

"You should know better. I love your pasta salad. It's a meal on its own. The corn and shish kabobs are a nice bonus, though."

"I just hope you can manage the corn with one hand. Should I spoon feed you? With all the pain meds they gave you, you're a little shaky."

"I certainly won't turn down your help."

Gemma sat down and dished both plates high before hauling a forkful into Lando's mouth. "What did Luke mean back at the hospital when he said he knew I wouldn't fall apart?"

Mouth full, Lando had to finish chewing before answering. "The truth? I wasn't sure you'd still want to be with me knowing what happened. I was afraid knowing I got shot might mean you'd decide that you didn't want to be with a cop."

She took his hand. "Oh, Lando. For a smart man, you're really dumb sometimes. I love you, cop and all. Don't you understand that? What concerns me right this minute is how you're coping after…after killing a man. Are you…okay?"

"It's never an easy thing to live with, especially over something as trivial as serving a restraining order. If Akin had simply taken it, accepted it, he'd still be alive tonight and able to see his kids at some point in the future. Now it's a forever decision he made when he ran."

Realization hit Gemma. "That wasn't your first time, was it?"

"No."

"Okay, change of subject, unless you want to talk about it."

"Do you want me to?"

"Totally up to you."

"Then no, I'd rather not."

While they ate, stars glittered overhead as nightfall spread out like a cozy blanket around them. Cicadas came out to join the crickets in a lazy serenade. A few frogs warbled their way into the chorus.

They finished their meal with Lando almost nodding off.

"Why don't I help you to bed? I'll come back later and do the dishes."

'I do feel sleepy."

"Demerol does that," she cracked as she helped him into the bedroom. After turning down the comforter, she helped him kick off his shoes, unbuttoned his shirt, and tugged off his jeans as he teetered on the edge of the bed like a drunk. She gave him a little shove into the stack of pillows and watched him fall back in a stupor. She tucked him in like a four-year-old, but doubted he'd even remember. Before she'd even left the room, he was out, snoring like a seasoned lush.

But she didn't feel like going to bed at eight o'clock. Something Suzanne had said earlier that day kept rolling around in her brain. She had to call Leia for confirmation.

"Can you talk? I mean I know it's almost closing time, but...I really need to know if you can remember all the guys Mallory has gone out with over the years, enough to put a list together."

"Now? You're kidding. That would take hours, maybe days."

"Then what about your mom? Would she be able to come up with a list like that?"

"Are you kidding? Mom knows all the dirt on everyone, names, dates, and she never forgets a face."

"Then I'll call her. Sorry I bothered you."

"No, that's okay. How's Lando doing?"

"Painkillers kicked in. I promise you he's sleeping like an adorable infant."

Leia snorted into the phone. "I'll have to take your word for that. I didn't know my brother was ever an adorable anything, least of all an infant. Look, I gotta run. Mr. Cathcart thinks we owe him a free dessert because we shoved him out the door. Go figure."

"Give him that two-day-old tiramisu I saw in the fridge the other day. That'll make him think twice about becoming a pest."

"Good thinking. A great way to pawn off the whole thing."

As soon as they hung up, Gemma punched in the number for Lydia. Fortunately, Lando's mom was full of useful information. They put together a list of Mallory's lovers and made up a list of questions about Mallory's life in general.

After ending the call, she went out to the backyard to gather up their dishes from the picnic table. Rufus ambled up, shoving his nose into her leg for some attention.

She sat down on the bench to rub his ears. "Things are getting complicated now, Rufus. We found a dead body and Lando got shot on the job. What are we going to do? I wanted to fall apart before I got to the hospital. But I didn't. I held it together and got kudos from Lando and Luke for my valor."

Tears streamed down her face as she put Rufus in a bear hug. "Little do they know I'm a phony. What if we'd lost him? What if he...? I couldn't handle it. Now I know exactly how Gram must've felt after losing Poppy. It must've felt like her heart had been ripped out manually to let him go."

Rufus whined and licked her face. "That's right, boy. From here on out, I'll be a rock. We both will. I'll be the best wife a cop has ever had in the history of cops. And you'll be the best dog. 'Course you're already the best dog in the world, aren't you?"

They sat there under the stars, breathing in the sea air.

The pep talk kept her from a torturous worry fest and gave her the incentive to finish the dishes before heading to bed.

She got undressed in the dark, then crawled beneath the covers, scooting as close to Lando as possible. Resting her head on his good shoulder meant she could watch him sleep. If she ran her hand over his chest, she could feel his heart beat, an affirmation that they still had a chance to make their life wonderful. If he'd survived a shooting, anything was possible.

Falling in love with him all over again was a glorious thing. A tune popped into her head from a high school talent show they'd once done together. She began singing, ever so softly into his ear the words to "Songbird."

She was still humming the tune as she drifted off to sleep, content that the man she loved was Lando Bonner.

7

Lando woke in a fog, blurry-eyed from the heavy dose of Demerol. Somewhere his phone kept dinging again and again with a string of text messages. His hand fumbled getting to the nightstand, trying to reach the off button to shut off the device before it woke Gemma. He picked it up, only to see that all the texts were from the same person, Jeff Tuttle.

Victim Rawlins: Sexual assault still up in the air. Found DNA underneath nails. Fought and scratched the person who attacked her. Lab results still pending for another week, maybe longer. No need to bug me today because I can't hurry them along.

Lando sat up and tried to clear his brain. Rolling to his left side brought pain to his shoulder and a reminder that less than twenty-four hours ago Ben Akin had tried to end his life with a .22. His quick reflexes had saved him, but left behind nasty scorched flesh where the bullet had seared his upper arm.

On the other side of the bed, Gemma struggled to come awake. Her cell phone kept trilling; the noisy device repeated the alert four or five times before she rolled over to put a stop to it. Sweeping a section of hair out of her eyes, she read the message. "I don't believe this. Luke sent me five texts to remind me to change your bandage, as if I didn't have the sense to do that."

Lando looked down at his arm and ripped off the tape and gauze. "There. Problem solved."

"What'd you do that for?" Gemma asked, scooting across the sheets to get a better look at the damage and inspect the wound for herself. "Lando, this looks awful. You can see the path the bullet took right through your skin."

He ignored her concern and nibbled the side of her jaw. "It's no big deal."

"It is," she countered as she bounced off the bed and headed into the bathroom. "Luke must've thought it was important."

She scoured the medicine cabinet for peroxide and Neosporin, and then grabbed one of the large bandages Luke had sent home with her.

She came back out in nurse-mode, hands full, and plopped down at the edge of the bed to work her magic. "I see now what your brother was worried about. It's red and puffy and oozing. This could leave an ugly scar. Is this the first time you've been shot?"

"I got nicked one other time on the leg by a drug addict strung out on heroin. He was shaking so bad his aim was way off. And Payce tasered me once when we were trying to arrest a drunk down at the pier."

"Tasered you? No wonder you and Zeb need each other." She took his chin. "Thank goodness for drug addicts with lousy aim. What does my patient want for breakfast?"

"You mean after a hot shower? I'd love an omelet with ham and cheese."

"Your wish is my command. Just try not to get your owie wet, though."

Before she could dash off, he grabbed her hand. "Maybe you should join me in the shower and supervise. I dreamed last night you were singing to me."

"That's because I was."

"*Songbird*. Why don't you help me get undressed, songbird?"

For an answer, she yanked his boxers down and led him to the walk-in shower. "God, you're gorgeous."

"That might be a first. I don't think I've ever heard you say that to me before."

She kissed his mouth, a deep, soul-rendering lip lock that ignited a fire. "From now on, we'll make love twice a day."

It finally dawned on him what had changed. "Maybe I should get shot…"

She put her fingers to his lips to stop him from finishing. "Don't say that. Don't even think that. I love you with all my heart. Don't take that away from me now, not after I fully understand how precious you are to me."

"I'm not going anywhere."

"No. You definitely are not. Not for at least twenty minutes."

Forty-five minutes later, she broke eggs into a bowl, and walked him through her evening. "I had a long talk with your mother last night."

"About my getting shot?"

"Although that topic did make its way into the conversation, it wasn't the main reason I called her. After talking to Suzanne Swinton yesterday, it occurs to me that Mallory had a constant string of men in her life. That should be your starting point. Not that I'm trying to tell you how to conduct your investigation or anything."

"Of course not," Lando said, giving her an effective eye roll.

"Hey, I'm just trying to help you while taking the heat off me. Your mother and I stayed up late last night comparing notes. One thing we couldn't figure out is what exactly Mallory did to make a living. What was her main source of income? Who did she work for? Lydia didn't know the answer to that any more than I did."

"Huh? I know Louise mentioned she was a pharmaceutical rep for a while until she got fired for selling the samples."

"Jeez. What other jobs did she have? I mean I haven't seen her work since I've been back. Lydia says she had plenty of money to blow around town at the bars, but never seem to be able to hold a job. Where did she get her money, Lando?"

"Beats me."

"So that'd be something else to check into. Lydia and I also put together a list of Mallory's...relationships. Lydia was able to come up with most of the men in town who knew her in the...biblical sense."

Lando chuckled. "My mother did that?"

"Yep. Over the years, she's seen Mallory drag a string of dates into the restaurant so often to eat and drink that it's a regular thing. Or was." Gemma handed him the list.

Lando perused the names. "Holy crap, this is every guy in town. And not all of them are single."

"Bingo. Married guy trying to hide his deceit might be a motive for murder."

"Could Mallory have been blackmailing some of these men?"

"Now you're getting on board."

"Mom even came up with the year Mallory went out with them."

"Not as precise as she wanted it to be, but close enough to start asking questions of said date. I believe that would fall into the category of old-fashioned police work."

Lando pressed a kiss to her lips. "I would've gotten around to digging into Mallory's personal life at some point, but this makes it so much easier. Thank you."

"No problem. Like I said, it's self-serving. Maybe when you go poking into her personal life, Louise will cut me some slack and keep her trap shut. Are you aware that yesterday she told sweet little Angela Fisher that I'm a witch who can put spells on people? Angela came into the store and asked me to conjure up a potion to get even with Tristan Phillips for calling her a bad name. Angela's twelve. Louise keeps telling anyone she sees that I'm a witch. And yes, you heard right. That's with a W not a B, a B I could live with, but labeling me a witch is just nuts. She's ruining my business."

"I plan on having a talk with her about that."

"It won't do any good, Lando. Louise will deny everything and blame it on her friends, who obviously have a grudge against me. I don't care for myself. I just don't want to have to let Lianne go."

"Are things that bad?"

"Not yet. That's why I'm trying not to reach that point."

"I thought the online website had increased sales?"

"It has. Twofold. Just not enough to cover overhead and expenses in the long run. Look, Lianne isn't going anywhere if I can help it. I just need to increase walk-in traffic. The sad part is I can't even count on people I've known for most of my life to help me out on that score."

With his good arm, he took her hand. "We'll think of something to turn things around."

"Are you going to work today?"

"Sure. Why wouldn't I?" He grabbed her around the waist. "You have something better planned?"

"I wish. Unfortunately, I have to go make decadent chocolate delicacies that no one wants to buy. I can give them away for free, but when they're for sale…"

"It's gonna work out, Gemma. I swear it will."

"We should probably put some effort into picking out the songs for the playlist for Saturday night. I wanted to run a couple by you by Whitehorse." She reached over and unlocked her iPhone, scanned the music library until she found what she wanted. "Canadian band, husband and wife singing duo. She has a great voice. He rocks guitar."

The rhythm and vocals for the song "Emerald Isle" filled the kitchen.

"I like."

"I thought you might."

"I'll get the band on board for a rehearsal Friday night."

"Is that enough time?"

"A couple of run-throughs and we should be fine. We aren't exactly playing the Hollywood Bowl." Checking his watch, he drained his coffee cup. "I need to take care of some stuff before getting to work."

"Will you be okay?"

"I'll be fine."

"Be careful out there, Quickdraw. Try staying out of the line of fire."

He kissed her with an intensity he hadn't felt since he was eighteen, making it last as long as he could before he had to go. "I'm always careful, don't cha know." He ran a thumb down her jaw. "Promise me you'll stop worrying about Louise."

"Why do you say that?"

"Because it's past time I did my job."

To make good on that promise his first stop was Claude Mayweather's ranch-style house.

For such a pretty summer morning it was a shame to start his workday off in such a fiery mood, but it couldn't be helped. Fact was, it was way overdue.

Peanut started barking before Claude ever opened the door.

"Hey, Chief, what's up?"

"I'm gonna ask you straight out and I want the truth. Did Louise tell you who she thought killed her daughter?"

Claude shuffled his feet and dropped his eyes before clearing his throat. "She thinks Gemma Channing did it, told me so within the first few minutes after you told her Mallory was dead."

"And did she ask you to make sure everyone else thought so, too?"

Claude nodded. "Well, sure. Gemma's the one who found the body. You tried to alibi her. Seems you've been compromised, Chief."

"No, I haven't, Claude. And that's what's pissing me off, that you think I have. Gemma didn't murder Mallory. I have the forensic evidence to back that statement up. You push me on this and I guarantee I'll push back. Hard. Stop the negative crap, Claude. Today. It ends today. Are we clear?"

"Gemma didn't murder Mallory?"

"No."

"Louise is wrong?"

"How many ways do I need to say it, Claude?"

"Okay, okay. I'll keep my mouth shut from now on out."

"You'd better tell the rest to keep their remarks to themselves as well. Or do I need to make my next stop Janet Delgado's place?"

"No, no, I'll take care of Janet."

"Good. I'm on my way to see Louise now. But if I have to come back here, Claude, I'm digging into your little group…digging into motive, putting you guys at the top of my suspect list because now I have to start wondering why you're spreading these malicious lies. Is it to cover up for someone in your group? See where I'm going with this?"

Claude's face turned white. "Yes, sir. I mean, no, no need to do that, Chief. I'll end this smear campaign now. I promise."

"You do that."

The Rawlins home was two blocks over. Lando pulled up to the curb and walked up to the little stoop. Holly answered the door still wearing her robe. "Is Louise here?"

"She's planning Mallory's funeral. Can I give her a message?"

"I'm not going anywhere, Ms. Dowell, not until I talk to Louise. I understand this is a difficult time for both of you, but…I need to straighten some things out. Today. Now."

"Let him in, Holly," Louise said from the end of the hallway. "What is it you want, Chief?"

Lando stepped into the foyer and didn't waste time getting to the point. "I want you to stop telling people that I'm covering for Gemma. You know it isn't true. I also want you to stop building a case against her. Stop spreading these vicious lies. Don't deny you're using your friends to do it either because I know better and I have proof. I've spoken to Claude."

"What if I am? I can't stop people from talking. Claude, too. And you can't do anything about it either."

"I can. And I will. You keep this up and you can look for another job. Over the years, you've racked up a list of complaints against yourself as long as my arm. This is an official warning. If you don't knock off these ugly things you're telling people about Gemma, if you don't put an end to it today, you're gone."

"You can't fire me over that, I'll go straight to the mayor. Fleet will reinstate me."

"Go ahead. Contact him. You have a very short memory, Louise. Fleet's one of those people who've been after me for years to get rid of you because of your abrasive attitude. And don't even try to get away with this crap by pushing it off on your sister, or anyone else. I know what you're trying to do. What I don't know is why. Maybe this is more than your hatred for Gemma. But I'll get to the bottom of it, eventually, even if it takes me into next week. For starters, I just spoke to Claude and he's calling Janet. Keep accusing Gemma, and I'll continue down the line with all your other friends until I've uncovered your real reason, the real point to all these accusations. You end this today or you're done working for Coyote Wells PD."

"Fine. But the truth will come out. And when it does, Gemma will go down."

"The truth? I'm not sure you'd recognize it. I have evidence from Jeff Tuttle that rules Gemma out completely. She was with me when Mallory was killed. I told you that Monday morning and you refused to believe it then. But you know what I think, Louise? I think you're *afraid* of the truth. You're afraid of the *real* story coming out why your daughter was killed. You know everything Mallory was into and you're afraid if you don't divide the town now you'll face public ridicule this time around. It'll be so embarrassing for you that you'll have to take drastic steps to save your reputation. Instead, you'd rather take the lead and blame Gemma than deal with the truth."

Louise slumped down on the bench in the entryway. "You'd really fire me?"

"Yeah. I would. But not to protect Gemma or anyone else. Ever since I took over this job from Caulfield, you've been an outspoken critic of mine. Didn't think I knew about that, did you? I've known it from the start, every lousy thing you've ever accused me of, or Payce or Jimmy or Dale, people have confronted me about it wherever I go in town. We're seven years into this, Louise, and our relationship is barely tolerable. From eight in the morning until you leave at five, you're a drain on department morale. I'm done looking the other way. I should've let you go seven years ago. But now when I look at you I see what I've been reluctant to see. There's something sinister about you, Louise, something off. It finally hit me this morning. If you're that unwilling to hear the truth about what really happened to your daughter that you'd make something up just to hurt someone else you've never liked, then I don't need you in my department. Not now. Not ever."

"So is that it? After working there for almost thirty-four years---I started when I was twenty---you won't give me another chance?"

"Would it do any good?" Lando asked. "Don't pretend I haven't asked you every year at review time to change your attitude. Where did it get me? You flew out of my office in a rage, headed to Thackery's Pub down at the wharf, and began to bitch and moan about how badly you'd been treated. You thought all those times I wouldn't find out? Nothing much happens here that doesn't get back to me one way or another. You and I both know this is nothing new. So don't pretend it is. I ignored it and that's on me. So here we are at the crossroads. Maybe it's time for you to walk away on your own, with your pension intact, and on your own terms. Otherwise, I'll put in the termination paperwork this afternoon."

Louise began to sob, "I'm sorry. I was just so upset about Mallory. She was my whole world. I lashed out at Gemma because she was still alive, and Mallory was gone."

Lando ran with the fake tears and turned it around on his dispatcher. "Sounds like you really are messed up. You should probably go see Dr. Rennick, the county shrink, before you retire. In fact, I insist on it."

"So you're forcing me out the door."

"This is your out, Louise. I suggest you take it. Retire and I won't fire you. It's your choice."

Lando glanced at Holly as he turned to leave. "Try talking some sense into your sister and see if you can convince her to keep her big mouth shut until I get to the bottom of this investigation. Do you think you can handle that?"

Speechless, Holly Dowell simply nodded.

"Great. Go finish your plans for the funeral."

8

Even though a few new customers had found the shop---Dr. Song had stopped in twice to replenish chocolates at the behest of her staff---by the end of the week Gemma could tell Louise's tactics had already taken their toll. Some of Gemma's regulars were keeping their distance.

"I hope you don't have to lay me off," Lianne lamented.

The statement made Gemma bobble the bowl she held. It was one thing to admit defeat to Lando, quite another to admit it to Lianne. These days, it wasn't in her nature to give up. "I won't do that. No need to worry."

"How can you not? We haven't had a customer all day."

"Then we'll do something else," Gemma said, trying to remain upbeat. She caught sight of Vince Ballard walking toward the shop. "Ah, see. Here comes the winemaker now. Maybe he'll buy out the store. I'll go into sales mode and get him to buy our entire line of truffles for his tasting room."

"Ugh. I don't like that guy. Do you mind if I duck into the backroom while he's here? Maybe take my break early?"

Gemma snickered. "Sure. Go ahead. Abandon me in my hour of need. Coward."

"Yep," Lianne muttered as she barely managed to dash into the storeroom before the bell jingled above the door.

"Hey, Mr. Ballard. How's it going?" Gemma called out. "Haven't seen much of you lately."

"I've been meaning to drop by. I never thanked you for finding out what happened to Collette, Marnie, and Marissa. I admit I certainly underestimated you."

"I underestimated myself and bounced back. Besides, by now you're bound to have heard some of the rumors floating around town. From Louise Rawlins. She thinks I killed Mallory. So far, she's winning the gossip mill. Customers have been scarce around here. Empty shop. Aren't you afraid I might put a spell on you or worse, put something sinister in the chocolate?"

Vince took a seat on one of the stools and reached into his pocket, pulled out a hundred-dollar bill and placed it on the stainless-steel counter. "You should hear what Louise says about me behind my back. That woman's gums have been flapping ever since I moved here. Once I bought the vineyard and started my business she called me every name in the book. Tried to run me out of town more times than I can count. Never could admit to the fact that her daughter is a genuine nut job and a wannabe felon. So you know what I say to people who listen to that kind of BS?"

"What?"

"Stick it where the sun don't shine 'cause you don't need their business. Now be a dear and give me two dozen of those strawberry-filled white chocolate drops and two dozen of those white chocolate truffles covered with macadamia nuts. Both go great with the tawny port I bottled last winter. You should come by some time and try a sample."

She didn't care if he did take it the wrong way, Gemma stretched her arms out and wrapped them around the man's neck. "Thank you, Mr. Ballard. I needed to hear that today, not to mention, I appreciate your business."

He chuckled and patted her arm. "That's another thing. You need to start calling me Vince."

"I can do that, *Vince*."

"What's going on here?" Paloma said from the doorway, rapping her cane hard on the floor. "Cut that out, you two! Do I have to be the one to tell Lando his girl has a yen for this washed-up old winemaker?"

Vince laughed. "Get on in here, you old sot, you troublemaker, you. Where've you been keeping yourself? Won't even invite me to supper anymore. My feelings are hurt."

Paloma took a seat at one of the tables. "Trying to stop missing Marissa so much and having a lousy time of it. How about you?"

"Same here. Life just isn't the same at the vineyard without Collette. Every morning when I pull into the lot I still expect to see her car there. And when I unlock the office door, I expect to see her sitting at her desk. Crazy, but I miss her something fierce."

Paloma stretched out her legs, letting her cane dangle on the back of the chair. "Have you found anyone to take her place?"

"No one can take Collette's place," Vince admitted. "Although I have gone through the motions and interviewed a few people. So far, I haven't found anyone who's the right fit."

So much sadness all around, Gemma decided. "You two need a refreshing chocolate soda. It won't completely take away the blues, but it will fix what ails you on a warm summer day. What do you say?"

"I'll fix them," Lianne called out from the hallway, fanning her face. "That storeroom is mighty hot this time of day. Putting away all those supplies got to me."

Gemma chuckled as she boxed up Vince's order. "I shouldn't have sent you back there in this warm weather in the first place," she cracked, doing her best to keep a straight face.

Lianne rolled her eyes and looked out at Vince and Paloma. "I did volunteer to rearrange the storeroom."

"What are you two prattling on about back there?" Paloma demanded. "Lianne's not the only one who's burning up in here. It wouldn't hurt to turn up the AC a notch. Your customers are sweltering."

"I wouldn't want that," Gemma piped up as she scooted over to adjust the thermostat. "It has been unseasonably warm along the coast this summer."

"Two chocolate sodas will help with that," Lianne crooned from behind the counter as she got busy.

Vince turned his attention to Lianne. "How are *you* holding up since Collette died?"

Lianne nodded toward Gemma. "This one's helped me tremendously the last few months. Without her, I might've fallen apart completely."

"It's mutual," Gemma stated. "Lianne came into my life at just the right moment. I guess we both needed a shoulder to cry on. In fact, I'll fix two more sodas and we can all sit down and console each other."

They passed the next hour laughing and talking---even reminiscing about Collette---so that by the time Vince left, he seemed in better spirits.

"I might've misjudged Vince," Lianne admitted as she cleaned up the table. "I might've been doing the same thing with him that Louise is doing to you."

"Same here. I'm ashamed to say there was a time I did think he murdered Collette *and* Marnie, maybe even Gram." While Vince had left in a better mood, Gemma noticed a lingering sadness in Paloma's eyes as if she wasn't even listening to the chatter anymore. "What's going on with you? Is everything okay?"

"I'm old and cranky, that's what's wrong," the elderly woman huffed out in a desolate sigh. "Did you ever…I don't know…think to ask me more about your father, more than you have?"

"I didn't think you wanted me to."

"Why on earth not? Aren't you even the least bit curious about him? What he loved? How he spent his time? He wasn't just a serial cheater, you know. He had some good points. He was a hard worker, a stand-up guy to his friends, a loyal person who would do anything for anybody."

"I didn't want to bring up a lot of sad memories for you. Asking intrusive questions about him is a sure-fire way to get you to tell me to shut up. Or worse, shut me out completely. I don't want that."

"But if you don't ask, then you won't know. I could die tonight and what I know would be lost. Do you want that? Don't you want to know the truth about what happened to your father the day he had that accident? As for me, I may never live long enough to know."

Gemma leaned back in her chair. "Let me get this straight. You want me to ask you about the day Michael died? Because I've wondered. Was he drinking? Was he upset about my mother putting pressure on him to leave his family? Is that what caused him to drive off that cliff?"

"All I know about that day is that Reiner Caulfield knocked on my door and said my son ran his car off the roadway and landed in that ravine. He insinuated that Michael did it on purpose. I never believed that. In fact, after that night, I never really took Reiner seriously about anything. And now that I know Caulfield did nothing when Marshall Montalvo killed his wife, I keep wondering about why he wanted me to think Michael took his own life that day."

"Lando said the official report didn't hold much of anything, not even a blood test to determine if he had been drinking. It did mention a bottle of vodka found on the floorboard, though. There are photos of the accident. I just haven't seen them yet."

Paloma's face softened. "So you were curious enough to ask Lando about it."

"Well. Yeah. I just didn't want you to know I was checking into it. And I didn't want to get your hopes up when I probably won't be able to learn anything of value anyway." She laid a hand on Paloma's wrinkled one. "I'm so glad I have you in my life. If you ever need to talk, even if it's three in the morning, pick up the phone and I'll be there for you."

Paloma's eyes watered. "I never thought Michael's cheating would have an upside. But you're it. Oh, I adore Van and my two great-grandchildren he and Nova have given me. Those kids are the light of my life. And Michael's daughter, Silby, your half-sister, loved playing the piano so much I can still hear the music coming off those keys. She would've been thirty-six next month if the leukemia hadn't taken her."

"I'm so sorry. I want you to know that I'm not trying to detract from your love for Van or his children. That isn't my goal."

"I might be old, but I'm certainly capable of loving all my grandchildren. I still take tulips out to the cemetery to put on Michael's and Silby's graves. But they'll come a time when I won't be able to do it. You should go visit your father."

Gemma wrapped her up in a hug. "I certainly will. When you go next time, I'll drive you out there. You're a wonderful woman, Paloma. I'm so happy you're my grandmother even if I'll never get to know my father."

"Who says? All you have to do is ask me anything. It would give me a chance to talk about him again. Which brings me to the problem at hand. I'll have to find the right time to tell Van about you."

"Will Van be upset?"

"Probably. He was just a baby when Michael died. He grew up without a father and he's resented it his whole life."

"Like me."

"Yes, the two of you have that in common, but you aren't nearly as bitter about it."

"I don't mind giving Van time to come around. I'm not sure what kind of sister I'll make, but I'm willing to try my best at having some kind of relationship with him."

"I'll make sure I tell him that," Paloma promised.

"I've even thought about changing my name to Coyote. Would you be opposed to that?"

"Not me. Van might have something to say about it though."

"Then I'll wait until I get to know Van before making such a drastic change. I wouldn't want him to think I'm moving in on his territory."

9

On Saturday nights when Fortitude played it wasn't unusual for the Duck & Rum to have a packed crowd. But for whatever reason, tonight it was jammed to the rafters. Whether it was curiosity over Gemma and Lando getting back together or not, no one could dispute the couple was still a hot topic around town. It was as if people were waiting for the fireworks to explode, a precursor to the breakup that would surely happen. Not everyone was convinced their relationship would make it to the end of summer.

Owner Adam Greendeer refused to confirm or deny there was a betting pool in place as to what date the train wreck would take place.

If Gemma or Lando had known that people were betting behind their backs, they would never in a million years have agreed to appear on stage.

But since it was a covert operation, a top-secret project no one discussed around them, neither one suspected anything.

Least of all Gemma.

Inside the bar's restroom, she reapplied her lipstick and re-brushed her hair for the third time. Looking at herself in the mirror, she was as ready to step on stage as she could get. She'd worn a silky, cream-colored dress with a sexy lace mesh top that brought out her golden skin. It had a little skirt that flared when she swished back and forth, which she planned to do a lot of tonight. Her heels had a strappy ankle wrap and a barely-there look that showed off the chrome nail polish on her shiny painted toes.

Confident she'd done her best to look the part of a cabaret singer, she exited the restroom to seek out her friends. On her march to the stage, she tried to make the rounds, asking as many people as she could to put in their requests. It was a habit the crowd seemed to appreciate. They often screamed out crazy song titles as if trying to stump the band. Everybody had a favorite tune they wanted to hear. It didn't mean Fortitude would oblige but it made for friendly PR. With Louise running her mouth, Gemma could use all the goodwill she could muster.

With an enthusiastic crowd like tonight's it didn't seem like Louise was winning the gossip war.

She caught up with her friends as they gathered around a large table near the stage to wait for the show to begin. Leia had persuaded her mother to join them along with Zeb's sister, Willow.

When she reached Lydia, she leaned in and whispered, "Better put in your suggestions now, Lando is pushing for moody ballads tonight."

Lydia narrowed her eyes. "I told him I expected to hear at least one Willie Nelson song. He knows how I love Willie. If he wants any more of my chicken fried steak, he'd better not disappoint."

Gemma pointed a finger at her and winked. "Lando would never disappoint his mama."

Luke waved her over. "Lianne said you were planning to sing a couple of songs from a Canadian band."

"We were, but rehearsal didn't exactly go as planned last night. I might try to wing it through one, though, depending how drunk the crowd gets."

Leia guffawed with laughter. "This should be a fun night. Is Lando even able to play guitar?"

"You know how he is. Just try and stop him," Gemma shouted over the ever-growing crowd. She spotted the band circulating---Jimmy, Dale, Bosco, and Radley, the drummer---making the rounds to build up enthusiasm. By looking at the four of them no one would ever guess their nine to five gigs consisted of hardworking jobs in law enforcement, bartending, and teaching.

Lando tapped her on the shoulder and swung her into a dance. "You ready to rock and roll, darlin'?"

"As ready as I'll ever be. Where've you been? You disappeared thirty minutes ago with Jeff Tuttle. Did Tuttle get the DNA results back?"

Instead of answering, Lando playfully began to nibble her neck.

"You're in an awfully good mood." She looked into his eyes and suddenly realized why. "By any chance, you didn't take any more of those pills just to get through tonight's performance, did you?"

But before she could get him to answer, Greendeer began his announcement. "Ladies and gentlemen...back by popular demand, here's what you've all been waiting to hear, Fortitude!"

That's all Gemma heard as she was pulled up on stage. Lando was so charged up for the first song, he'd picked something to get the crowd rocking. He went into a wild rendition of "Snow (Hey Oh)" by the Red Hot Chili Peppers. A strange choice because he couldn't have picked a tune more difficult to maneuver through the changing riffs and chords. With a still-healing left arm it was as if he'd had a miracle recovery.

That's when she knew. It wasn't Demerol he'd taken.

Jimmy had no problem keeping up on rhythm guitar, nor did Bosco on bass. Dale held up his end on the keyboard with a spirited accompaniment. Radley was perfect on drums. But as she looked out into the crowd she scanned faces, wondering who exactly had supplied Lando with speed.

What was he trying to prove anyway, she wondered as she sang backup on "Pretending." Their third offering provided Lydia with her Willie Nelson fix. Lando's soulful "Always on my Mind" rendition seemed perfect with its lilting melody for slow-dancing.

But by the fourth song, "Just Breathe," Lando slurred a few of the lyrics. Covering for him like he'd done for her in other performances, she neatly saved the tune by embellishing the chorus. No one in the audience seemed to pick up on the flub and it didn't faze Lando.

By the fifth song, Lando had started sweating under the lights, which wasn't all that unusual with the heat emanating directly from the spotlight. But this time he was giving off enough energy to light up a stadium. When he belted out "Running on Empty," it might've been less than a simple tune and more like a sign he was about to crash.

Jimmy noticed something was off and slid across the stage to get Gemma's attention. They exchanged speculative looks. Okay, so she wasn't the only one who felt like Lando was on something other than a music high. She lifted a shoulder and got the same response back from Jimmy. Neither knew what to do about it.

To slow things down, Lando surrendered vocals on "Black Velvet" and let her contralto take over. All the while she belted out the lyrics she kept an eye on him. Afterward, he seemed to rebound, going into overdrive on the next song, the hard-driving "Sympathy for the Devil."

"This wasn't on the playlist," Jimmy noted in a whisper.

"He's in his own zone tonight," Gemma said. "Let's just try to keep up and get through this."

They took a break at the halfway point giving Gemma the opportunity to steer Lando off stage and into the hallway. "What is up with you? I want to know who gave you the speed."

"What? I'm just in a good mood. You said so yourself."

"Lando, don't screw with me. What did you take?"

The other bandmates had followed them into the corridor, surrounding Lando in a circle. "Yeah, we'd all like to know," Jimmy demanded. "What are you on tonight?"

Lando held up his hands in a defensive posture. "Okay, okay. Suzanne Swinton might've given me some of Buddy's vitamins to help get me through the set. She said taking two always gave Buddy a burst of energy. So I took four."

Gemma burst out laughing. "So a cop took amphetamines from a former alcoholic slash addict's wife trying to get rid of her hubby's stash."

"Best cure for coming down off that is pot," Dale offered. "Only marijuana cache I know about is the bundle we have locked up in the evidence room back at the station."

Jimmy nodded. "Still sitting there after we busted Medford Davis in May."

Gemma cleared her throat. "Guys, I don't think having the chief of police smoke pot to come down from his high is a good idea."

"I guess not," Dale said, rubbing the stubble on his chin. "What do you suggest then?"

Gemma blew out a breath. "That we get through the show and let him come down naturally at his own pace."

"That could take twenty-four hours," Bosco provided. "Course he already has a good two-hour head start."

"We could shorten the second set," Radley suggested. "But then folks might wonder why and start asking questions."

"He did get shot this week," Gemma began. "We could always use that as an excuse."

"Should we confront Suzanne?" Jimmy asked.

Gemma made a face. "I'm not sure drawing attention to it is a good idea. Not tonight anyway. Will we make sure she doesn't hand those things out to another unsuspecting schmuck? Oh yeah. Just not tonight. Look, stay with him while I get Luke's attention. Luke needs to check him out before he goes on again."

"Good idea," Bosco muttered as he tried to keep Lando standing still in one spot. It wasn't easy. The guy kept trying to climb the wall.

A few minutes later the hallway got even more crowded when Luke appeared.

"There's a storage room back here," Gemma directed. "Let's take him in there so you can look him over."

It didn't take long for Luke to notice how Lando's muscles were twitching. "His pupils are like grapefruits. How much of that stuff did Suzanne give him?"

"He took four is all I know. What the milligram count was of each I have no idea, but it must've been potent stuff because it kicked in almost immediately. We could always go ask her."

"I doubt she knows," Luke said as he checked Lando's pulse. "It's probably some crap Buddy picked up from Joe Petrillo, the resident drug dealer until Zeb and Lando busted him in a joint sting back in April."

"There's irony in there somewhere," Gemma stated. "Look, I don't want you to mention this to anyone. If your mother or Leia asks, could you downplay this and blame it on his shoulder?"

Luke frowned. "I guess, but don't you think everyone will wonder what's up with him? I mean, even if you hadn't come to get me, I could see something was wrong. I mean look at him. His heart's racing like he ran a marathon." Luke bopped his brother lightly on the face.

"Hey, what'd you do that for?" Lando demanded, ready to fight. "I'm just standing here."

"I ought to do worse than that for taking unknown pills from somebody like Suzanne. You should know better."

"I had some pain in my arm and Gemma didn't want me taking more Demerol. Plus, I didn't want to disappoint the crowd."

"That's because you love playing rock star every Saturday night," Luke muttered, turning to Gemma. "I think he's fine, other than feeling like he's soaring higher than Neil Armstrong for the next few hours, I think he'll live through this."

"So should we just let him back on stage?"

"Try to contain his mood swings. And get ready for the spiral downward. Not to mention the headache he'll suffer afterward."

Gemma grinned and took Lando's chin in her hand. "You're gonna pay for this and there's nothing much I can do to help you. Are you sure you want to go back out there? We could leave now and make up an excuse."

"Leave? I don't want to leave. I have more songs to play."

"Okay, but don't say I didn't try," Gemma uttered, cutting her eyes toward Luke. "I guess we prepare for the second coming of Elvis because he definitely doesn't want to leave the building."

The second set was even livelier than the first as Lando danced, pranced, and strutted his way into the rock 'n roll hall of fame. Every time he swiveled his hips like Elvis, the crowd roared louder. The only upside was that he was using up a lot of energy. The faster he boogied his way into the record books, the quicker he would touch down.

That began to happen near one o'clock when they closed the set with three classics to end the night a little early. Gemma and Lando were near the tail end of "Stand by Me" when his voice began to fade and tremble. She and Dale quickly took over vocals.

As customers cleared their tabs, Lando's head began to pound. He swayed, and Jimmy moved in with Bosco to help him off stage before anyone noticed. Except for Luke and Lianne who met the band backstage.

"I need to wait until the place clears out before getting him to the car," Gemma suggested. "I don't want anyone to see him in this condition."

Jimmy and Bosco continued to shoulder Lando's weight onto their own and walked, half-dragging him, down the hallway and back to the storage area.

"Why all the secrecy?" Jimmy asked. "The entire Duck & Rum just witnessed him max out his rock star persona. I don't see hiding out in here doing much to help the situation."

Gemma wouldn't be dissuaded. "But now he's coming down off the high, something I don't think he'd want people seeing. Give it twenty minutes before we get him into the car and get him home."

Leia and Zeb chose that moment to show up in the wings. "What on earth is wrong with him?"

"Long story," Gemma said. "You guys go on home. We'll see you tomorrow."

"Sure, see you guys tomorrow bright and early," Leia said in a cheery voice. "Shadow Canyon awaits."

Twenty minutes later, Gemma had shooed the others on home. It was Luke who stayed around to help her get Lando outside to the parking lot. Slow and steady they walked him across the pavement. With each step, he looked like he might pass out any minute. "I hope we can still make it tomorrow but don't count on it."

"He just needs a good night's sleep. But if you have any problems, like if he should have difficulty breathing, get him to the ER. Don't wait," Luke cautioned.

"Don't worry, I'll keep an eye on him the entire night," Gemma vowed.

Zeb had doubled back and hustled to take over for Gemma on her side, taking the burden off her. "He's sure not showing any signs of pain. Why's he so shaky?"

"He's tired," Gemma snapped, unwilling to admit to him what Lando had taken.

She let Zeb and Luke settle Lando into the passenger seat. "I think we're gonna head straight home."

"Probably a good idea," Luke said as he skirted the front of Lando's cruiser. "Want us to follow you?"

"Thanks, but we'll be okay." She waved goodbye to her friends and turned to close the car door. She spotted a man standing in the shadows. She let out a sigh of relief when she saw it was Van Coyote. "I didn't know you were here tonight."

Van swayed on his feet from too much alcohol. "I had a long talk with my grandmother earlier this evening. She told me what you think, about that cockamamie story you gave her. She told me what your stupid mother claimed happened with my father. I got news for you, lady, I'm not standing around letting you weasel your way into my family. There's been no DNA test to prove we're related. Nothing to confirm anything. So don't go getting your sights lasered in on my grandmother's dough. You got that?"

Van stepped closer. "Stay away from my grandmother. I don't care if you are the police chief's girlfriend."

Lando heard his name or maybe it was the threat and started pushing open the car door. But Gemma put all her weight against it to keep it closed, holding it in place so he couldn't get out. The last thing Lando needed tonight was to get into an altercation with a taxpayer, especially since he was still hyped up on uppers. So far, she'd been able to hide it from everyone at the bar and intended to keep it that way. While Van might be loaded on God knows what, people weren't depending on Van Coyote to keep the peace.

With a sadness that started in her throat and inched down to her belly, she watched her brother stagger off to a black pickup truck parked at the far end of the lot. The angry red aura she saw emanating off him scared her just a little.

She felt like running after him to keep him from driving. But in his state of mind she doubted it would do any good. Instead, she took out her cell phone and dialed 411. Directory assistance gave her Van's number at home.

When a woman's voice answered, Gemma went into her spiel. "This is Gemma Channing. Sorry to bother you so late but I thought you should know Van just left the Duck & Rum and he's been drinking. I don't think he should drive."

On the other end of the line, she heard Nova suck in air. "Did he confront you? I told him not to do that. I'm so sorry."

"Let's just say my first encounter with my brother didn't exactly go like I'd hoped. Nova, I just don't want him to get into an accident. That's why I'm calling."

"My kids are sleeping, but I'll run over there and pick him up. Is there any way you can stop him from getting in that truck until I get there?"

Gemma bit her lip. "I don't think so, but I'll give it a shot. If I hurry I might be able to block his exit with the car. After all, I am sitting in a police cruiser."

"Great. Do that and I'll be right there."

Gemma hit the gas and circled the lot, positioning the SUV behind Van's pickup.

"What are we doing?" Lando asked as he slumped against the passenger side door. "Who were you talking to on the phone?"

"Just sit tight and no matter what that guy in the pickup says or does don't do anything stupid. He's drunk and we're waiting for his wife to show up."

"Don't worry. I don't feel so good. My head hurts like a freight train's running through my brain."

"I bet it does," Gemma muttered as she kept an eye out for Nova.

Van didn't take kindly to seeing a police car pulling up behind his truck. "What the hell's going on here? Get out of my way. I gotta get home."

Gemma rolled the window down a few inches, so she could yell at him. "Not until your wife gets here to drive you home."

"You called my wife? Why? I'm perfectly capable of getting myself home."

"Sure, that's what all the drunks say."

"Who you callin' a drunk?" Van shouted as he jumped out of the vehicle.

"I'll handle this," Lando said, fumbling for the handle on the door.

"No, you won't," Gemma stated, grabbing his arm. "You're staying put. We're just gonna sit here and play it cool for the next few minutes."

But cool wasn't on Van's agenda. He let out a string of curses peppered with a string of insults.

Tired of listening to the racket, Lando tried to get out of the car again. "That's it. I'm arresting this dumbass for disturbing the peace."

"That dumbass is my brother," Gemma reminded him as a car horn blasted out to her left. She spotted Nova behind the wheel of a subcompact Kia.

Nova was in no mood to argue or take any guff off her husband. "Lock up your truck and get in the car, Van. Now!"

"Aww, honey. I could've driven home," Van said, swaying on his feet. "She didn't have to bother you like this."

"Look at you! I left two babies at home asleep and I'm not gonna sit here and argue with you when it's almost two in the morning. Now get in the damn car!"

This time Van did as he was told.

Nova sent Gemma a wave as she put the Kia in reverse. "Thank you for not letting him drive home like this."

"No problem. We'll talk later."

Nova smiled. "Yes, I reckon we will."

"Do you guys have to talk so loud?" Lando complained as he held his aching head in his hands. "Mind telling me again what that was all about?"

Gemma put the car in gear and roared out of the lot. "Just a little icing on an otherwise really crappy night."

"Hey, I thought the show went great," Lando stated.

"You would, since that handful of Buddy's extra special bennies gave you the ability to walk on the ceiling or at least feel like you could. By the way, the crowd really went for your Mick Jagger impression. Better hope there's no video of that available if anyone ever wants to replace you as the top cop."

"I did a Mick Jagger impression?"

"Oh honey, not only did you do Jagger, you tried Chuck Berry's duck walk. I will say you put more effort into it than Michael J. Fox ever did in *Back to the Future*. But that's little comfort if your enemies ever get wind of it. Trust me. You're gonna want to confiscate any video of tonight. Period."

"Why?"

"Because you don't often see a police chief parade around like he's on crack."

10

Lando paid dearly for his mistake. The next morning his head still felt like a wrecking ball kept smashing into the side of his skull.

At six-thirty when he tried to pick up his phone from the nightstand to check messages, his hands shook so hard he dropped the device and it slid underneath the bed. After spending ten minutes trying to retrieve it, his body sweated like a man working construction in a hundred and twenty degree heat in the middle of Death Valley.

Though he had puked several times already, Gemma insisted he drink water to hydrate. She arrived back in the bedroom in time to see him teeter and sway on his feet.

She shoved him back into bed and took the phone out of his hand. "Dale and Jimmy will manage anything that comes up today. They know you're still drugged out and in no shape to help with any emergency right now."

"I'm not…drugged out."

She put her fingers to his lips. "Shh. Don't argue."

"What about the trip to Shadow Canyon?"

"Don't worry about it. You're in no shape to ride a horse."

"I can do it," Lando insisted as he instinctively burrowed under the covers.

Rufus trotted in to rest his head on the bed in a show of sympathy.

"Really? So bouncing up and down on a horse is preferable to staying in bed and sleeping it off. Better use today to recover or else Monday will hit you like a freight train."

"You go ahead. Go without me. You don't have to stay here and babysit me."

"I like babysitting you, especially when you do something truly stupid."

Lando made a face. "Don't remind me. Do you have to talk so loud?"

She ran a hand over his damp forehead. "Sorry. Get some sleep. Maybe we'll catch up with the others later."

He grabbed her hand. "No really, go without me. I'll just…lie here…and die…alone."

"Luke says you just feel like you're dying."

"It'd be nice if my brother gave me something for this nasty headache."

"He did caution against taking any of the Demerol with speed any time soon. It's a great way to experience respiratory failure firsthand or bring on a heart attack."

"Don't worry. I'm not planning on taking anything stronger than an aspirin."

"Let's hope not. I wouldn't take any pills from Suzanne for a while either. Dale went over there this morning and confiscated Buddy's stash. All of it. Well, supposedly all of it. Turns out, Buddy kept a small amount of acid in there that wasn't marked. Buddy admitted to Dale that Suzanne could just as easily have given it to you because she had no idea what it was. So who knows what you actually took."

Lando groaned and rolled over.

Gemma closed the bedroom door and went into the kitchen, where she texted Leia that they wouldn't be riding anywhere, not today. She scrambled eggs and was just about to sit down to have breakfast when the doorbell rang.

Rufus beat her to the door and stood wagging his tail, waiting for it to open.

Lydia held up a basket filled with jam and bread---croissants wrapped up in a bright red cloth to keep them warm. "After that spectacle last night I thought Lando could use some of my homemade prickly pear preserves. Besides, I finally got the truth out of Luke. He said Lando was strung out on speed."

Gemma chuckled. "Listen to you. What would you know about speed?"

"Oh, please. I was young once."

"Come on in. The thing is, he's sacked out and probably will be for the rest of the day."

Lydia patted Gemma's hand. "More for us then."

"The coffee's hot and the eggs aren't as good as the ones you make, but there's plenty."

Lydia unpacked the basket and held up a quart-sized jar filled with purple liquid.

"What is that stuff?"

"An old remedy for a hangover. Cactus juice."

"You're kidding? You're gonna try to get Lando to drink that? Lots of luck."

Lydia snickered. "He is a tad on the picky side, isn't he? The juice from the prickly pear wards off all kinds of toxins. Natives have known about its powers since they started using medicinal plants thousands of years ago. It's one of the best natural ways to fight off the effects of booze by detoxing the liver. We're about to find out what it does after too many amphetamines. We'll let him sleep a little longer, take our time eating breakfast, and then make him drink as much of this as he can hold."

Gemma unscrewed the lid and took a sniff. "Smells good, actually."

"Go ahead, try some," Lydia prodded. "It's good for what ails you. I ought to know, I've been using it in salads and vinaigrettes at the restaurant since I took over running the kitchen. Never had one complaint. But that's my little secret. It's a wonderful, all-around fruit that's overlooked for its health benefits."

Gemma sniffed the contents again before taking a tiny sip. "Wow. Not bad." She took another swig, this time bigger. "Tastes a little like watermelon, only sweeter."

"Flavorful and good for you," Lydia said, sounding like a commercial. She plopped down at the table. "You watch, this'll have my boy up and like new in no time."

"Was it just Luke who sent you over, or did Leia find out, too?"

Lydia dished up eggs, piling them on her plate. "We cornered Luke this morning and tortured the truth out of him. You should've told us last night. We knew something was wrong by the way Lando acted. Leia was the first to sound the alarm this morning. Plus, she knew how much you were looking forward to seeing Shadow Canyon, and when you cancelled, red flags. With all this going on with Louise, who could blame you for wanting a peaceful afternoon? It's a perfect place to spend a lazy summer day. Who knows? You might even catch a glimpse of Aponivi."

"You think so?"

"I don't see why not. The keeper of truth often appears on summer days as a dust devil, roaring through the canyon walls right before a monsoon hits."

Gemma checked the weather forecast on her phone. "No rain on the horizon…at all."

Lydia waved off the comment. "Monsoons can appear out of nowhere. Aponivi showing up seems to bring them on. But he's also a bit of a weather forecaster himself…in life, about life. He's known to make a person see things they don't want to see, make them aware of things they never knew."

"Like bad weather's coming?"

"Weather is a metaphor that means a lot of things. Aponivi acts like a window into a person's past and his future based on that past."

Gemma grinned at her once-upon-a-time mother-in-law. "Now you're talking in riddles, Lydia."

"I suppose I am. You'll have to see him for yourself to judge. Leia didn't want you to miss a chance at an encounter. And if my miracle cure doesn't work, I'll sit with Lando until he feels better."

"That's ridiculous. He's a grown man who's been taking care of himself for years."

Lydia smiled. "That's right, which means he doesn't need a babysitter, not you or me. If Luke thought there was a chance he'd have a serious reaction from those pills, he would've admitted him to the clinic to keep an eye on him."

"So you think I'm overreacting?"

"It's sweet that you want to make sure he's okay, but I don't think Lando Bonner needs a nurse."

"I know you're right. The fact is I freaked out the other day when he got shot. I decided I wanted to be the best wife…I mean, girlfriend that any chief of police has ever had. He mentioned he thought I might not be able to handle his job, danger and all. I admit it gave me pause. I mean, look what happened to Ben Markham. Ben died because he stopped some crazy nut for speeding out on the highway. Knowing how fragile life is, I want to prove to Lando I support his career no matter what, no matter how dangerous it is."

Lydia's face showed real concern. "Just be yourself, Gemma. It's all anyone can ask of someone they love. Don't try to be someone you aren't."

"But...I want him to know I...I love that man more than anyone else in the world. I always have. I want to show him I can be a steady rock every time he walks out that door to face...whatever risks are out there."

"You've certainly matured from that girl who married my boy when she was eighteen."

"Let's hope so. Do you really think you'll get Lando to drink that stuff?"

"Never underestimate a mother. Wanna bet on it?"

"Sure. Twenty bucks says he won't let that pass his lips."

"You're on."

After breakfast, Gemma stood back and let Lydia make her case to a grumpy, irritated man, who basically just wanted to be left alone.

At first, Lydia's pitch for her super cure didn't convince the stubborn Lando of anything. And there was no amount of arm twisting that worked.

"Mom, I told you before that stuff is not for me."

"Don't be such a baby. Do you want to stay in bed all day and waste such a beautiful Sunday? Wouldn't you rather man up and take something that'll make you feel better? Don't you want to spend your day off with Gemma outdoors instead of curled up in a fetal position?"

"Shaming me into drinking that vile stuff won't work," Lando grunted. "However...if it'll take away this pain in my head...maybe I'll risk it."

"You won't know that until you drink it," Lydia insisted. "I'm not trying to poison you, for goodness sake. I'm your mother."

Lando blew out a breath. "Fine. Hand it over."

Gemma watched as he downed the entire jar in one long gulp.

The stuff made him belch as he handed the jar back to his mother. "Satisfied now?"

"Of my three kids, you always were the most obstinate child I had," Lydia grumbled. "Now sit back and let that work its way through your system. Let me know when you start feeling better."

It took most of the morning for Lando to act like his old self again. His stomach had settled down enough that he ate two pieces of toast spread with prickly pear jam and drank a pot of coffee. He had to pee a lot, but other than that felt less wobbly. His head had stopped throbbing about an hour after he drank the wonder juice.

By ten-thirty, they waved goodbye to Lydia and left Rufus taking a morning nap in his doggie bed. Zeb's place was a short drive away.

The compound known as Long Shadow Stables sat among the rolling hills between Shadow Canyon and Fire Mountain. The views from all sides were breathtaking and worth the trip. A cluster of Spanish-style ranch houses and casitas dotted the landscape, giving each member of the family a place for private quarters. The ranch hands slept in a state-of-the-art bunkhouse with six bedrooms that could accommodate a dozen workers. It had a communal kitchen, a dining room with a long farmhouse table, and a rec room for unwinding after a long day or relaxing in front of a flat-screen TV.

Gemma made the turn onto a long driveway that twisted and curved its way up to the main house before veering off toward the paddock.

The gang had already gathered near the corral when she pulled her Volvo into the parking lot.

"Looks like we haven't missed much," Lando remarked.

"Getting a late start, though. At least they waited."

Luke greeted them with his usual good nature. "Glad to see the rock star didn't croak."

"I hope you don't use croak in front of your unfortunate patients," Lando sneered, glaring at his brother. He channeled his sour mood into a further insult. "And you call yourself a medical doctor. You couldn't give me anything to get me up out of bed, and yet our mother mixed up some concoction our forefathers used a hundred years ago and had me up on my feet in no time. Here I am, fit as a fiddle."

Luke was in no mood to take guff off his brother. "You're saying you wanted me to hand out drugs to you? Since when did the police chief become such a pill-popper?"

"Bite me," Lando snarled.

"Didn't improve your mood, I see," Luke grunted. "That would take another miracle drug, I suppose. A shame our forefathers couldn't find a cure for your bad temperament."

Leia stepped between her siblings to calm things down. "Guys, could we just, for one day, not do this. Gemma and I want to enjoy this. And so does Lianne. Don't ruin this trip for us."

Duly scolded, Lando cleared his throat. "Sorry. You're right. I'm still a little edgy."

"Well, knock it off because I wanted to show you guys the horse Zeb bought for me," Leia announced. "Zeb found her living on a ranch in Modoc County. Her owner died, and all the ranch stock was auctioned off last month, including all the horses. That's her over there by the water trough. Her name's Buttercup. She's feisty and spirited and I absolutely adore her. Isn't she the most gorgeous animal you've ever seen?"

Gemma followed Leia's gaze and started walking toward the paddock where a beautiful buckskin quarter horse had turned to graze. Buttercup had a yellowish-golden body, a tan mane, and a black tail. "You're right, that's the most stunning horse I've ever seen."

"Isn't she though? She's my engagement present instead of a ring and I couldn't be happier. Zeb and I are taking the big leap. Do you think we're crazy?"

Gemma grabbed her friend in a hug. "I think you're following your heart. Not a thing wrong with that. I'm so happy for you."

Lianne appeared from the barn, holding the reins of a docile Rudy, a beautiful strawberry roan that had belonged to her sister Collette. "Glad you guys could finally join us. What's going on?"

Luke wrapped his arms around his sister. "Leia and Zeb are getting married. I'd say it's about time they stopped hiding from everyone and made it official."

Lianne bounced on her toes. "That's huge. When's the big day?"

"We haven't set a date yet," Zeb explained. "We were thinking sometime in the fall."

Lando clapped Zeb on the back before getting his chance to put Leia in a bear hug. "I don't think you could do any better than this guy."

Leia rested her head on Lando's shoulder. "I'm so glad you feel that way. I was…afraid of what you'd say."

"Why wouldn't I be happy for you? I've gotten to know Zeb a lot better over these past few months. He's a good guy, comes through in a backup situation, too. What more could I ask for in a brother-in-law? Then again, I like the other side benefit, having another cop in the family."

"Someone who knows what they're doing," Zeb added, rubbing his hands together. "Time's a-wasting, people. Pick your horse and let's saddle up."

Gemma went with a gentle mare, a black beauty named Gypsy with white leggings all around while Lando picked out a black and white paint they called Bandit, who usually saw little exercise during the week, if any. Bandit didn't have an owner paying his room and board. He'd been abandoned and left wandering in the desert. No one knew how long Bandit had gone without food or water. By the time the Longhorns took him in, Bandit had been starved down to skin and bones.

Zeb's younger sister, Willow, had nursed him back to health starting him on small meals. She'd gradually increased his feed over time and in eight months with plenty of tender loving care had brought him back to full strength. She was on hand to give Lando some advice. "Don't be surprised if he's skittish through the part of the trail that's the scrub. The area might bring back bad memories of the desert for him, so reassure him with a few pats on the neck that you don't intend to abandon him again. Remind him that not all people are abusers. And don't over-pace him."

Lando rolled his eyes at the young Willow, a year out of college and on the bossy side. "I know how to take care of a horse."

Willow ignored his comment while rechecking the bridle and girth. She ran a hand down each of Bandit's legs before she was satisfied the horse was ready to ride. A bit reluctant, she handed the reins over to Lando. "While that's probably true, every horse is different. Every horse has a different story. You would remember that about them if you rode more often. Bandit has been damaged beyond belief. All I'm saying is go easy on him. Don't expect too much of a bond right away."

Lando stared at the horse-lover, noting that Willow put everything she had into her job. Her raven mane might've been secured down her back in what had started out as a tight braid but was now a rather messy loose bundle that flopped around as she readied the horse for riding.

"Stop worrying, mother hen," he commented. "Bandit and I will get along fine. I've never mistreated a horse in my life and can't stand people who do it."

Willow's head snapped up, her dark eyes flaring. "I never met the man or woman who mistreated Bandit, but we see a lot of abuse in this business. You never get used to it. Some horses we can help. Others have to be put down. Still more are out there at the mercy of their cruel owners. The good news is we're able to shelter those we rescue who've had it rough until they can find a forever home of their own. But some never do. I go off the edge when I see humans mistreat an animal."

Gemma leaned into Bandit's nose to rest her head there. "So Bandit is available if someone wanted to buy him?" For emphasis, she poked a finger in Lando's ribs. "Hear that?"

Willow's face broke into a wide grin at the implication. "Are you in the market, Gemma, or trying to persuade Lando?"

"A little of both. What's the story on Gypsy?"

"Her owner died. Gypsy came to us through an auction. She's such a gentle lady, we always put her in the group the school children ride. We have a lot of school districts that come out here for field trips three or four times a year. This being summer, Gypsy hasn't seen much action lately."

"I'll take good care of her," Gemma promised. "And look after Bandit as well."

Zeb noticed Luke studying a bay sorrel. "This big guy loves a day trip, but rarely sees one. His name's Jocko. His owner rarely comes to see him. It'd be a treat if you'd get him out of the corral before he forgets how to be a horse."

"Sounds like a good fit for me. What are you riding these days?"

Zeb went over to a champagne-colored colt with a sprinkle of freckles and big amber eyes already saddled and raring to go. "Didn't you know? I fell in love with Zander about a year ago. He'd been abused for who knows how long. He still has the scars from being whipped. But Zander's the smartest horse I've ever owned. Aren't you, boy?"

The horse responded by nuzzling his owner's chin.

Zander took the lead, followed by Buttercup, Rudy, Jocko, Gypsy, and Bandit. They started off through the flat Genesee Valley, through the rolling hills known as Gawonii Creek, and up the incline that would ultimately lead to Shadow Canyon.

Summer wildflowers thrived among the stalwart sagebrush, scattering the trail in blasts of color. Orange poppies grew alongside fiery paintbrush, while blue snapdragons stood at attention like regimental soldiers.

With walls a thousand feet in height, the canyon trails followed the meandering zig-zag of the Corona River until its forceful current met up with a tributary stream, a place where striped bass and trout were plentiful.

Gemma remembered that as teenagers they'd camped out overnight along its banks to catch their suppers---six pounders were the norm, enough to feed four people.

"How is it we completely stopped coming out here?" Leia asked as she looked around at the cathedral-like stone walls. "I'd forgotten how peaceful it is out here."

"These rocks are still considered sacred to our people," Zeb noted. "And if you're camping out here for any length of time, you can still poke around in the dirt and find shards of Indian pottery where villages once stood."

Gemma was too much in awe of the place to ruin it with a bunch of chitchat. She rode in silent reverence, enjoying the pinyon pine and black cottonwood that popped up along the trail. When it squeezed off, narrowing into a slit, they rode single file through the rocky pass, heading further along the rutted pathway.

Gemma could feel the past all around her. She could see it in her head. The struggles of the tribes for survival. One or two images popped up, a single man and woman trying to get away, to run as fast as they could before the enemy caught up with them. And then, out of nowhere, a horde appeared, coming straight for her—ghosts growing in numbers—men, women, and children carrying bows and arrows, knives, and anything else they could use for a weapon.

But bows and arrows were no match against Winchesters. Behind her, she caught the sounds of hoofbeats. Soldiers carrying rifles approached an encampment along the riverbed, mostly made up of women, children, and the elderly who'd remained behind while their warriors went to hunt for food. The slaughter that ensued was difficult to watch.

Unable to make the vision stop, Gemma was forced to witness the destruction firsthand until nothing remained except the smell of smoke and the odor of burning flesh. She couldn't believe the carnage. Nothing left of the village remained except a wailing infant, frightened and sick, crying somewhere in the distance. The images made her sick to her stomach. She had to hold tight to the saddle horn to keep from falling off.

Gypsy must've sensed Gemma's sorrow, because the mare reared up in a skittish display as if a snake had slithered across the dirt.

Gemma held the reins tighter, leaning down to whisper reassurances in the horse's ear. She stroked the mare's neck. "It's okay, girl. Settle down. It's okay. I'm sorry I upset you. From now on, I'll try to block out those terrible scenes from the past."

"You okay?" Lando asked.

"I'm fine. Out of practice is all."

Once they reached the river, the horses waded through the shallow water to the banks on the other side. The landscape here was dotted with big-leaf maple, red alder, and knobcone pine, and a forest filled with lots of hidden secrets.

"It's a shame we didn't do this yesterday, so we could set up camp and stay longer," Lando said.

"Maybe if you didn't always have to play rock star every Saturday night," Luke began, "we could've taken the opportunity to do just that."

"I like music," Lando stated in his defense. "Sue me for enjoying that side of my life on what's practically the only amount of time I have off."

Losing her patience with them, Gemma snapped, "Do you guys have to pick on each other when we're spending the afternoon in such a beautiful setting? Look around you. Imagine our forefathers hunting for game, taking care of their families, or trying to maintain a sense of normalcy while waiting for soldiers to attack at any moment. There, over by that cave, a mother and her three children, babies really, lost their lives trying to hide from a massacre. I might be late to the party, not having known about my native roots until recently, but at least I know when to appreciate the moment. And this is it. If all you guys want to do is argue, then go off by yourselves. Because your bickering is ruining it for the rest of us."

Lianne kicked Rudy into a faster pace, coming up alongside Luke. "She's right. Either stop squabbling or head back. Fight there. Your choice."

It was Luke's turn to make amends. "Sorry. I apologize for the rock star comment."

"That's okay," Lando grunted. "I suppose a part of it is true."

Zeb and Leia led them up a steeper trailhead, and then down into the gorge that ran along the stream. The riders could hear the babbling brook long before it came into view.

"If you two promise to be good, we could at least camp here for the afternoon," Leia suggested. "It'd be a great place to eat the roast chicken I brought in my pack. And Zeb is carrying the rest of the food in his saddlebags."

Lando set the paint into a faster trot. Bandit responded by scampering up the hill where he could look down into the valley below. "I could eat and the horses could take a water break. But here's an idea. There's our old campsite up ahead near the fork in the river. How about we stop there? It offers more grassland before the woods take over."

After some discussion and then agreement, they moved on to set up their camp in a better mood than when they'd left. They gathered wood and kindling for the fire pit, already established by other hikers and overnight campers.

A stirring in the trees forced Gemma to remember what had happened in the nearby canyon, the massacre of an entire village. "There's lots of history here and not all of it good," she said as she studied a colony of finches setting up house in a patch of thistle.

Picking up on a vibe, she headed off in the direction of the cave entrance she'd spotted on the side of a small overhang.

Lando grabbed her arm. "Where are you going?"

"Exploring. I thought I'd check out that opening and see what's in there. Wouldn't it be great to scout out the area like we did when we were kids?"

"After we eat I'll go with you."

"Sure. I guess it can wait."

Surrounded by woods, they settled back for their meal and watched a family of rabbits scurry out of a field of clover, taking cover in an adjacent meadow where a patch of cabbage had taken over the sage.

In the shade of the canyon walls, Zeb helped Leia set out their buffet of food on a rock and took out a six-pack of beer. He tossed Lando a can of soda. "No alcohol for you, buddy."

Lando caught the Orange Crush right before it hit his face. "Fine by me. I'm off all that stuff anyway, at least for a while. My head still feels fuzzy."

Lianne popped the top on her beer. "I find it hard to believe Suzanne and Buddy didn't get arrested for giving the chief of police speed. If that had happened in Portland…"

"And in the middle of a murder investigation no less," Luke stated. "If I didn't know those two so well, I'd say the whole thing worked to Louise's advantage."

Chewing her lip, Lianne looked confused. "But Suzanne said she couldn't stand Mallory. So why would she help Louise embarrass Lando?"

"She wouldn't," Gemma supplied. "Suzanne is one of the few on my side. And she adores Lando, always has."

Lando took a gulp of his soda pop. "Doesn't matter. As soon as my head clears, I'm thinking about arresting both of them for possession. Dale already impounded ample evidence to do it, a ready-made excuse to throw them in jail."

"But you won't do that," Gemma pointed out. "It wouldn't hurt to steer Buddy into a rehab program. That's the difference between Coyote Wells and the big city---we take care of our own. Luke, you should go see Suzanne and suggest rehab for Buddy, make sure he gets there and stays there until he's on the road to a real recovery."

Luke gave her a broad smile. "Good idea. But Lando should come with me and put a little fear into Buddy to make sure he follows through. Suzanne will go along with whatever Lando recommends."

"Don't be so sure of that," Lando stated. "Do you have any idea how many times I advised her to get a restraining order on Buddy. Every time he hit her, I'd use the same speech. In each instance, she always forgave him. Which is why getting Buddy into rehab isn't a bad plan. I'll do my part."

"What's the word on Gafford?" Zeb wanted to know. "Is he the one who killed Mallory?"

Lando shook his head. "I spent the better part of a day checking out his alibi, talking to every co-worker that I could. It seems he's been in Crescent City for two months now working on a construction project that's just getting started, building a new apartment complex. He comes back occasionally to check on his cabin, but mostly stays close to the work site. The last time he came to town was Thursday when he hooked up with Mallory. His supervisor says he was back at work first thing Friday morning."

Leia raised a brow in challenge. "But Crescent City isn't that far from here. He could've come back to town during the festival on Saturday and Sunday and gone unnoticed. Gafford had the weekend to bum around his cabin."

"Not according to his supervisor. The guy says Gafford was in Crescent City exactly where he was supposed to be. Sunday night Gafford played poker until almost midnight in one of the motel rooms belonging to a co-worker. After that, he headed off to his own room. Gafford has at least five witnesses who say he was with them all evening. At the time of the murder Billy Gafford was losing at cards."

Gemma finished off her chicken, sealing up her trash in a plastic bag. "It wasn't Gafford who killed her. I told Lando that when I saw her arguing with another man that night, that didn't fit his description."

"You did? Where?" Luke said in wonder. "That's amazing. What did he look like?"

Gemma chewed her bottom lip. "It was nighttime. Mallory was standing on the beach with a man who looked familiar, like someone I've seen around town. But it was dark, and I didn't get a good enough look at him." She eyed Lando before adding, "It was foggy Sunday night so I couldn't have gotten a clear view of him anyway. Maybe next time, I'll do better."

"Next time," Lando grunted.

Leia elbowed her brother in the ribs. "She did play a huge role in solving the murders last month so if I were you I wouldn't give her any guff about 'seeing' anything."

"I'm not giving her guff," Lando protested. "I'm impatient. I want to get this thing resolved and get Louise out of my hair for good."

"I can't believe you threatened to fire her," Zeb said. "That's long overdue."

Gemma stared at Lando. "You didn't mention that. She'll go ballistic. She'll likely sue you…for something."

"She won't sue anyone. I have a list of complaints filed against Louise that go back years. She tries a lawsuit, she'll lose."

"I hope you know what you're doing," Gemma uttered. "It's been my experience that most people don't win against Louise Rawlins."

Fascinated with the topic, Lianne stoked the worry. "Why is that?"

Leia swallowed her last bite and started cleanup. "Because she's fearless when it comes to taking anyone on, and she seems to have deep pockets to pay for lawyers. Which begs the question, where does she get her money?"

Gemma thought about that and turned to Lando. "Does she make that kind of salary, enough to blow on attorney's fees?"

"Hell, I don't make that kind of money. She even mentioned a few times that she has her house paid off, so there's no mortgage for her to worry about without a job."

"That's what I thought. Anyway, getting back to what I saw. Mallory was fighting with this guy, *and* she was still fully dressed while doing it. Sometime after that things must've have taken a turn toward violent. I don't think she lived long after that."

Lando got to his feet to help his sister pack up. "The thing is, Mallory isn't the first female that died on that same stretch of beach. There's another case that happened years ago on Caulfield's watch. A girl whose remains were found just beyond the bend where the riptide becomes dangerous during high tide."

Gemma's eyes widened. "Is that the case you wanted me to look at, the one you mentioned last Sunday night?"

Lando shifted his body weight to look at Gemma. "That's the one. The girl couldn't have been any older than fourteen. What breaks my heart is that after all this time, she's still a Jane Doe. Caulfield never ID'd her. Not sure if it was from laziness or ineptitude. Either way, I can't find her killer if I don't even know where she came from or who she is."

Gemma's sigh was laced with sadness. "Jane Doe should get justice, even after all these years. No one deserves that. What happened to her remains?"

"The county paid for a plot. She had a simple burial with no headstone, just a marker that says the date she was found."

"That's so sad," Lianne added. "There has to be a way to find out who she is."

"Don't forget about Chloe Pendleton," Zeb declared, looking around at the canyon walls. "Hikers found her remains out at Spirit Lake, less than two miles from where we are now. She'd been strangled, her hyoid bone snapped. That's one of my unsolved cases and it doesn't have anything to do with incompetence or laziness on my part. I ran down every single lead that came my way, only to hit a brick wall at every one of them. It's been five years now and I still don't have anything solid. I don't know why a young store clerk from Reno was found on the Rez. She had no known connection to the area, no relatives here, no one I could locate." He looked at Gemma. "Maybe you could…you know…come into the office sometime and go over that file."

Gemma hugged her knees to her chest, an amused look on her face. "Guys, I hate to remind you, but I'm not exactly a psychic detective, at least not yet. I didn't even see fog on the beach in my Mallory vision. Who's to say Mallory didn't argue with a woman? So far, my visions haven't exactly instilled confidence."

"Hey, I believe in you," Leia said. "And anyone who doesn't should be ignored."

"Absolutely," Lianne added. "That's why it wouldn't hurt to delve into both case files. You're on a roll, or is it a streak? You don't mess with a streak. Am I right?"

Luke bumped her shoulder. "You are indeed. Not to mention, the five of us believe in Gemma's ability. That's all that should matter."

"It matters a great deal," Gemma responded. "But I have a business to run, candy to sell. Some people in town still think of me as 'that turncoat who left to live in Snob Hill.' I'm not sure what they'll think after Louise gets through claiming that I'm a witch. Certain people around here seemed to have accepted Gram's psychic abilities. But a witch? I doubt they'd see that as a step up. Sometimes I don't get people at all."

"Your grandmother didn't solve murders," Lando pointed out. "To some people Marissa simply helped them through life. Add in homicide to that and people are easily spooked."

Zeb squinted into the setting sun making its way over Fire Mountain. "I hate to cut this party short, but we're losing the light. We should probably start heading back before it gets too dark to negotiate the trail, especially for Bandit and Gypsy."

"But we didn't get to go exploring," Gemma pointed out. "I wanted to check out that cave."

"Sorry. But the horses come first," Zeb said with authority. "If you plan to come back, get an earlier start."

Gemma settled into the saddle with regret. But she knew she'd be coming here again at the first opportunity. Hesitating so the others would go first, she held Gypsy back so that she'd be bringing up the rear.

One glance over her shoulder, she stared for as long as she could at the canyon. An eerie wind whistled through its corridors of hard stone walls. She thought of Aponivi, and decided that he must be thinking of her.

"I'll be back," she muttered. "I'll come back so you'll have to show me more, more of the past, more of what I don't know."

"What are you mumbling about?" Lando asked.

"Nothing. Just seeing the spiritual side of this place and feeling its power for maybe the first time in my life."

11

That night, as they lay in bed, Lando took Gemma's hand. "What did you see out there today that made you so sad?"

"The people who came before us had it rough, didn't they? Did you know about the massacre at Shadow Canyon?"

Lando kissed her hair and brought her closer. "A sad time for our people. Our own Trail of Tears. We were lucky. At least the government let us hang around our native land and didn't ship us off to Indian territory."

"Oklahoma," Gemma whispered. "It hurts to think how many people died on the trip there."

"Then don't think about it," Lando suggested. "Nothing can remedy that hardship or put a pretty spin on it. Best not to dwell on the past. Any past."

"You're a complicated man, you know that? Not two weeks ago it was you dwelling on our past, not the good stuff, but all that negative."

"Let's not talk about that either. Besides, I'm really not that complicated. I like to keep things simple and on a roll. I'm thinking about buying Bandit."

"I knew it! I could see the love you had for him in your eyes."

"He's a sweet horse. Did you see how he and I moved together? Not once on the trip did he falter. After what he's been through, that's nothing short of amazing."

"He and Gypsy got along well. Did you notice that? I'm thinking Gypsy would love to take me back out to Shadow Canyon, especially if she belongs to me."

Lando tickled her ribs, making her squirm next to him. "Want me to call Willow or do you want to handle it?"

"I'll let her know tomorrow." Her mouth twisted in questioning fashion. "Lando?"

"What?"

"If Billy Gafford isn't the right guy, then who killed Mallory?"

"I think between the two of us, we'll be able to find out the truth."

"You mean like Sherlock Holmes and Watson?" She slapped him on the arm. "Don't you dare call me Nancy Drew. You do that again and two can play. I'll start calling you one of the Hardy Boys."

Lando grimaced. "No self-respecting cop or grown man wants to be known as a Hardy Boy."

"Okay, then what?"

"What's wrong with keeping it simple? Bonner and Channing."

"Better, but what about Bonner and Bonner? I used to be anyway. We make a good team."

"We do."

"What's bothering you? You seem distracted."

"I don't know. I keep thinking about motive. Something just doesn't add up with Louise and Mallory, never has."

"I take it you aren't talking about their bitchy demeanor, are you?"

"Nope. First thing tomorrow morning I'm going to get a judge to issue a financial warrant, then make a trip to the bank."

"You know, I might be able to see more about what happened that night if I had something of Mallory's to hold in my hand to touch. I'm sure there are lots of things inside her house that would help me do that."

Lando rose up on one elbow to make sure he could see into her eyes. "Are you suggesting I let you into her house to poke around?"

"Well, it would certainly be better than asking Louise to let me in there. We could sneak in tonight and no one would know."

"I'd know."

"They do that kind of stuff on TV all the time."

"That's TV crap, pure fiction. And they also get caught every single time."

"We wouldn't. I'm sure of it. You're the chief of police. Who's going to catch us?"

"Gemma, I'm not taking you into the victim's house and that's final."

"Where's your sense of adventure? Sometimes I don't understand you at all."

"Right backatcha. I'm the top cop in town, not a randy teenager full of raging hormones who'd let you talk me into doing just about anything and everything. That's crazy talk so just put it out of your head."

"You're saying our randy youth was all me? Selective memory, Mr. Bonner. You used to be bold, not afraid to go wild and..."

"Wait a minute. I went wild Saturday night and got blasted for it."

"Lando, you got high on pills. I'm talking about your natural instinct to go wild along the many stages of the rest of your life. Big difference."

"I don't see what letting you into Mallory's house has to do with me going wild. I really don't want to hear any more about it. I have a long day tomorrow and I need to get a full night's sleep. That's the end of it."

Which is why she waited for him to get into a deep sleep before sneaking out of bed and getting dressed. She signaled to Rufus for absolute quiet as she snuck into the closet to pull on a black pair of leggings and a black hoodie.

She left Rufus in the bedroom as she tiptoed out into the foyer where she'd left her riding boots. Pulling those on, she grabbed a penlight and a crowbar from the utility room and stuffed them down into a backpack.

She slipped out the back door to walk the three blocks to Mallory's little bungalow in the fog. Sometime during the night, a thick mist had moved inland. It swirled around her legs with each step she took, curling over the concrete, making the sidewalk disappear.

Hoping to conceal this little outing, especially from Lando, she slid into the alleyway and stuck to the shadows.

Kamena had made it clear that touching an item from a person might divulge more information. That meant all Gemma needed was a hairbrush or maybe a piece of clothing she could hold in her hand to see deeper into Mallory's Sunday night. What had the woman been up to right before her death? And if it worked out, she'd get major bonus points if she discovered what Mallory had been up to long before that. If she could shed light on Mallory's deepest, darkest secrets, Lando would surely forgive her for this little covert operation.

Mallory had always maintained a mysterious persona about everything she did, and Gemma intended to poke and prod until she uncovered what was behind it.

The houses along Sands Point were all dark, not a single light in any of the windows. Better cover, thought Gemma as she darted across the street---and almost fell on her face when she spotted a police cruiser parked at the curb.

There was Dale Hooper sitting behind the wheel, keeping an eye on the place like a voyeur. Was it at the behest of Lando or had Dale decided to do this on his own? She supposed it didn't matter. Either way, Dale was the obstacle to getting in there without getting caught. With the cop at his post, once she got inside, if she managed to do it at all, she'd have to find her way around in the dark with only her flashlight as a guide---no turning on lights of any kind.

Then it dawned on her. Was there a security system in place? An alarm that would go off and wake the entire neighborhood the minute she pried open a window?

Realizing she hadn't thought this through very well, she tried to push away the negative energy, tried to rely on her instincts more. But the main thing that ran through her head was the embarrassment Lando would face if she got caught in the act.

She'd just have to make double sure she didn't get busted. With any luck she could locate an unlocked window and slip in without Dale seeing a thing.

Scurrying around back, she clung to the side of the house and inched her way along the flower bed. At the entrance to the backyard, she struggled past a patch of overgrown hollyhocks, almost five feet in height, that blocked off the back door.

Interesting, Gemma thought as she stood on the patio trying to determine whether Mallory had installed a monitoring system. Unable to spot any wiring other than an ancient phone line attached to the outside wood, she clung to the back of the house until she found the smallest window, one that had four old-fashioned frosted panes that had to belong to a bathroom.

She tried pushing up on the frame, but it wouldn't budge. With the slightest bit of pressure, she used the crowbar to hit one pane of glass dead on in the center, so that it shattered into a spider of eight pieces.

She sucked in a breath and waited for the sound of an alarm to blast out into the night. But the only sound she heard was the crickets chirping in unison guarding the flowerpots.

She blew out air, and began to chip away at each crack, trying to make the least amount of noise. After clearing the glass off the frame, she reached in with one arm and unlocked the latch.

Positioning the window up as far as it would go, she heaved herself over the frame and shimmied through the pitch-black opening, dropping down into the tub on the other side, landing on her hands. In the dark, she had to kick the wall to right herself and stand up. Losing her balance, she reached out to steady herself with the shower curtain, only to have the rod give way and collapse on her head before it banged against the wall and ultimately landed on her foot. All before she ever crawled out of the tub.

She got out the little flashlight, so she could see how to navigate her way over the rim. One foot over the edge and then another and she was standing in front of the vanity. Surprisingly tidy, the room was small and cramped but spotless.

If she got lucky, the bathroom was as far as she'd have to go. All she needed was one personal item from the victim and then she'd skedaddle back home, no one the wiser.

Gemma spotted a small canvas pouch with a tan on brown pattern resting on the toilet tank and snatched it up. Perfect, she thought, as she tossed the makeup bag into her satchel.

Tempted to explore Mallory's domain, she had her hand on the bathroom door to go further when she changed her mind. She really didn't want Dale to catch her looting like a thief, so she backed up, wedged herself through the window once again and dropped, feet first, on the grass outside.

She heard muttered voices. It was Dale having a conversation with someone.

Gemma panicked when she realized Dale was out of his patrol car and standing between the houses talking on his cell phone.

Dale's presence prompted a dog to start barking in the yard across the alley, which triggered a skittish homeowner next door to turn on her porch light. From that vantage point the spotlight zeroed in on Mallory's backyard, lighting it up like Christmas morning. It was clear the watchdog and the blazing light prevented her escape from either direction.

Dale came around the corner of the house to check the grounds, his phone still glued to his ear doing no more than a cursory look around.

She had to get out of there and fast.

Ducking down out of sight, she crawled on all fours into the thick patch of hollyhocks to wait until calm returned.

Sitting there, hugging her knees, she didn't realize until this minute how dedicated Dale was at his job. He stood not ten feet away like the queen's guard, unwilling to move from the palace.

Gemma felt tiny insects landing on her bare flesh and then scuttling up her limbs. It was all she could do not to flail them off or worse…bolt out of there.

After ten minutes of bug bites she wanted to smack Dale with her backpack. Just go already, she wanted to shout. She had to wait another fifteen minutes for him to finish his conversation and go back to his cruiser.

After several minutes went by, impatient at the situation, she slipped out of the flowers and headed for the side of the house. Hugging the wall, she tried to make herself as skinny as possible while letting the shadows hide her. She made her way to the front corner of the house, hiding behind a line of juniper. From the bushes, she kept her eye on Dale, waiting for her opportunity to make a break for it. When Dale bent down to retrieve something from the floorboard of his car, she took off running in the opposite direction.

Somewhere in the distance she heard another dog set up a din, but by that time she was halfway to the end of Sand Point. She darted down the alleyway, took a right at the corner and ran like hell toward Peralta Circle.

After letting herself in the back door, she went into the laundry room and got out of her dirty clothes. She tossed them into the washer and used the utility sink to sponge off the sweat and grime from her caper. The water was a cool reprieve from the insect bites. She hunted down a bottle of aloe and slathered the lotion all over her ankles and hands to stop the itching.

Before heading to bed, she stuffed the backpack behind the dryer, then tiptoed her way down the hall and opened the bedroom door.

Half expecting Lando to confront her, she was grateful to find him sleeping like the dead. Rufus, however, was wide awake. The pooch lifted his head and acted like he'd been waiting up all this time for her return. Like a disapproving father, woman's best friend stared at her in disappointment, as though he would forever know what she'd done. The eagle-eyed canine continued giving her the stink eye as she got undressed and slipped under the covers.

When Rufus kept up his judgmental gaze, she raised her head toward the dog, mouthing the words, "Go. To. Sleep. Everything will be fine. You'll see."

12

During breakfast there was no mention of burglary, theft, or breaking & entering. Although Rufus still acted as if he knew she'd committed illegal trespass and hadn't forgiven her for it.

Gemma looked on as Lando devoured everything on his plate as though he hadn't eaten for days. "I see your appetite's back."

"These are the best scrambled eggs I've ever tasted. And the pancakes are good, too. What made you decide to cook such a spread?"

Guilt.

But she kept that big dose of emotion to herself. "You certainly didn't have trouble sleeping last night."

"Nope. Slept like a rock." Wiping his mouth with a napkin, he pushed back his chair and carried his plate over to the sink. "I hate to eat and run, but I need to track down Judge Hartwell before he leaves for court to get the ball rolling on that warrant."

"Louise finds out and you'll be toast."

"Unless Hartwell and Louise run in the same circle, discretion is a judge's mainstay. He's supposed to keep his mouth shut."

"If you say so, but Louise has her long tentacles in everything around here. Keep me posted. Promise me you'll at least give me a head's up if she decides to go vigilante."

"Will do." He placed a kiss on her mouth, and left whistling his way out the door.

She slumped against the counter, her hands hiding her face. "Oh. My. God. I cannot keep doing this. Sneaky is not my strong suit. I should never have gone over to Mallory's house and taken that…"

She dashed off to the utility room to retrieve the reason for her guilt. She ran her hand behind the dryer and yanked up the backpack. Digging into its depths, she pulled out the makeup bag. She wasn't sure how this worked. Was she supposed to open it or just hold it in her hand? To hell with this, she thought, unzipping the bag.

"Oh, my God. It's all hundred-dollar bills." She dumped the contents out onto the dryer and began to stack them as she counted out one hundred and eight hundred-dollar bills for a final tally of ten thousand eight hundred dollars---stuffed in a makeup bag left on Mallory's toilet.

And not a single vision had popped into her head during the count. So much for Kamena's directive.

"Now what?" she muttered out loud, glancing over at Rufus, who wagged his tail from the doorway. "Yeah. Yeah. I know. No way I can keep this from Lando now. I'll have to hand this over as evidence. I know. I know. I was a fool for getting involved. Stop looking at me like that."

She scrubbed both hands over her face. "What have I done? When he hears about this I'll be lucky if he doesn't run me out of town."

Slipping back and forth into panic-mode, Gemma went to work,. The secret she harbored couldn't be shared with anyone until she talked to Lando. Which meant the heavy heart and guilty conscience weren't going away anytime soon on their own.

Knowing Lando was at Judge Hartwell's getting a warrant, she couldn't very well barge into the judge's house and hand over the evidence she'd obtained…illegally. She'd have to wait for Lando to get done at the bank and get back to his office before unloading the cash on an unsuspecting cop who just happened to be her lover. Her explanation had to be stellar. Which meant she had maybe two hours at most to work on her story.

Her mind wasn't on making sea salt and caramel truffles but on coming up with a good excuse as to why she'd felt the need to break into the victim's house after being told to stay away. It was way too late for regrets. She already knew she should've listened to him when he refused her request.

The more she thought about her predicament, the more furiously she ground the cacao beans into powder. Somewhere between the whir of blending butter and sugar, doubt crept in and lodged in her chest. Could her troubled soul and guilty conscience cause a heart attack? Because her chest kept tightening until it was difficult to breathe.

When Lianne stuck a sharp nail into Gemma's ribs to get her attention, Gemma practically jumped through the plate-glass window next to the kitchen prep area.

"Don't do that!" she shouted. "Never do that when a person is deep in thought."

"We have visitors," Lianne explained, jerking her head toward the front door.

Gemma turned her head to see a trio---Elnora Kidman, Natalie Henwick, and Ginny Sue Maples---making their way to the counter. She cut her eyes toward Lianne and wiped her hands on her apron. In a low voice, she warned Lianne, "If Louise sent the librarian to warn me about the lynch mob she rounded up, run out the back door and save yourself. Don't go down with the ship."

"They do look serious," Lianne remarked in a whisper.

"Let's see what's on their minds." Gemma turned her attention to the ladies. She tried to make her voice as upbeat as possible. "Haven't seen you guys in here in a while. What can I get you today? Paloma swears the Mayan truffles are first-rate."

"A bag of those would be great," Elnora said. "But we aren't here for the chocolate. The Happy Bookers held a meeting last night---minus Holly Dowell, of course, who tells us she's dropping out. Anyway, those of us who are left voted to open the door to new members."

"People keep dying," Ginny Sue added in a flat tone. "We've dwindled down to an embarrassing few. Before anyone else croaks we'd like to get our membership up."

Elnora frowned at Ginny Sue's presentation. "While I might not have put it quite that way..." the librarian continued, "we want you and Lianne to join our little book club. Leia, too, if you can talk her into it."

"And anyone else you can persuade," Ginny Sue finished. "I'm working on a few people myself, but it seems no one has time to read anymore, which is just sad."

Natalie cleared her throat. "Reading is so much more enjoyable than sitting around and watching those ridiculous reality TV shows that are so popular these days. To get our membership up, we need fresh faces, people who will actually read the material and be able to contribute to the discussion."

Elnora nodded. "Marissa used to be the driving force for all of us. She'd send reminders as the meeting drew closer. And we could always count on Collette to keep us organized. Marnie, bless her heart, would suggest the best reading material she'd hear about from the faculty at school. But after losing those three, we're on the brink of disbanding."

"We don't want to do that," Ginny Sue lamented. "Every community should have a vital and active book club. It's what separates us from chaos and lawlessness. If this town can't muster up the membership for a little ol' book club, then we're doomed as a society."

"You're not doomed. I'd be honored to be a part of it," Gemma said when she could finally get a word in. "Leia's super busy, but I'm sure she'd be happy to contribute. She loves to read."

Lianne piped up, "And as a newcomer, it'd be a great way for me to meet more people. Thanks for including me."

Elnora's face lit up, beaming along with the other two women. "Then it's settled. Our first meeting is next Thursday evening at my house. At that time, I'll get your email addresses and pertinent information for future meetings. Ten days should give you plenty of time to read our next selection, *Morning Splendor* by Lorna Garrison, four hundred and fifty pages of vivid descriptions from the Great Depression. As a former schoolteacher, Lorna has a way with words. She wrote a number of period pieces, delightful books that make for perfect escapism from what we're dealing with now. No murder in any of her books at all."

Ginny Sue put her elbows on the counter and leaned over the edge. "As much as Elnora adores the storyline, I'm on the fence so far, but then I've only read five chapters. The setting is Alabama right before World War II. To be honest, I find the story a bit dry and dull. The only redeeming value for me is the old southern recipes the author peppered throughout the pages that might actually be a kick to try sometime."

Natalie scooted onto a stool. "Well, I think it's a perfect choice. Since we've been dealing with all this murder lately, Elnora and I agreed we should try something a little less…stressful. Lorna's story isn't just charming, it's uplifting. Something we could all use around here in spades."

"Sounds fascinating. I can't wait to get started," Gemma said, sounding not the least bit convincing since it wasn't her kind of book. "Anyone need chocolate to help with all that stress?"

Natalie all but swooned. "You read my mind. While I'm here, bag up a half a pound of those strawberry-filled white chocolate things I saw on your website."

"I'll take the same," Ginny Sue said. "But throw in some of those dark chocolate vanilla crèmes. My sister's down from Medford, Oregon, and she's eating me out of house and home."

Gemma chuckled as she and Lianne bagged up the orders.

After the women left, Lianne turned to her employer. "Do you suppose that it was Mallory all this time who's been preventing the others from asking you to join? Especially in light of the fact that it was your grandmother's club to begin with. For some reason, Mallory didn't want you taking Marissa's place."

"Could be. Did you notice Elnora is wearing her hair different? New haircut *and* she got rid of all that gray."

"I heard that it's because she's dating Ansel Conover."

"The widower who always carries that metal detector around wherever he goes?"

"That's him."

"I think he used to be a professor at UC Davis. I'm sure I had him for a basic science course freshman year. Something about archaeology, I think."

"He does love to dig in the ground. I saw him the other day on the same beach where Mallory died."

Gemma made a face. "Lando won't be happy to hear that. In fact…" She wanted to tell Lianne about the makeup bag, but Lando needed to hear it first. Just as she'd decided to head to the police station, Paloma came through the door dragging her cane on the floor.

"So did the Happy Bookers make you guys an offer?"

"They did, and we accepted."

"Good. Now that that's settled, I want to apologize for my grandson's behavior Saturday night. Van is a hothead these days. Nova and I can't for the life of us figure out why he's so angry all the time."

"Would a chocolate soda help?" Gemma asked with a wink.

Paloma grinned. "It couldn't hurt. You don't seem to be too upset by the nasty scene Van caused."

"My mind's been on other things."

Lianne wiped down the counter more out of habit than necessity. "Gemma's been toying with the idea of taking music lessons."

Gemma sent her friend a knowing look. Bless her heart, Lianne was changing the subject at just the right moment. She slid the soda in front of Paloma. "Here you go. I considered the piano for about two seconds until I decided it might be too difficult and switched to learning how to play the guitar. Standing on stage strumming I should be able to handle. Although now that I think about it, we have way too many guitar players in the band."

Sipping on her drink, Paloma leaned back in her chair, enjoying the flavor of the chocolate. "There's nothing quite like an old-fashioned soda on a warm summer day. You know, Silby's piano is just sitting there gathering dust. You might as well have it."

Gemma stared at Paloma. "I couldn't possibly take your daughter's piano."

"Why not?"

"Because it wouldn't be right."

"Silby would've loved knowing her half-sister got some use out of it."

"Really? You think so?"

"I knew my granddaughter. She was a generous soul with an amazing talent. I've no doubt that had she lived she would've been a first-rate concert pianist. All these years, it's been a constant reminder of what I lost. Take the piano, Gemma. You'll be doing me a favor."

"I'll think about it. I'm not even sure I have an ounce of talent."

"Well, you have a wonderful voice. Let me know what you decide."

It was already noon by the time Paloma left, and Gemma realized she hadn't called Willow about Bandit and Gypsy. While taking out her phone, the makeup bag tumbled out of her purse, dropping to the floor.

Lianne bent down to pick it up. "Nice bag. Really nice. Huh. This looks just like the one I saw Holly Dowell fidgeting with during the Sun Bringer Festival."

"Are you sure?"

"I'm positive. It was right here in the shop. Holly came in to get two chocolate crème sodas and while she waited she redid her makeup, right over there at the corner table. It kinda annoyed me because I thought she should've gone in the restroom to fix her face."

"There's probably a dozen of these bags floating around town."

"Are you kidding me? Don't you know what you have there? That's no ordinary bag. It's a four-hundred-dollar Fendi cosmetic bag, probably from a line they carried a couple of years ago."

Gemma rolled her eyes at the ceiling. "How do you know this stuff and I don't?"

"I used to wait tables at a trendy restaurant, remember? I saw all different kinds of women parading their handbags around for everyone to see, showing off high-dollar Hermès' bags or Gucci."

"I should've known if it belonged to a Rawlins it'd end up being much more than just an ordinary makeup pouch sold at a superstore."

"The question is, how did you end up with Holly's cosmetic bag?"

Gemma grimaced and sucked air between her teeth. "I wish I could tell you, but I can't. Sorry. I'm in enough trouble with Lando already."

"Say no more. I don't want to know the dirty details."

Gemma started off toward the office in the back. "I need to put this in a safer place than under the counter. Look, I need to call Willow about Bandit and Gypsy. Lando and I've decided to buy them."

"That's so cool. Now we'll all be able to ride any time we want."

"Yeah, well, when Lando finds out what I've done, I might be riding alone."

The police station had been a hotbed of activity all morning long. Payce had been poring over all the evidence and logging it into

Mallory's case file while Lando spent hours at the bank obtaining copies of Mallory's account activity.

Jimmy, the only man on patrol, had radioed in several times, commenting about the small turnout at Mallory's funeral. He was standing at the cemetery giving Dale the play-by-play. "I bet there's not even fifty people here."

"That really isn't surprising considering Mallory wasn't all that popular."

"Why aren't you home in bed? Why are you still hanging around the station after your shift ended?" Jimmy asked, still eyeing the people who'd showed up at the gravesite. "You were up all night."

Dale's heart raced with worry. "Does Lando know you sent me over there? To Mallory's?"

"I texted him Sunday afternoon about it but didn't hear back until later. He may want to switch us around."

"That's what I thought. I need to speak to him about something important."

"You didn't mess up, did you?" Jimmy chided. "I mean, all you had to do last night was watch a house. Even Payce couldn't screw that up."

It was something Dale didn't need to hear right now. He was very much afraid he'd already let down the entire department. In fact, he wasn't even sure he wouldn't get fired over it. He glanced through the photos he'd taken with his camera phone this morning and wondered what it meant. If he'd missed something vital last night it would be the end of his career as a cop.

Nervous, Dale ended the call with Jimmy and paced the lobby until he finally got his chance to speak to Lando when the chief stepped through the double doors and headed to his office.

"What's up? Shouldn't you be home in bed?"

Dale trailed after Lando, following him all the way to his desk. "That's just it. I need to speak to you. Right away. Now. It can't wait."

"Okay. If you're planning on telling me that you and Mallory were a thing…a hot item…I'll need a written statement to that effect and you'd have to…"

"No, nothing like that." Sheepish and nervous, Dale handed the boss his cell phone with the pictures he'd taken that morning.

Dale began to ramble as Lando stared at the images. "I don't know how it happened. I don't know how to explain it. But when I did a walk-through of Mallory's house before clocking out this morning, I found the bathroom window broken and the shower curtain bunched up in the tub. I know it wasn't like that when I started my shift. I know that's why Jimmy sent me over there to make sure nothing like this happened. Honest to God, I don't know how it got that way, Chief. Honest I don't. I swear I didn't see a single soul there all night."

Lando turned a visible shade of gray before anger took over. "It isn't possible," he uttered under his breath as he dug through the photos Payce had taken a week earlier at Mallory's house. Every room had been accounted for, every angle covered outside, every window and door captured in still photographs like a pro. He'd done everything by the book. Payce had done a thorough job making sure every inch of Mallory's house had been represented in the crime scene photos, locked in and preserved for all time.

Lando skimmed through the pictures until he found the ones from the bathroom, a pristine bathroom window. Not even a crack in sight. "I think I can explain it. Go home, Dale. Get some sleep."

"Do you want me back over there tonight?"

Without answering, Lando left Dale standing in his office as he stormed out and headed to the chocolate shop. He'd built up a solid head of steam when he opened the door and spotted Gemma talking to Lianne. Grabbing her by the arm, he yanked her into the small room she used for an office.

"What the hell were you thinking? I can't believe you broke into a victim's house like that. Do you realize you could jeopardize my entire case over this little stunt?"

"I know you're angry, but…if you'll just…listen…"

"I passed angry ten minutes ago. I'm more like livid now. What is it with you? I tell you about procedure and you just ignore any semblance of due process. You cannot go around doing that just because you feel like it, just because you think you'll get some stupid vision out of it."

"If you'll just let me explain and tell you about what I found, maybe you won't be so mad…"

"I don't care what you found. Whatever it is, you came by it illegally."

"You will. I found a very expensive makeup bag that had ten grand stuffed inside it."

"What did you say?"

"You heard me. Cash. I counted out one hundred and eight, hundred-dollar bills. That's ten thousand and eight hundred dollars. I found the bag on the back of the commode on the toilet tank."

"Wait. The thing is I just went through the crime scene photos. I'm certain…"

Without letting him finish, Gemma went into apology mode. "Look, I should've listened to you last night and stayed put. I'm sorry I didn't. I never should have gone in there. I know it now and I promise I'll never do anything like that again."

Lando began to pace in the small confines of the office. There was something not right about this whole thing. But Gemma kept talking.

"What are you thinking?" she asked. "Say something. Yell at me. Anything. I know I was in the wrong here and I'm sorry. I'm apologizing."

He put his hands on his hips and stared at her. Another emotion moved through him, something akin to pure awe of what she'd managed to do. "I can't believe you got past one of my guys without him seeing a thing."

"Don't be too hard on Dale. He almost caught me. Maybe he would have if he hadn't been talking on his phone."

"You're saying he was distracted? He's not getting paid to talk on his cell phone. And you should never have set foot in that house."

"Even though I found in excess of ten thousand dollars?"

"About that. It's weird Payce's crime scene photos don't show that makeup bag there the day Mallory died. Monday morning Payce and I got there around eight o'clock. It wasn't there."

"What are you saying? It had to be right there in plain sight. Payce must've missed it."

"Pictures don't lie, Gemma. I had Payce shoot the entire house eight or so hours after the murder, taking each room one by one. It's what crime scene techs do to capture the evidence and preserve whatever comes up down the road. I'd say this is a biggie. The window wasn't broken. That's how I knew you'd been the one to go in there. Only you would think you could get away with something like that and not get caught. And then I looked at the other photos from inside the bathroom. The back of the toilet is clear in the pictures Payce took, completely clear of clutter, completely clear of anything. Nothing there on the toilet tank at all. Get it now?"

"That doesn't make any sense. That's impossible."

"Neither does you going into that house. Does it even matter that you've put me in an awkward position? How do I explain this to Dale? Or more importantly, to the county attorney? How do I explain obtaining ten grand from Mallory's house that could be useful at trial but was obtained by my ex-wife in a compromising, breaking & entering sort of way?"

"Of course it matters to me. What can I do to prove it to you? And at this point I'm a lot more than your ex."

He ignored her comment. "Let's see this cash."

Gemma reached under the desk and pulled out her purse. She unzipped the makeup bag and handed it off.

He stared at the money inside.

"I just found out from Lianne that Holly Dowell has this same type of bag. You might notice the white stuff clinging to the money? If I'm not mistaken that white powder is cocaine residue. Maybe Mallory died as the result of a drug deal and Holly was somehow involved."

Lando's forehead crinkled in thought. "Or it was planted to make us think Mallory was involved in drugs. If this bag does belong to Holly, she must've known we'd eventually stumble on it and see the white powder, and then assume drugs were involved."

"Why would Holly want to make us believe that?"

"I don't know, Gemma. But now that you've handled this bag over and over again, I doubt Holly's prints are even on it. Or anyone else's. Yours certainly will be. Add that to a list of things I'll have to explain to the D.A."

Gemma winced. "Sorry. We could just ask Holly if it's her bag."

"We? You're kidding, right?"

"Ah. So no more Bonner and Bonner crime-fighting team, huh? That was certainly short-lived."

Lando rubbed the back of his neck. "In what perfect world would we be considered a team? Team players trust each other. They don't go out and do stuff behind the other person's back. You went to all this trouble to get a vision, so after all this, what image did you get exactly?"

An embarrassed look crossed Gemma's face. "Not a thing. I was too distracted by the ten grand to pay attention to any vision that might've popped up on my radar."

"Serves you right."

"I did it to help the case," she pointed out. "The least you could do is show a little gratitude."

"Oh, no you don't. You aren't dragging me into guilt when it's you who's in the wrong. Way in the wrong. Does Lianne know about the ten grand?"

"No, but she recognized that I had a bag exactly like Holly's."

"What a mess. I have to figure out how this money got inside that bathroom after Monday. Whoever put it there had to have access and maybe a housekey. I can tell you this. There were no signs of forced entry when we there hours after the murder."

"Couldn't you look at it this way? You might never have found the bag of money if not for me, not for weeks or months."

"That's some screwed up logic there," Lando admitted. "But there is truth in it."

"Why was Dale guarding the house anyway? What was he doing there? It surprised the heck out of me."

"Jimmy was working dispatch Sunday when a tip came in that hinted someone would be trying to get into Mallory's house. He put Dale on it, just in case. It's not what I would've done initially but…it's too late for that now. It seems we've all been had."

"Maybe not. They probably wanted you to go in there and look around so you'd discover the money, manipulating the course for the investigation. I'm the one who got had, not you. While you were spending Sunday recouping from Buddy's pills, I kept thinking how I could get hold of anything that belonged to Mallory. If that bag is really Holly's, then maybe that's why the vision thing didn't pan out."

"Interesting. I didn't even know about the tip until late Sunday night when Jimmy sent me a text message about it. By that time Dale had already been there for hours. I decided to leave him there. What could it hurt? But stationing Dale outside where he says he didn't see anything was a waste of time."

"Not necessarily. I might not have been there all night, but I can confirm there was no one around when I was there. Although…"

"Although what?"

"I did hear muttered voices over Dale's conversation. At the time I thought it was coming from the house next door. That might be why Dale didn't hear anything either. So did you find out anything weird about Mallory's finances?"

"Other than she was flush with plenty of cash? Not really. Other than a few large transfers back and forth in the past few months, she paid bills and bought groceries as usual, nothing much out of the ordinary."

"Define plenty."

"About four hundred grand."

"Holy cow. That's…plenty all right. So are we good?"

Grabbing her around the waist, he nibbled the side of her jaw. "If I get to keep my job, we're fine."

"And if you get fired?"

"Get ready to make it up to me. Big time. Me with no job, you'll have to become my sugar mama. My ego's gonna need a lot of stroking."

She laughed until her belly hurt. "We're both screwed then. My chocolate shop isn't making the kind of bucks to be anyone's sugar mama. But I'll sure give it a whirl. How are you at grinding cacao beans?"

13

Louise Rawlins stormed up the steps of the police station working up a good head of steam. Payce body-blocked her, preventing the dispatcher from marching down the hall straight to the Chief's office. "Get out of my way, Payce Davis. Your scrawny ass won't be able to stop me. I'll slam your sorry butt to the floor if you don't get out of my way."

"What's the problem, Louise?" Payce said, trying to keep her from going any further.

"I want to see that no good rat you call a chief of police. Get him out here, I'm not taking no for an answer."

Her eyes narrowed into slits as Lando came into view. "Someone broke into my daughter's house from the bathroom window. I want the city to pay for fixing it. Do I need to point out that you should be keeping a better eye out for things like that?"

"I'm glad to see you, Louise. Come into my office and we'll talk in a more private setting."

Louise glared at Payce before making her way down the hall to Lando's office. "I'll take a check now, if you don't mind…for the damage to that window."

"Take a seat, Louise. Get comfortable," Lando prompted as he plopped down in his own chair. "As it turns out, I do mind. You should know that this morning Judge Hartwell signed a few warrants. And by a few, I mean all kinds of documents that allow me to dig into Mallory's financial records, her computer, her phone archives, social media posts, even a blank search and seizure if the situation should present itself. You demanding money from the city is a situation, Louise, a curious situation. Since Mallory's cell phone was missing from the crime scene, I'm in the process of going through her phone activity---both landline and mobile. And something strange popped up. Her cell phone carrier was kind enough to give me a snapshot of the most updated calls made from her phone. I find it interesting that someone used Mallory's cell phone as late as Sunday to call and talk to Jimmy, claiming to have a tip. That so-called tip was to warn us that someone would try and break into Mallory's place."

"So? The killer probably did that. There must be something in there he wants. Or she wants. Something valuable."

"Are you stating for the record that you aren't in possession of Mallory's phone?"

"Of course not."

"Is Holly?"

"Not that I know of."

"Since you stormed in here, maybe you can answer a few questions that I've been curious about, stuff that will eventually get checked anyway. What exactly did your daughter do for a living?"

"Since losing her pharmaceutical job she's been unemployed. But she had a few prospects in the works, a few headhunters had recently contacted her about some very good openings in sales."

"Would you say your daughter had an active social life?"

"Mallory was beautiful. She attracted men. Sometimes the wrong sorts of men. Did you check out that Billy Gafford?"

"I don't think it was Billy. Until this is over, and I find the killer, promise me that you and Holly won't go near Mallory's house again like you did just now."

"But the window..."

"I'll get the window fixed. This afternoon if possible. I'll find who did this, Louise. I promise. Just please stop making it more difficult for me with all the false accusations. I realize you're hurting and one way to handle grief is to lash out. But try to keep the innuendo and opinion to a minimum. It might work to embolden the killer. And we don't want that."

Louise licked her lips. "All right. But if you can't get the job done, you should know that I'm prepared to bring in the best private detective out there I can find to do what you can't."

"I understand. So noted."

After Louise left his office, Lando leaned back in his chair and wondered how his dispatcher could afford a high-priced attorney *and* a big-ticket detective without sweating the cost. Where was she getting that kind of dough? Not once in his tenure as chief had he ever wondered about an employee's integrity enough to dig into their background. Until now. He'd inherited Payce and Louise from Reiner Caulfield's time in office. He'd hired Jimmy and Dale himself after sending the two men to a rigorous, extensive training program in Los Angeles before handing over the keys to a patrol car. But now, he decided he needed answers to Louise's mystery money. It might be a simple enough explanation if she inherited wealth from a relative. He'd have to dig a lot deeper into her past. And to do that, he'd need an extensive look into her background, one that went back further than the obligatory seven years.

"**Y**ou're late," Gemma said as she sashayed her way to the door to crush Lando in a hug. She had to make things up to him and decided that would take an extra dose of sweetness. She made a grand gesture toward the dining room table where a buffet waited. "I thought we'd celebrate. It isn't every day we become horse owners."

"We're entertaining? Tonight? Because we bought a horse?"

"Two horses."

Lando spied the food. "Who else is coming? There's enough shrimp cocktail here to feed twenty people. You couldn't have given me a heads up?"

She patted his chest as she took him by the arm. "I know you've had a long, tough day, but I couldn't talk Willow out of doing this or her parents. For the Longhorns selling a horse is a big deal. Selling two is a reason to party."

"Apparently."

Her lips curved. "Be grateful I talked them into having this soiree here tonight instead of out at the compound. Otherwise, you'd be getting into bed a lot later. This way, when it's all over, you can walk into the bedroom and collapse."

He nibbled on a crab puff and began to realize there was an upside to hosting an impromptu get-together. And the way Gemma looked in a shimmering summer dress was beyond a windfall. "How'd you put all this together after working all day?"

"Lydia and Leia. Who else works this kind of magic in the kitchen on the spur of the moment? Your mom's outside with Rufus playing fetch. Your sister will stop by after she closes up. It seems running that restaurant is an endless cycle of hard work. I don't know how your mom ever did it by herself."

"She had three kids she used as child labor," Lando deadpanned. He remembered those days of what seemed like nonstop orders and a sink full of never-ending dirty dishes and smelly pots to scrub. He thanked whatever lucky stars had given him the courage to pursue law enforcement. That pluckiness meant he didn't have to spend twelve hours standing at a grill, every single day, seven days a week, smelling like a grease pit. "My mother always said she loved not having to work for anyone else. But there were times I thought she'd drop where she stood from exhaustion. She did everything from bussing tables to figuring out the menu and then following through with all of it."

"It wasn't all that bad," Lydia proclaimed as she let herself in the side door with a worn-out Rufus in tow. "Owning a restaurant just wasn't for you. You never really got the hang of food service, even though I did teach you how to cook a steak on a grill like a pro."

Lando went to the fridge and pulled out a beer. "Didn't say I couldn't put together a decent meal when it counted, but all the other stuff that goes with running a restaurant had absolutely zero appeal."

When the doorbell rang, Gemma let in Zeb, followed by the entire Longhorn family. Willow trailed after her parents, Theo and Rima, who'd brought a fistful of freesia.

"These are lovely," Gemma began, sticking her nose into the bouquet. "Thank you. I'll use them as a centerpiece for the table. Come on in and make yourselves at home."

Theo looked around the living room and nodded his head in approval. "It's a good day to rejoice when people get themselves a horse. Horses are the key to connecting with our ancestors, with nature, with life in general." He walked around to the fireplace and stopped. "I see you kept Marissa's things mostly intact. It's good for her spirit."

Rima swatted her husband on the arm. "Theo is old school. I'm sure Marissa won't mind when you get ready to make some changes. Her spirit will be just as happy as long as you're happy. That's what she wants more than anything, to see her granddaughter make it in this world content and doing what you love."

"My Gram had a definite bohemian side to her that I've come to embrace. Let me show you the solarium where she grew all her fantastic herbs. I'm even trying my hand at growing lavender in pots. Who knew I'd love taking up gardening so much?"

"I'll show her around," Lydia offered, looping an arm through Rima's. "Unless you'd rather start on the buffet first?"

"Not yet. I'd rather see how the orange mint I gave Marissa turned out. I gave her fresh cuttings a week before she was murdered. She'd planned to debut a new ganache and she hoped the orange mint would provide just the right flavor."

"Orange mint? I don't remember seeing any pots with that in it," Gemma supplied.

"I'll show you what it looks like," Rima offered. "Maybe you'll be able to create that ganache after all."

As the women headed off to the sunroom, Luke and Lianne arrived carrying a stack of books, all copies of *Morning Splendor* they'd either checked out at the library or purchased at the bookstore.

"These are for the new members of the book club," Lianne explained as she slipped her pile onto the hall table.

Luke did the same, dropping his stack next to hers. "If this isn't enough to go around for everyone, don't bother trying to find any more because we gathered up everything available in town. Neely at the bookstore said she could order more, but since it's out of print, it'll take a special order to get anymore from a supplier out of Denver."

"Passing several books around will also work," Gemma said, "depending on how many new members we get. You didn't have to do this, Lianne."

"Yeah, I did. You guys have been great to me since I moved here. It's my way of giving something back. I mean, look at all this food. I didn't even have to cook tonight."

"Trust me, that's a blessing," Luke stated with a grin. "What Lianne does to eggs is not for the faint of heart."

She punched him on the arm. "I didn't grow up in a restaurant like you did with a knack for cooking. I serve food to customers, not prepare it."

Luke nipped her around the waist and danced her over to the buffet. He captured a stuffed mushroom from the tray and dangled it near her mouth. "It's okay with me if you never learn to whip up a decent stew. You have other more interesting talents I prefer."

"I do, don't I?" she said, laughter in her voice.

"We needed this," Lando told Gemma, piling his plate high with steak fajitas. "After the kind of stressful day I've had, it's always good to relax around friends and family."

Gemma stared at her ex. She knew that look well. "You had a run-in with Louise."

"I did, but I'd rather not talk about it and ruin the evening."

She rubbed his shoulder. "Understood. And when you go to Zeb with the problem, whatever it is, I'll completely understand that you shared it with him and not me."

He cut his eyes to hers. "How did you know I planned to do that?"

"I'm a witch slash psychic, remember? If only I could use my impressive gift to figure out where Marissa put the orange mint she got from Rima last spring. Rima couldn't find it either. But she's given me an idea, one that could lead to a totally new dark chocolate cheesecake flavor."

Leia came in after everyone had picked up their appetizers and drinks, slamming the door behind her. "You know what infuriates me about this town?" She didn't wait for anyone to answer and didn't act like she expected anyone to offer a rejoinder. "I'll tell you what I hate. Louise came in tonight with the mayor. That Fleet Barkley is a piece of work. Those two got into a huge argument and when I pointed out that they were bothering the other diners and needed to keep it down, they turned on me. Then when I asked them to take it outside, what do you suppose they did next?"

"They didn't take it outside," Lando suggested.

"No, they did not. Instead, they banded together and acted like they were suddenly best friends, criticizing me for my aggressive approach to a customer, claiming that I overreacted."

"Louise and the mayor, coming together in public? That doesn't sound like Fleet."

Leia whirled on Lando. "I swear if I didn't know better I'd think the whole thing was a setup, a phony fight they used to make the restaurant look bad. I'm telling you something is definitely going on between those two. They were downright cozy afterward, making up by ordering an expensive bottle of wine and finishing it off just before closing time."

Gemma set down her plate and angled toward Lando. "Sounds like Louise is actively going behind your back to rally Fleet to her side, making sure she doesn't get fired."

"But Fleet has gone out of his way, especially over the last few months, to tell me how much he couldn't stand her. His disdain for her goes back years to when I first took over as chief. Not to mention all the times Fleet showed up in my office reiterating how Louise was a pain in the butt, which is almost daily. He hasn't shut up about it since I've known him."

"After tonight, I wouldn't believe anything that comes out of Fleet's mouth. Playing dirty is what Louise does. This proves it because the mayor seems to have had a change of heart about all of it. Little weasel," Leia breathed out as she turned to inspect the buffet. "How'd the shrimp cocktail go over?"

"As you can see by the empty platter, it was a big hit," Gemma replied and got a nudge in the ribs from Leia.

"Grab something to drink and meet me out on the patio. Bring Lianne and Mom with you. Better ask Rima and Willow if they want to join us. I wouldn't want hurt feelings if my future in-laws think we're talking about them."

Gemma did as she was told and rounded up the females, herding them outside under the stars.

Leia had already removed her shoes and stretched out on the lounger, staring up at the sky.

"What's up?" Gemma wanted to know as she handed Leia a glass of Ballard chardonnay. "What's so important that we're out here so the men can't hear us?"

"Oh, that. I just wanted to get off my feet. And it's a beautiful night, too pretty to be stuck inside. That being said, we may have a problem. Now that I've settled down and replayed the whole thing, maybe that disagreement wasn't staged. I heard a spattering of what Fleet was angry about, something to do with his father, something that happened a long time ago between Louise and Aaron. Fleet kept accusing Louise of putting pressure on him, withholding information, and being unreasonable."

"Why would Fleet care about what his father did at this point? Aaron Barkley's been dead for five years or more," Lydia pointed out.

Rima nodded. "At least. Some people say he was a shady character with a questionable past. I know for a fact Aaron had some type of connection with Louise that goes way back to when she first arrived in town, back thirty-four years or so ago. She couldn't have been more than nineteen back then."

Lianne was quick to speculate. "An affair maybe?"

Rima seemed uncomfortable talking about it but decided to take a seat in one of the other deck chairs. Idle chitchat wasn't her style. But Rima decided this might be the perfect opportunity to finally open up. "Maybe at first, but a lot more than that by the time Louise and Aaron had been in town a couple of years, at least that's how it looked to me. I was a year younger than Louise back then. I remember coming into town and seeing this brash, rude woman flit from one job to the next. One week she'd be working at the dry cleaners and the next waitressing at Captain Jack's Grill."

Leia traded looks with her mother. "You're kidding? Louise used to work for the restaurant?"

Lydia's eyes got bigger. "I'd completely forgotten about that. But like Rima said, it wasn't for long, three weeks maybe, before Louise was off doing something else. She finally settled down when she went to work for Coyote PD."

"If you remember Louise back then you probably remember that truly awful summer in 1984. I was home from college. The worst summer in my life began in June, everything around me seemed to shatter in heartache. It changed my life forever. I remember asking, why do these terrible things keep happening."

"What terrible things?" Gemma prompted.

"For one, the car wreck that killed my older brother, Hank Montoya, out on the old logging road, not the section where those women were buried in the spring, but the spur that connects to the Interstate. It's a little farther away from town. That spot they call Dead Man's Curve."

Goose bumps ran along Gemma's skin. She heard herself speak the words, "The ninety-degree hairpin curve."

"Yes, that's the one," Rima said in agreement. "I'll never forget the evening Chief Caulfield knocked on our door with the news, telling us Hank was gone. I was devastated. My whole family was. I remember going to his funeral and watching Donna, my sister-in-law, sitting there with my two little nieces on her lap. Hank's death took away a piece of me, took away my spirit, took away the head of our family. His death put more of a strain on us. We were already struggling on the reservation. We counted on Hank's income just to eat. That was before Theo. I wouldn't meet him for another year, wouldn't move onto the compound with the Longhorns for another year after that. Before Hank died, college had been a struggle anyway. Not with grades, but with money. There never seemed to be enough of it. After he died, I wasn't sure I should continue. My mother insisted I try, though. So I took a job in the cafeteria, cleaning up, washing dishes, anything I could do before my first class started. I look back on that summer as a turning point, not because of the hardships, but knowing I'd never quite be the same again. Ever. I stopped being a naïve kid the day Hank died. Life changed when we lost him."

Willow put a hand on her mother's shoulder for support. "Tell them about the other thing."

"Well, that's also around the same time a young girl was found dead on the beach, something that I took to heart, another something I had a difficult time getting over because it happened so close to when Hank died. I couldn't help but wonder what was going on around town. Why all this death all of a sudden?"

Gemma sat down next to Rima. "Are you talking about the fourteen-year-old Jane Doe?"

"Yes. However, at the time, no one was sure how old she was. Caulfield never found out her name or where she came from. To this day I still go out to the cemetery every June and bring extra flowers, some for Hank's grave and some for the unknown girl."

"How close together were they, the deaths?"

"A week apart, as I recall. I guess I was still reeling from Hank's death when the girl came up dead. It seemed so surreal at the time."

Gemma squeezed Rima's hand. "I'm so sorry. I had no idea."

Leia got up and went over to her future mother-in-law. "I'm sorry, too. I had no idea this discussion would lead to making you feel so sad."

"It was a long time ago. But sometimes things happen that are so hurtful, the pain never truly goes away. I was very young and impressionable, and in such a dark place that when the second deadly accident occurred it really pushed me over the edge."

Gemma and Leia traded looks. "There was another accident that summer?"

"Same place as Hank's car wreck out on Lone Coyote Highway, at that hairpin curve. Another car ended up in the ravine. I had to go to another funeral that August for Lindsay Bishop. After that, I remember thinking it was one of the worst summers I'd ever had here, and I love it here. I was so glad to see it come to an end, though, so I could leave Coyote Wells and get back to school, that I made up an excuse and left a week early before Labor Day."

"Mom's family might've been dirt poor, but she got a full scholarship to Oregon State," Willow said with pride, resting her hand on her mother's shoulder. "Graduated first in her class and came back here to teach."

Rima patted Willow's hand. "I do love the area. That's why I never moved away. And then I met Theo and we started our own family. But I don't like looking back to that summer when everything seemed so fall apart."

Back inside, the guys were still standing around the buffet, nibbling on what was left.

"So it's just like middle school all over again," Theo began, "guys in one part of the house, girls in the other. Or in this case, they're outside gabbing. I've never seen my wife so chatty."

Lando gazed through the sliding glass door and grinned. "Look at that. For once, Gemma seems to be listening. That's gotta be a first. God knows she doesn't listen to me."

"Lianne, too," Luke said. "Whatever they're discussing, it must be fascinating. Lianne's hanging on every word."

"They're bound to be talking about us," Zeb offered as he dipped a chip into the guacamole. "Women are notorious for sharing every detail of their lives on any given day."

"Ain't that the truth," Theo stated. "But your mother is rarely so animated. Look at her. She's dabbing at her eyes. Maybe I should go see if she's all right."

Through the glass, Zeb studied his mother. "I bet she's talking about Hank. She only gets that upset when she remembers her brother. Hank died before I was born, out on that stretch of road they nicknamed Dead Man's Curve. She doesn't talk about him often, but when she does, she gets all weepy just like she is now."

Theo scratched his chin. "I bet you're right. Rima's never gotten over losing her oldest brother. Even though Hank was an alcoholic and drank like a fish, she thought he hung the moon. It was inevitable that he'd end up losing control of his car that day and crashing into…something. His car rolled over twice before it hit the bottom of the ravine and stopped. It shoulda caught on fire, but it didn't."

Lando's ears perked up. "That was a bad spot to be driving drunk."

"Blind stinking drunk. And yes, it was. That was before I met Rima. But a year later she was still distraught, still haunted by Hank's untimely death."

Lando filed the information away in his brain and took that opportunity to take Zeb aside. "I need to talk to you."

"About what?" Zeb asked, dipping a chip into a cheesy, spicy concoction.

"I may need your help with something." He went into his plan on how he intended to learn more about Louise.

"And this intensive background check, you think it'll provide a motive for Mallory's murder?"

"Ultimately, yes. I need to do this on two levels. Computer and lots of legwork."

"Let me guess, I'm the legwork."

"For now, yeah." Lando told him about Gemma's find.

"Holy cow. I always suspected Mallory was into something illegal, just never caught her in the act. Where's the ten grand?"

"Locked up for safekeeping."

"You mad at Gemma for going in there like that?"

"I was. But as she pointed out, we might not have found the money if she hadn't gone rogue. I hate it that she does things like that, though."

"I hate it that Leia works like a dog at the restaurant. But it's her thing, what she loves. We can't change who they are, we can't alter what's in their DNA."

"I'm not sure sleuthing is in Gemma's DNA. Part of me is blown away that she got by Dale like she did and the other part wants to slap the cuffs on her to teach her a lesson."

"I'd be careful teaching Gemma a lesson. There are bound to be consequences. I tried that once with Leia and your sister didn't speak to me for almost a week."

Lando chuckled. "Thanks for the tip. Some days I think things between us are going great and then she does something like this. Putting my job in jeopardy has to stop. It's reckless. What if Dale had spotted her? She could've been shot. She doesn't even take into account what could've happened out there in the middle of the night."

"Then make it clear in cop terms. Was she that good at B&E or was Dale just sloppy?"

"Good point."

"I thought you'd planned to keep Dale away from any job that had to do with Mallory."

"Jimmy sent him over there. This case is already so messed up I don't think it matters much."

"When do you want me to start this legwork?"

"First thing tomorrow or whenever your schedule allows, the sooner the better, though."

"For a chance to get something on Louise or Mallory, I'll make time."

Later, while she was getting ready for bed, Gemma went over Rima's conversation with Lando. As she slathered lotion on her face and arms, she hit the high points. "That's three fatal accidents we know about at that same spot in the road."

"The high fatality rate no doubt played a major role in the state's shutting it down and re-routing the highway away from the coast."

"Did anyone profit from that decision?"

"You're suggesting that someone staged those car accidents in an attempt to lobby the state to alter the northward route out of town?"

"Maybe. Although when you say it like that it does seem preposterous."

"Hank and Michael both worked for the casino. Maybe there's a connection there."

"So you do think three accidents are more than a coincidence?"

"It bears checking out. Who's this Lindsay Bishop?"

"No idea. But when all this went down Louise hadn't been in town long enough to make tried-and-true lasting friendships."

"Every town has a backstory. We just need to find out what ours is."

Gemma scooted closer. "I want to go back out to Shadow Canyon."

"To see what's in that cave?"

"Among other things. I feel drawn to the area, similar to how I felt about Mystic Falls. My grandparents had a connection to these places. I can feel it in my bones."

"I could tell that by the photos in the entryway. Your grandfather had a knack for photography. And not just when your grandmother was his subject."

"He did, didn't he? I wonder if he ever encountered Aponivi on his trips into the countryside. I'm sure he and Marissa knew about Kamena. There's a photograph I found that shows Mystic Falls in all its glory. If you look close enough, you'll see the outline of a figure standing in the spray, a misty form. It's a dead ringer for Kamena. Which means she was there the day he took the picture, watching, observing."

"Imagine, Kamena in spirit form giving a shout out. Your grandparents must've been aware of the history. I wonder why he didn't sell his photos?"

"Probably sentimental reasons."

"Can the trip to the cave wait until the weekend? I don't want you going out there alone."

"I'd prefer to go sooner. I need to see what Aponivi wants me to see."

He rolled on top of her to nibble her throat. "And what does the holder of truths want to show you that can't wait until I have time to go with you?"

She yielded as he traced a line to her mouth. "I'm sure it's something important. But right this second, you're distracting me."

"That's the plan. I'm tired of talking about Louise and Aponivi."

She reversed their positions. "Then let's don't."

14

After Lando left for work the next morning, Rufus set up a din of barking and wouldn't stop. The dog shot toward the front door. His tail-wagging was the big giveaway. Her pooch had a habit of doing that only when someone came into the courtyard that he wasn't sure about, someone he'd never seen before.

Through the peephole Gemma spotted Van Coyote standing halfway into the quad, between the fountain and the stoop. Apparently he hadn't found the nerve to make his way up to the front door yet.

Gemma calmed the dog and opened the door, startling her half-brother.

For several long seconds, they stared at each other. It was Van who broke the awkward silence.

"I owe you an apology. I was pissed after Grandma's talk. Saturday night I took Nova out for dinner. Afterward I persuaded her to stop by the Duck & Rum for one drink. I knew you'd be there. I was hoping to confront you because I was still bitter about my dad. Our dad. I kept throwing back tequila. Nova suspected what I was up to, especially when you went up on stage. She knew I was waiting to have it out with you. Nova tried to get me to leave with her then. But I wouldn't listen. When we were sitting at the bar, I started spouting off to her. She said I was dead set on making a scene, embarrassing her, so she finally got fed up and left me there to stew. Our night out turned into an almost-divorce situation. I love my family. My kids mean everything to me. Nova said if I didn't come over here and apologize she'd pack up the kids and move back in with her mother on the Rez. I don't want that, so here I am. What do I need to do to make this right?"

Gemma pulled him through the doorway. "Your apology is enough. Look, I just want to get to know you. That's all. Is that such a bad idea?"

"No, of course not."

"Good. Because I've never had a brother before. I'd like to know what that's like before we start fighting with each other. I'm sure we'll have disagreements over the years, but...I'd like to be your friend."

"I could live with that."

"Okay then. Because I don't want your grandmother's money. My Gram left this place to me. I have a roof over my head, a business, a job I enjoy. Plus, I'm in love. To tell you the truth my life is better than it's been in years. I don't need Paloma's money. It's all yours when that time comes. Let's hope that doesn't happen for twenty years yet. Your grandmother is well aware that my Gram took care of me in her will. That's why I reminded her that she should take care of you the same way. It's not about Paloma's money. It's about what she holds in her heart. That's my heritage, the one I didn't know anything about until my mother decided to be honest for once in her life."

"It was mean of me to say all that. I'm sorry I did it in such a horrible way."

"It's okay. Half the town thinks I'm a witch. I doubt you said anything that equaled that. How about some tea? I made a pitcher, added lavender and honey to it. It's good. You should try some."

"So you aren't still mad at me?"

"I was never mad at you, Van. And even though I mentioned to Paloma I might look into changing my name to Coyote, I wouldn't---not if it meant embarrassing you in any way. I would never do that unless you said it was okay first."

Van lifted a shoulder. "Thanks for that. But he was as much your dad as he was mine. I won't stand in your way if that's what you want."

She looped her arm through his. "Thank you. I'm not sure what I'll do yet. We could sit down together and discuss it with Paloma. She's offered me your sister's piano. How would you feel about me taking it?"

"It's gathering dust in Grandma's living room. If that's what she wants, I'm fine with you taking it off her hands. I'm pretty sure seeing it there every day makes her sad. And my kids aren't interested in playing the thing." Van blew out a nervous breath and ran a hand through his hair. "I should probably text Nova that we're okay now. Otherwise, she might be gone before I get back."

"She wasn't really serious about that, was she?"

Van took out his cell phone. "I don't know. When Nova makes up her mind about something, she usually means it. She's the one who told me not to waste my money on the betting pool at Greendeer's place."

"What betting pool?"

Van twisted up his mouth. "I've gone and stepped in it now." Over iced tea and vanilla cookies with chocolate glaze, he told her about how the betting pool worked. "Bettors around town were supposed to pick a date and time for when you and Lando would break up for good. Everyone seemed to think it would happen soon. They kept expecting a big blowup between you two every Saturday night that would surely end it all. For some people it was great fun. They wanted to be there to see it happen firsthand. Greendeer was in on it, right there behind the bar, holding the cash, which I'm told has reached almost two thousand dollars. Not a small pool when you think about it. But Nova said you guys looked awful happy up there on stage and I shouldn't waste my money with it. She thought it was a stupid thing to do."

Gemma's anger rose in her throat, but she tried to tamp it down. If Louise's witch rumors hurt, hearing about the betting pool was the ultimate slap in the face. "Does Lando know about this?"

"No idea. I don't think so. No one was supposed to let the cat out of the bag. Don't tell Greendeer it was me, okay?"

"Your secret's safe with me. But I'm not promising what Lando's gonna do to Greendeer when he hears about this. What a rotten thing to do."

To prove that point, after Van left, Gemma decided she needed to tell Lando about it in person to measure his reaction against hers. She was so furious she needed to walk off her anger anyway. She clicked the leash to Rufus's collar and headed out the door.

She didn't get far. Two steps away from the flower bed, the vision stopped her in her tracks. The scene next to the fountain was like a play where all the actors knew their lines well and played their parts like professionals.

Five people stood before her, all wearing ski masks and pointing AK-47s at either her or the house, she wasn't sure which. They were all swearing, cussing, yelling instructions, and roaring out a sting of orders. She heard gunfire, rounds and rounds went off as glass shattered.

It was so real she glanced back to see if the weapons had hit their mark and destroyed all the stained glass above the front door. But there was no damage at all. Windows were intact. No bullet holes, no breakage, no broken glass scattered on the cobblestone walkway. Nothing was out of place.

When she turned back toward the fountain, the five people were no longer there.

Shaken, she plopped down on the bench next to the cairn. "What did I just see? Think. They had their faces covered for a reason. What were they so upset about? And what were they shooting at?"

She noticed Rufus staring at her like she was a crazy person. "I'm all right, really I am. Don't look at me like that. I just witnessed something horrific, but I have no idea what it means. Just give me a minute. I'll be all right. I will. And then we'll go see Lando at his office."

But she was still shaky when she got to her feet. The walk to the police station was on wobbly footing and still-trembling legs. Payce must've noticed something was off because he immediately stood up from behind the desk where Louise usually sat.

"You okay? You look like you've seen a ghost."

"I don't know. I think maybe I did. Is Lando here?"

"Yep. Studying crime scene photos in his office. That's all he does these days."

She wasn't sure she could hold up to seeing Mallory's dead body again. In fact, she wasn't even sure she should mention the crazy thing she'd just seen. After all, she didn't even know where or if it fit into the case at all.

The walk down the hallway seemed to take forever, as if she had to tread through molasses to get there. Rufus seemed to understand and pulled her through the thick of it.

Lando seemed to sense something was amiss because the door to his office opened before she could knock. "Are you okay?"

The question brought her back to the reason she was there. "Not really. Did you know Adam Greendeer is running a betting pool, speculating on when we'll break up? According to Van, people all over town are betting against us. That's why we've had so many people showing up on Saturday nights. They want to be there to see it all go down, the big fight that leads to the big break up. They want to see it happen in person."

"What? I thought Van wasn't speaking to you."

"He came by to apologize. Nova made him. We're cool now."

"So your brother gives up Greendeer's money-making scheme? Because I know he's bound to be taking a cut."

"Do you realize we went up on stage and people have been…?"

"Laughing at us? Yeah, I get that."

"How long do you suppose this has been going on? We should do something to get back at Greendeer. But what?"

"We should plan something really devious."

"Like a pretend breakup in a very public place," Gemma suggested. "You don't think our friends knew about it, do you?"

"Should we feel them out or just plain ask them?"

"If we ask outright then they'd know we were faking the breakup. That would lessen the revenge somewhat. Come on, what am I saying? I don't believe for a minute Lianne or Leia would bet against us like that, not Luke or Zeb either. Look, it might've been my idea to fake it, but I don't want to pretend to break up, not for anyone, not even for revenge."

"Neither do I."

"Then what do we do? Because I'm not singing for Greendeer ever again."

"Maybe that's it. We don't have a contract or anything on paper. Fortitude is free to perform anywhere we want. We just won't show up next Saturday night."

"Oh, no. Adam needs to know why. And he needs to get your band's name off his marquee like…right now."

"Agreed. Want to come with me?"

"Are you kidding? I wouldn't miss the look on his face when we tell him. Let's go."

On the ride to the bar, Gemma prodded. "You've been super distracted lately. What gives?"

"I can't locate Louise's personnel file. I searched every drawer in my file cabinet. Hers is the only folder missing. Then I went down to the basement where we keep the old records. I spent two hours hunting through every old carton I could find just in case it had been misplaced. Then I poked through a storage room filled with more boxes. I came to one very disturbing conclusion. Louise's personnel file hasn't been lost, it's been obliterated. It isn't anywhere in the building. It's gone on purpose. I suspect she took it for a reason."

"Which means she's hiding something."

"Zeb and I have been digging into her background. Her credit file begins when she arrives in town. That stuff Rima mentioned about how Louise showed up here at the age of nineteen is mysteriously accurate. Zeb's been prodding more information out of his mom, trying to pick her brain about what she remembers. It's as if Louise Rawlins never existed until she arrived here."

"Did you check to see if she had any connection to Marshall Montalvo?"

Lando's eyes widened. "That's an interesting road to follow."

"Since Montalvo pretty much owned Reiner Caulfield, who's to say he didn't have a great deal of influence over Louise---chief of police and dispatcher---working with Montalvo."

Lando pulled the cruiser into the almost-empty parking lot of the Duck & Rum. "What's the plan? I say we threaten to take our act over to Bodie's Outpost."

Gemma made a face. "That's not exactly our kind of crowd, music-wise. They like their Country and Western old-school, leftover from the sixties. I suppose I could practice my Patsy Cline. But no one sings like Patsy so I'm sure it'd be a major disappointment. I might be able to do a few Dolly Parton cover songs. And you'd have to…"

"Listen to you. Greendeer wouldn't know we'd be bluffing."

"Why are we bluffing, though? I mean this guy took bets behind the bar about us ending our relationship. Adam's holding the money, money that people gave him in the hope they were guessing the exact date that we'd split up. That's cold, Lando. Cold."

"Then I guess we end our association with this place and Greendeer."

As he reached to open the car door, Gemma grabbed his hand. "There's always us putting together a new venue. We could open our own place."

"You're looking at six months to get a liquor license. Minimum. Do you really want people listening to us when they're sober?"

"Ouch. That'll put a ding in my ego, however accurate. Then we have to teach Adam Greendeer a lesson about betting against us."

"Agreed." Lando let himself into a hall of empty tables. He spotted Adam sitting at the bar going over his books.

"Hey, what brings you guys by this early in the day?"

"Deceit," Gemma uttered between clenched teeth.

"Is it true you've been running a betting pool about us breaking up?" Lando began. He saw the answer in Adam's eyes. "That's what I thought. We just came by to tell you to get another act for Saturday nights. We're done."

"Now wait a minute, don't be so hasty. I'll give you guys a raise if you stay put."

Gemma folded her arms across her chest ready to do battle. "No deal. We know now we can't trust you…about anything."

"Look, it was all in fun. What my customers do is none of my business as long as I don't catch them doing anything illegal on the premises. I'm a live and let live kind of bar owner. The clientele is here to drink and have a good time. You guys provided the good time, the good-natured fun."

"You took money and bet against us," Gemma continued.

"The pool wasn't even my idea. Harry Ashcomb came up with it."

"Harry? Why would the pharmacist take an interest in whether we broke up or not? What does it matter to him?"

"It was a joke," Adam said, trying again. "It doesn't mean anybody is laughing at you guys."

"It kinda sounds that way to us," Gemma explained. "Put yourself in our shoes."

"Okay, okay. Would you stay here if I told you something about Mallory that might help ID her killer?"

Lando narrowed his gaze. "Greendeer, are you telling me you have information and haven't mentioned it before now? And you're only doing it because we're threatening to leave? I've known you how long? Why would you do that?"

"Because I don't want to get mixed up in all this just like I didn't want to get involved with all those women going missing back in May."

"I'm seeing another side of you, Greendeer. I don't like it. All this time I thought you were an upstanding kind of guy. You're the one who helped me ID Rance McIntire by his American Express card. But right now, I'm with Gemma on this. I can't bring the band in here every Saturday night knowing you're so reluctant to do the right thing unless you're backed into a corner with no options."

Desperate now to save his entertainment from walking, Adam blurted out what he'd been keeping to himself. "Denise Coolidge saw Dale with Mallory the night she was murdered. There. Now you know."

"Dale Hooper?"

"Yeah. Dale your patrol officer. Now, will you reconsider?"

"We'll think about it," Lando said as he stormed toward the door.

15

"There's probably a completely innocent explanation," Gemma drawled as she followed Lando outside.

"Then why the hell didn't he mention it to me when I asked about his relationship with Mallory? If it meant nothing he should've been up front," Lando grumbled as he scooted behind the wheel.

"I don't know, but I'm sure he had a reason. You should probably calm down before talking to him."

"Oh, I don't intend to go banging on his door in the middle of the day without getting more information. Nope. I'll wait until he goes on duty tonight and catch him unaware. While he's sitting at the dispatch desk, I'll talk to him then. He'll be closer to a jail cell."

"Ouch. That's sneaky."

He cut his eyes to her. "Like someone else I know. Want me to drop you at the shop?"

"Sure. Where are you headed?"

"Someone has to ask Denise Coolidge about what she saw the night Mallory was murdered."

"Wait. I've changed my mind. Instead of taking me to work, now's a good time to look over that Jane Doe file you wanted me to read."

"Now? I really wanted to be with you when you went through that."

"I guess it can wait then. Something's been bothering me about that conversation I overheard…when Dale was on his cell. If you feel this strongly about confronting Dale, you need to look into his cell phone records and see who he was talking to that night at Mallory's house."

"Good idea. If I don't kill him first."

"Lando, you've known Dale all your life. Dale didn't kill Mallory."

"Then what's he hiding?"

"Maybe he's into something he can't get out of, maybe he's in over his head."

"He could've come to me any time with a problem. He knows that."

Gemma rolled her eyes at that. "Sometimes…how shall I put this? You can be a tad difficult to talk to."

He pulled the cruiser to the side of the road and angled in his seat to stare at her. "Is that why you go behind my back most of the time? Because I'm so difficult to talk to?"

"I go behind your back because you're stubborn and so am I. There's stuff I feel strongly about doing and…let's face it…you try to tell me what to do. We're like two opposing sides butting heads. I think we're getting better…other than that misstep I took going into Mallory's house."

"Going? Really? Call it what it is. Breaking and entering, theft, and then pretending the next morning that everything was just fine."

"I said it was a misstep on my part. The truth is I don't think you're a team player. You like everything to go your way."

"Don't turn this on me. You admit what you did was wrong. I'm in the middle of a very sticky murder investigation where I've called out the victim's mother trying to protect you."

"You're right. I'm sorry. I get caught up. Maybe that's what's happened to Dale."

He shook his head. "I can't look at Dale as a friend as long as he's holding back. If he won't come clean about Mallory I can't help him unless he's honest with me. Look, I acknowledge I might possibly be hard to talk to at times, but in my defense, I'm the one who's ultimately responsible for catching the bad guys. It's on me if Mallory's killer goes free."

"I understand that. And it weighs heavily on your shoulders. I'm just trying to help you out, not hinder you."

"I get that. How about if I drive you to the station, you stay in my office and read the file while I go see Denise. Then when I get back, we'll discuss what's there."

"Sounds like a plan."

Denise Coolidge was a single mom with two kids who worked at her family's grocery store called Two Sisters' Food Mart. She was at checkout when she saw Lando walk through the double glass doors and head right for her checkout stand.

Lando eyed the pretty brunette who was checking out Janet Delgado.

"Adam told me you'd probably want to talk. Adam and I are cousins. I'm not sure a lot of people know that."

"Yeah. I'm aware. Is there some place we can talk privately?"

"Don't mind me, Chief. Go right ahead and talk," Janet suggested. "I've still got half a cart to unload."

"That's okay, Mrs. Delgado. I can wait for Denise to finish up."

Denise snickered. "No problem. I'll get Joan to cover for me while I take my break. Meet me in the breakroom in ten minutes."

True to her word, Denise appeared ten minutes later at the back of the store where her aunts had added a little room with a table and chairs and a refrigerator. Carrying a can of Diet Coke and a bag of Cheetos, she took a seat at the table.

"You know why I'm here. Adam says you saw Dale talking to Mallory the night she was killed. Why don't you walk me through what you saw?"

"Nothing much. The festival had just wrapped, and I was bone-tired from running after my kids and working a double shift the night before. On top of that, I still had to work that Sunday night until closing. I'd bought a jug of milk and several boxes of cereal and was toting them out to my car when I heard loud voices coming from the end of the parking lot. I look over in the dark and what do I see? That no-good Dale Hooper having a row with his girlfriend right in front of me. It pissed me off."

"Why?"

"Why? Oh, jeez. Don't tell me you're one more person in the dark about us. Fine. I can see by your face you didn't have a clue. Last spring Dale came sniffing around and stupid me thought he might be serious about having a relationship. I even let him spend the night a couple of times when my ex had the kids. Next thing I know he's going out with Mallory Rawlins behind my back. I told him if that dyed platinum hair is what he wanted, then he shouldn't bother coming around me and my kids anymore. And then that Sunday night I see them arguing."

"Didn't it make you happy that they weren't getting along?"

Denise popped the top on her soda and sighed. "Maybe a little. Okay, a lot. But it did make me realize those two deserved each other. Fine by me."

"Was the argument physical? By that I mean…"

"I know what physical means, Chief. My ex wasn't exactly the calm type in a fight. And yes, Dale had her by both arms and he was screaming at her to listen. But Mallory wasn't having any of that. You know Mallory. She was right up in his face, going toe to toe about something. Right then, I thought to myself that I'd lucked out. That's a side to Dale that he didn't show me those few weeks we were together. But at least I'm glad I saw it for myself. Otherwise… Because now I know there's no future for us. None at all."

"Had he indicated there might be?"

"We'd been talking again during that first week after he screwed up. After taking Mallory out on that date and getting caught, he seemed remorseful about it. We even talked this past Sunday night about taking up where we left off. He called me very late, woke me up to talk about getting back together."

"When he was on duty?"

"Yep. He was begging me for another chance and I kept saying no. He wasn't happy about my answer."

"I have to ask this next question. Don't take it the wrong way. But were you so angry with Mallory because of what she did with Dale that you could've killed her?"

For the first time Denise's lips curved up. "No way. Mallory's not worth it. My way of thinking is this, Chief. If Dale was stupid enough to get mixed up with her, then let them at each other for the long haul. I don't want any part of a guy who finds Mallory attractive. My kids are the most important thing to me right now. Don't get me wrong, Chief. I liked Dale. I do. I liked him just fine. But I need a man who doesn't cheat every chance he gets just because he can. I had that with my ex and I'm not going back to those days, not for anybody. He could look like Brad Pitt for all I care, and I'm not interested if he can't stay home with me at night."

"Good for you. Stick to that and…"

"I'll spend my old age alone…probably," Denise finished for him. "But a girl's got to take care of herself and her kids first. I don't go putting any man before that."

Lando awkwardly patted her hand. "You'll find someone who deserves you, wait and see."

Denise stared at the wall behind Lando's head. "I'm not sure that kind of man exists. But I sure don't intend to be anyone's chump ever again."

Gemma sat in Lando's office with Jane Doe's file folder spread out, so she didn't miss a line. Information was scant. It was as if the young woman barely existed. It was the autopsy that held the most clues. The coroner estimated her age at no more than fourteen years. She'd died from asphyxiation. She had a purple ring around her neck where a rope or a chord had been used to strangle her to death.

"What could a young girl have done to make someone so angry?" Gemma wondered aloud.

Her head was still buried in the document when Lando walked in. "Have you solved Jane Doe's case yet?"

"Very funny. Have you solved Mallory's?" she shot back.

"Did you know Dale had been dating Denise since last spring?"

"Hmm. Well, I saw her sitting in the audience once at the bar, looking adoringly up at him while he was on stage. Does that count?"

"Dale broke that girl's heart."

"What? Are you telling me Dale went out with Mallory when he could've been with Denise Coolidge? What was the guy thinking? Denise is so…"

"The opposite of Mallory?"

"Exactly. Why do men prefer that makeup-laden, face-painted, faux artificial hair when they could have a perfectly darling brunette. I'm so disappointed in Dale."

"Not half as much as I am. I have to spend tonight grilling him about where he was, especially since Denise says the argument she heard got physical. He needs an alibi and I don't think he has one."

"Wow. He went from dating Mallory once to going out with her more than that to arguing with her the night she died. How did we get here, Lando?"

"Simple. Dale lied. What have you learned about Jane Doe?"

"Not much. Did Caulfield look for any missing persons back then? Because there's not a single notation in the file that he ever sent out an inquiry."

"I don't think Caulfield did a damn thing except get the girl buried. Once I read the file, back seven years ago, I put out feelers to other law enforcement agencies, going first statewide and then national. Got inquiries back but nothing that matched her description or her age."

"Does that mean she was a runaway?"

"Not necessarily. Caulfield could've put down the description wrong. It's not unheard of when you do sloppy work."

"But a forensic anthropologist could use facial reconstruction to create a composite drawing. I read about it on my phone while you were out."

"The exorbitant cost for that is more than our little town could pay."

"But she needs to be identified, brought back to her family, wherever it is."

"I'm not arguing with that."

"What if I found a way to raise the money for it? Would you agree to exhuming her remains for the facial reconstruction? I'd suggest using these autopsy photos but they aren't all that great. I mean, just look at the angle. You can't even tell what her face looks like the way they took the picture."

"I noticed that. Sure. If you find the bucks for it, absolutely. We'll exhume her remains and hope for the best."

16

It left a hole in his gut, or maybe it was his heart, to suspect a friend he'd known forever of murder. But he had a job to do.

After supper, Lando headed to the station, his anger bubbling underneath the surface the closer he got. Once he pulled up and parked, he had to get himself under control.

Taking several deep breaths, by the time he walked into the lobby, his temper had calmed down enough to question his best friend and band mate and someone he'd trusted.

He found an unsuspecting Dale sitting behind the front desk with his feet propped up in an incline position. "Slow night?" Lando asked.

Dale immediately brought his chair upright. "Chief, what are you doing here? Is everything okay? I didn't hear anything over the radio."

"I need to see you in my office," Lando directed as he waited for Dale to walk ahead of him down the hallway. "And everything is definitely not okay. I had to calm down just on the ride over here. Do you know why?"

Lando moved behind his desk, only to spot Dale already beginning to sweat.

"You found out I talked to Mallory the night she died. And you're pissed."

"Shows, huh? I just want to know why you couldn't be man enough to tell me yourself. Why lie unless you were trying to hide the fact that you killed her?"

"I didn't."

"Convince me."

"Mallory's a hard woman to say no to. She kept bugging me to go out with her."

"Even after you'd started dating Denise?"

"You know about Denise, huh? I screwed up there. Now Denise won't even give me the time of day, let alone a second chance."

"Yeah, your love life is in the crapper, but that doesn't help me understand how you got involved with Mallory."

"One Saturday night not long after I started dating Denise, Mallory shows up at the bar. She hangs around the stage, but I don't think much about it until later. I'm in the parking lot loading up my speakers and equipment in the back of my truck and she starts crawling all over me, telling me how much she enjoyed the music, how much she'd always wanted to be with a musician. By this time, I'd had a couple of beers…maybe more…and…well…Denise had her kids that night."

"She couldn't get a sitter so that was a built-in excuse to cheat on her. Is that it?"

Dale's face turned a shade of red. "I guess it was. Anyway, I took Mallory back to my place. You know the routine. I tried to break it off with her the next day, reminding her that we had nothing in common. But she refused to go away. Then, Denise found out. You know how? Mallory walked right up to her at the checkout stand at the grocery store and told her everything. Denise couldn't break up with me fast enough. I was furious with Mallory and kept trying to track her down just so I could tell her to knock it off. I finally spotted her that Sunday night walking from the store. I had it out with her then and there and told her to leave me alone, that I didn't want anything else to do with her. You know what she did? She laughed in my face and said she was no longer interested. The damage had been done. And she didn't care if I'd lost Denise over it."

"Perfect, now you've handed me the motive. What time was that?"

"Nine-ten to nine-twenty maybe."

"At least that jives with the witness statement I have."

"There was a witness?"

"Oh yeah. The coroner says Mallory was murdered sometime between ten and eleven o'clock. You see how bad this looks, Dale. Where were you during that timeframe?"

"I told you where I was the Monday after it happened when you asked me the first time. We'd all been pulling double shifts for three straight days during the festival. I was exhausted like everyone else. I finished up patrol and went home. Jimmy will vouch for the time I went off the clock."

"Okay, but you also told me that you'd only gone out with Mallory one time. That was a lie. So why should I believe you now?"

"Because I'm telling you the truth. At ten o'clock I radioed Louise that I was headed home. Jimmy overheard my signoff because he radioed back that he was also on his way home. Once I reached my apartment, I cut the TV on and watched the A's game that I'd DVR'd. Feeling like a total loser, I grabbed myself a beer and wallowed in a good dose of self-pity about how Mallory had played me. I'd lost Denise and I was upset about that. I tried to watch the ballgame until the A's ace pitcher got rocked for four runs in the third inning and I lost interest. I must've fallen asleep on the sofa after that. Next thing I know it's morning and my cell phone is lighting up with a call from Payce telling me that we had a situation on the beach. Mallory was dead and…and then all hell broke loose."

Lando slumped over his desk and rubbed the back of his neck. "I'm gonna need your DVR. It might've just saved you from a murder rap. But in the meantime, this isn't exactly a tough call, Dale. As of this moment, you're suspended with pay until this investigation is finished."

"But we're already short-handed. What will you do for officers?"

"I've already asked Zeb to loan me a couple of his men. I need your service weapon, your police ID and your badge."

Dale hung his head but obliged by handing over his Glock and police credentials. "I'm sorry I disappointed you."

"Yeah. So am I."

Gemma settled into bed to wait for Lando and clicked on the radio. Tonight, the local station, KYOT, planned a tribute to 90s rock. From eight to nine, it was the Pearl Jam hour followed by

Green Day. Gemma didn't want to miss it. She sank back into the pillows and opened one of her grandmother's journals for a little bedtime reading.

Thanks to her Gram's written directions, she'd found fifteen diaries hidden inside the cairn next to the fountain. But in the last leather-bound book, Gram had divulged another hiding place, one where she'd put the others, the ones written *after* Jean-Luc's death, the ones that had come after Gram had sealed up the cairn. That surprise hidey hole had been a sealed-off panel in the back of the kitchen pantry. It was like Marissa had fashioned her own treasure hunt many years before her death.

Gemma was happy to play Gram's game. Maybe because each journal provided her with an insight into a woman she'd thought she'd known. The joke was on her. Marissa had held back secrets, little gems that gave her a glimpse into her grandmother's everyday life, a family history Gemma had under-appreciated or ignored altogether. Some entries were simple reminders that her grandparents had had an uphill battle from the start.

Those early years here were a struggle. Fortunately for us Jean-Luc was lucky enough to find work as a carpenter until the chocolate shop took off. In our second summer here, we were able to buy a secondhand vehicle, a fixer-upper as the seller called it. Jean-Luc used it to haul around his tools. It was an old '57 panel truck, a broken-down mess if you ask me that backfired every time he started out for work in the morning. But ever the optimist, my stubborn husband was not to be taken for a fool. That Frenchman worked night and day on the engine until he got it running like a top. He even painted advertising on the side that read, "The Coyote Chocolate Company." Everywhere he went people asked him, "What is that?" And he would go on and on about my exotic recipes for making chocolate candies. Eventually the advertising paid off and people all over the county began showing up at the store.

Maybe that's how we made so many friends, Jean-Luc and me. It seemed there were always people finding our little hamlet and deciding to stay. The beach was a huge draw for them I'm sure. Like Darren and Paige Bryerson, tourists down from Boise, Idaho, who decided to make this place home after driving through here on their way to San Francisco. They found a friendly place they fell in love with and they decided to pack up and move here for good.

People like the Bryersons might've moved to be closer to the ocean, but I tended to gravitate to Fire Mountain or Mystic Falls. On the other hand, Jean-Luc had his preferred places, too. Shadow Canyon and Spirit Lake were his favorite spots to getaway. We'd squabble about where to go on the weekends, even sometimes flipping a coin to decide. There was always so much to do and see, so many places we found to picnic or just spend a day hiking. Jean-Luc would always document the out-of-the-way spots with his camera. He took so many pictures he started selling off a few, first at the Farmers' Market and then later getting a booth at the local swap meet.

We enjoyed our new home tremendously and enjoyed each other even more. As much as we loved Coyote Wells, the town wasn't perfect, not by any means. We found that out the hard way when things began to happen that scared us. It all started one summer when Genevieve was little. Terrible things began to happen. People I knew turned up dead.

Gemma heard a car pull up outside. A peek from behind the drape revealed a tired Lando walking across the courtyard.

Flipping the dial on the radio to off, she marked her spot in the journal and put it away. "How'd it go?" she asked when Lando tiptoed into the bedroom. "I stayed awake to hear what happened with Dale."

Lando plopped down on the bed and toed off his shoes. "That was the hardest thing I've ever had to do."

"How'd he take getting suspended?"

"Dale acted totally defeated," he said while he removed his shirt and jeans. "If I didn't know better, I'd think Dale was set up."

"Really? How so?"

"Just a gut feeling. Think about it. Dale signed off that Sunday night less than an hour after the argument with Mallory. Anyone could've seen him pull into his apartment complex parking lot. That ten-grand showed up while he was there in front of the victim's house."

"After the anonymous and rather mysterious tip came in while you were out of the office---that didn't make any sense---and prompted Jimmy to send Dale there in the first place," Gemma added, beginning to follow the line of logic.

"Knowing full well I wasn't at the station and wasn't part of the decision-making process."

"Because you were out of action due to those pills Suzanne gave you. Maybe someone out there wants to weaken your position, strip you of your allies, and try to make you look bad. Weird. It's almost like every step since Mallory died has created chaos, the old divide and conquer approach."

"And that's why I love you. I love being able to run this stuff by you, run these crazy theories I have in my head. You seem to always pick up on my train of thought."

She ran a hand across his back. "Glad I'm your sounding board. I like the idea of that. While you were gone I read one of Gram's diaries. Like Rima, she mentions a summer when terrible things started happening and people she knew died. It's eerie knowing that two women during that time were spooked enough to talk about the experience---Rima in the present, and Gram mentioning it in her journal. It makes me wonder if others in town would remember it the same way. Were they afraid they'd be next? Were they afraid to go out at night?"

"We could ask around."

"I think I will. So what do we do about Dale?"

"Make sure his DVR kicked in when he said it did."

"There's a record of that?"

"You bet. It's not a rock-solid alibi, but at least it backs up his activity that night after he signed off."

"Why would anyone want to frame Dale, though?"

"The same reason they're trying to pin it on you. Muddy the waters until you don't know which way to row toward shore."

"Did you tell Dale about Greendeer?"

"Never came up. Why?"

"I think I'll stop by his place in the morning and let him know we still support him."

"You have that kind of faith in Dale even though most people in town will think he killed Mallory? You'd still want to be around him?"

"Hey, before that, they thought it was me. Besides, someone has to tell Dale about the band. And moral support always helps a person feel better, especially when they're getting kicked around."

17

Moral support came in the form of a bag of chocolates and a large mocha espresso over ice.

By eight o'clock the next morning Gemma stood in front of Dale's apartment on Harbor View across from the middle school. She had to knock several minutes before Dale answered the door. When he did, he looked out of sorts. "I brought goodies to make you feel better."

"You're incredible. Thanks. Come on in."

She entered a small living room where classical music drifted from a 1950s Packard Bell console stereo, an old system that played vinyl records. One wall of shelving held Dale's massive collection of albums. The excess lined the floor and other bookcases.

The rest of the room was a music lover's paradise. An upright piano sat in one corner next to an electronic keyboard. She glanced at all the posters on the walls, each one depicting famous piano players. She wasn't sure which face took up more space, Wolfgang Amadeus Mozart or Elton John. She shoved the mocha in his hand. "You, my friend, are an interesting collector."

"I like old records and sheet music and books about musicians. I'm surprised you're still talking to me."

"Oh, please. We don't think you killed Mallory."

"Really?"

"Stop being stupid."

"But Lando suspended me."

"With pay, same as he did with Louise. You boffing Mallory puts you in the 'connection to the victim' category and gives you an immediate pass to stay clear of the case. Period. End of story. Stop feeling sorry for yourself."

"But I let Mallory play me."

"Everyone gets played at one time or another. Mallory was an artist when it came to manipulation. Learn from it. Do everything you can to make amends to Denise. She's a keeper. Although don't be surprised if she never lets you get within ten feet of her again."

"I don't think I have to worry about that. She won't return any of my calls. And when she hears I've been suspended, she'll never speak to me again, not even in the grocery store."

"So you'll shop at the Kwik Mart from now on. Big deal. They have great tamales there anyway. The owner comes from Santa Fe originally and makes the best in town. Don't tell Leia I said that."

That last part finally brought a smile out of Dale.

"Giving you a pep talk isn't the only reason I stopped by. It's about the band." She told him about Greendeer's betting pool. "We're gonna have to find another venue. Did you know about what he was doing?"

"Not me. But I bet Bosco did. Bartenders always know the juiciest gossip."

"You're right and he never said a word to clue us in."

"Are we really leaving Greendeer? That would be awkward for Bosco. Where would we play? Bodie's Outpost is old-time country with a lot rougher crowd than at the Duck & Rum. That only leaves Thackery's Pub. And we all know Louise staked that place out as her own a long time ago."

"You're right. Greendeer did offer us a raise not to leave, but you should know he sold you out without a moment's hesitation. Greendeer is Denise's cousin. And she was the witness who saw you fighting with Mallory."

"Ah, and she told Adam. Jeez, I've burned a few bridges cheating on Denise, haven't I? So what do we do about Fortitude?"

"I don't know. Meet and take a vote, I guess. I just don't like the idea that Greendeer started that pool. It's like he was waiting on the sidelines for Lando and me to break up. The entire bar was taking bets on it. I'm not sure I have the same enthusiasm for singing that puts money in Adam Greendeer's pocket knowing that."

"I'd miss the band---playing was always our escape from our jobs---but I understand how you feel."

"Look, I don't want to be the reason we don't play. If you guys come to a decision, I'll abide by whatever it is."

"Okay, I'll get in touch with Radley and Jimmy. I'll save Bosco for last."

"I suggested a different venue of our own, but Lando says that would require money, filling out a lot of paperwork to get a liquor license, and waiting a long time for it to happen."

Dale's eyes widened with interest. "But we'd have complete control then. That's not a bad plan."

"Maybe. But right now, it's nothing more than a once a week gig. I doubt it would be financially practical in the long run to have our own place. What will you do with your time off until this thing is over?"

"Get some practice in on the keyboard, I guess, and go to work at the body shop for my dad. That's the sort of work I was doing when Lando approached me about joining the force. I certainly screwed that up."

"Stop it."

"It's true. That's what my dad will say. That's why I refuse to sit around twiddling my thumbs. It'll drive me nuts just sitting here."

"Having you nuttier than usual is no good," she teased. "Look, I gotta run. Don't get down on yourself, Dale. Everyone has setbacks. Before you entered the picture, the rumor mill was all about me killing Mallory, remember?"

"I do. But no one really believed that."

"You'd be surprised. Now buck up and don't get so down on yourself."

"Thanks, Gemma, for dropping by. I feel a lot better about things."

"Good to hear it. Let me know what Bosco has to say for himself. Okay? I'm curious how he'll explain not mentioning the pool. It would've been a joke then. Now, it's not that funny."

"Don't worry, I'll get to the bottom of it."

She turned to go and stopped. "Paloma offered me a piano. I've been thinking about taking lessons. If I take it, would you be able to show me a thing or two about the keyboard in your spare time?"

"Me teach you piano? I'd love to."

"Great. And I'm not trying to take your place in the band. I just thought I'd make Fortitude a little better if I was more musically inclined."

"You have a voice most people envy. You don't need any more than that. But I'm a real believer in branching out music-wise. Everyone should love music as much as I do."

"You know, you could always teach piano. It's just a thought, you know, if..."

"I get it. If I never get back on the force, I'll need to think outside the box. You'd be my first student ever."

"Are you telling me a girlfriend or two never nagged you to teach her a song?"

He smiled again. "Maybe. But you'd be the first to actually want to learn."

She left Dale's place and headed out to Zeb's stables. If she didn't take the ride out to the canyon today, she'd miss the opportunity to go alone. The weather was nice enough and she didn't feel like dodging Lando any longer. For days, he'd nagged her about not going alone. But it was simple---she didn't want to wait for the weekend. She wanted to do this herself. In fact, it was essential that she encounter Aponivi alone, just as she had with Kamena.

Inside the barn, she saddled Gypsy herself and did everything she could to avoid encountering any of the stable hands. Climbing aboard her horse, she led the way outside. Just when she thought she'd succeeded in her subterfuge, she spotted Willow waving her down.

"Taking her out for a ride in the middle of the week? How wonderful! Want me to come with you?"

"No need. You're probably busy and I've been hoping to get Gypsy all to myself for a little one on one time."

"Super. I wish more owners did that. Any special destination today?"

"Uh, maybe out to the canyon and back, just a jaunt to get some exercise. It's a beautiful day for a ride."

Willow frowned. "That trail's a little rocky. Are you sure you want to go it alone?"

"Positive," Gemma said, kicking Gypsy into a trot toward the same path she'd taken on Sunday, leaving Willow with her mouth agape.

It felt good to be outdoors in the fresh air and even better to sit atop her own horse and ride into the wilderness. Somewhere a plover called to its mate.

Scrub brush lined the trail as the ridgeline---beautiful layered rock formations---beckoned on either side. Serpentine outcrops helped form a landscape that could only be described as a stony, greenish- to bluish-silver overlay of boulders, the color changing depending on where the sun hit the wall. The height of the cliffs made for the perfect natural shelter from the elements, shade in the heat of summer, a buffer against the harsh northern winds in winter.

Her sense of history kicked into overdrive. She imagined a band of brothers and sisters camping in the shade of a manzanita and the forest of thick gray pine.

A red-tailed hawk swooped down from its nest, momentarily startling Gypsy.

"Whoa there, girl. It's okay. He won't hurt you, he's just looking for lunch."

She crossed through a rocky, mossy wash and up a steep incline where penny grass waved in the summer breeze. There in the middle of the field was a herd of whitetail deer, nibbling their way across the meadow.

Approaching the arroyo where the cave could be seen from the trail, she guided Gypsy down into a narrow gulley, following the winding banks of the rambling brook.

She stopped to let Gypsy drink from the stream before moving on through the thick copse of gnarly pinyon pine. They made it past the yucca and onto a flat extension of the canyon where the cave waited, its mysterious formation carved out perhaps centuries earlier.

Dismounting, she wrapped Gypsy's reins around the branch of a redbud tree and grabbed a flashlight out of her saddlebag. While making her way toward the entrance, she had time to think about what she wanted out of this trip.

The cave had to be a significant place for her native ancestors, a refuge used for lodging during a storm, a spot where babies might've been born, a place for lovers to hide away for some alone time.

She wasn't prepared for the bats that burst out of the blackness barely missing the top of her head. Ducking just in time, she realized this certainly wasn't the same kind of serene experience she'd had at Mystic Falls. Kamena had offered comfort. Confronting the holder of truth wouldn't be for the faint of heart. The fact that she was no quitter kept her from chickening out altogether.

The cave was smaller than it looked, cramped in size and smelly. The musty odor came from a slow trickle of water that dripped down from somewhere above her head and streamed across the rocks to form a small pond.

When a snake slithered across her boot, there was an instant of panic before she decided this dank place had nothing to do with Aponivi.

As soon as she stepped out of the cave, a wind kicked up. Even though the sky had been an Easter-egg blue not fifteen minutes earlier, it was now cloudy with blue-black storm clouds forming to the west.

"Is that rain moving in? That's all we need right now," Gemma lamented to Gypsy as she untied the reins. The horse whinnied in response. As if in warning, the mare shied away, ready to bolt.

Gemma patted the pony's ribs to settle her down and then rested her head on the horse's mane. "Easy, girl. It's just the wind whistling through the canyon."

She'd barely gotten the words out when the gust picked up in strength, whirling, scattering leaves and dirt around them. An upsurge of hot air felt like someone had switched on an oven. The force magnified, creating a vortex.

She held onto Gypsy as the powerful gale took over, blowing her off her feet. The swirling jet of air became night, encircling her and the horse.

As the brown haze churned around her, a strong voice called out. "I am Aponivi. Kamena has told me of your existence. There's no reason to be afraid. Your quest comes through me. From this moment forward, I open my mind and heart to you. You must do the same. Learn to trust your instincts. Always be on guard against false witness, for people around you depend on the truth."

She tried to get her mouth to work but nothing happened. Not until she realized the dust had settled and she could let go of Gypsy and be just fine.

"I need to see who murdered Mallory Rawlins. That's part of my quest---to find out the truth of what happened. Please help me find the truth."

"You have already seen the truth. Accept the dark past. Right the wrong that's been done."

The voice faded but the image it produced became crystal clear. She saw the same five people she'd seen in her vision in the courtyard at her house.

They stood before her, those five, carrying weapons---high-powered AK-47s. Their faces were hidden behind black ski masks, menacingly pointing the guns at…something in front of them. As gunfire rang out, Gemma even ducked to keep from getting hit. She heard swearing and cussing as one of the men yelled instructions. The sound of more gunfire pinged off metal. Round after round shattered glass. The shards littered the concrete roadway.

The wind suddenly calmed and the five men with guns vanished. Daytime returned. She caught the sound of birds chirping away in the redbud as if nothing had happened.

She heard a voice, its familiar angry tone droned in her head. She looked up to see Lando riding Bandit, making his way toward the cave.

"What are you doing out here by yourself? I told you to wait."

"I needed to do this…alone. Was that so terrible? I knew you didn't have time. I'm fine. I'm a grown woman, perfectly capable of riding to the canyon by myself."

"Oh really? You're white as a sheet. What's wrong? What happened?" Lando growled.

She dropped to her knees. "I'm just a little shaken. I saw it twice, the same scene. I think it was a robbery, but it was outdoors, on a highway maybe. What kind of robbery is outside like that?"

"What are you talking about? You saw two visions of the same thing?"

"Five men, all wearing masks, carrying AK-47s, shooting at…I don't know."

"Come on, baby. Let's get you back. I really came out here to give you hell for not waiting until the weekend. I'm sorry."

"S'okay. Let's not argue about this right now."

"Can you ride?"

"Absolutely."

He gave her a hand up and then lifted her onto Gypsy. "But for the record, even Theo Longhorn said it's not a good idea to go riding alone. Ever. Too many hazards. Anything could happen on the trail. Good thing I went looking for you. Lianne told me you rode out here. Then Willow confirmed your destination."

"Stop preaching at me, okay? I heard Aponivi's voice and then saw those five men with guns. It was like I was in the middle of a war zone. Just like before, I thought they might be shooting at me."

"Like a premonition?"

"No. Like something that already happened a long time ago. Aponivi mentioned I needed to right a wrong."

"Correct an injustice? What does that mean?"

"Beats me. I'm thinking of giving up this quest, this pursuit to enhance my psychic ability. I might've aced law school, but this is a whole new ballgame. When it comes to ancient shamans, I'm in over my head."

"Did you get anything out of the cave experience at all?"

"From Aponivi? No. Where Kamena was all warm and fuzzy, Aponivi was downright…scary."

"As a kid, the stories about Aponivi were always kind of creepy to me."

Gemma finally smiled. "Knowing that somehow helps. Were you really worried about me, enough to leave your investigation and come rushing out here to find me?"

Lando blew out a pent-up puff of air. "Murder makes any cop jittery about the safety of his significant other. Are you feeling any better?"

"I am. Thanks. On the ride out here, I realized this trip holds a lot of memories from when we were kids."

"Campouts and picnics."

"I remember the first time we came out here with Luke and Leia. We were probably eleven at the time. You told me this story, a legend about a great warrior named Wee-taw-wah, the spirit of the coyote, who protected a young maiden named Moonbow while she gathered water at a stream."

"Not quite the way I remember it," Lando corrected with a grin.

"Then talk to me, Lando. Make me forget what I saw back there."

"As the story goes, Moonbow was the daughter of a great chief. She woke up one morning and decided it was such a beautiful day that she'd weave her baskets down by the river. She walked all the way out to the nearest stream and found a rock next to the bank where she could easily braid sweetgrass and enjoy the birdsong without a worry in the world. Hours passed, and she had no idea she wasn't alone. Nearby a young warrior from a rival tribe had been watching her from his perch on a cliff. His name was Wee-taw-wah and he was so taken with the young girl's beauty, with her skin, with her eyes and her hair, that he couldn't look away. He spent hours watching her weave her baskets until he noticed movement in the trees. That's where Wee-taw-wah spotted a phantom, something sinister, watching the young maiden work. The watcher kept sneaking up on the young beauty from the other side, getting closer and closer. Wee-taw-wah saw the thing shapeshift into an innocent-looking maiden, ready to fool Moonbow. But the brave warrior knew the girl, the real girl, was in trouble. He called out to his spirit guide, the coyote, for help. Coyote immediately picked up the phony maiden's trail. Wee-taw-wah himself leapt into action, crawling down from the bluff to make his way as fast as he could down to Moonbow to save her. Meanwhile the enemy was ready to strike. Wee-taw-wah took out his bow, aiming his arrow straight into the shapeshifter's heart. Moonbow cried out with alarm until the phantom shifted back into his demon-like self. Moonbow was so grateful to Wee-taw-wah that she took him back to her village to meet her father. Whereupon, Wee-taw-wah asked for the lovely maiden's hand in marriage."

"You tell it so much better than I remembered. Why didn't you ever mention Aponivi to me back then?"

"I did. Over the course of our childhood, I tossed in Aponivi several times here and there. You just weren't paying attention."

"That's the same thing Leia said to me about Kamena."

"Then it must be true. Back then you weren't interested in learning native ways. Don't try to pretty it up. That cave you're so fascinated with was once earmarked as a make-out spot. But you wouldn't go in there. You said the place was too rustic."

"Rustic? It was downright creepy and an unacceptable place to stay for long, let alone make out. And if we've been in there before, why not mention it last Sunday?"

"Is it too much to expect that you'd remember all the times we spent out here?"

"I think it might be. Have you given much thought as to who you'll get to replace Louise?"

"No idea. Know anyone who needs a stable income with benefits?"

"As a matter of fact I do. Maybe Lianne would like to interview for it."

"Lianne? I thought she loved her job."

"She does, but it isn't exactly stable income. I can't promise I'll still be in business six months from now or that I'll ever be able to offer her benefits. She'd be better off with a regular job."

"What does Lianne say about this?"

"She doesn't know I'm out here pushing for her to take the job."

"It doesn't matter. You're getting way ahead of yourself. Louise won't go away without a fight. And suddenly her most vocal advocate is Fleet. I don't quite get his change of heart, but it's pretty obvious he's in her corner now. Up until a few days ago he hated Louise."

"My guess is money. Louise is offering him some type of financial incentive for his support."

"Whatever happened to good, old-fashioned ethics?"

"Out the window, significant other."

"Hey, I don't know what we are from one day to the next. As you pointed out, you're more than my girlfriend, more than my ex. But we don't live together. Some days I'm confused about where we're going."

"What's confusing about us? We love each other. That's the bottom line. Why do we have to declare anything else like we're filling out a box on an application? We shouldn't have to do that. Thanks to you, I'm wearing my wedding ring made from a moonstone rock that came from this very canyon. That says it all."

"It does?"

"We have a long history together that no one else comes close to recreating. We know each other's deepest thoughts. We're each other's best friend. Why does it have to be anything else?"

"If you're happy then I guess I am, too."

"You don't sound like it."

The trail narrowed down but on a steep incline where only one horse could get through the opening. Lando took the lead on Bandit, cuing him into a trot to get up the hill. Gemma did the same with Gypsy.

"I'm just caught up in this case. It's making me crazy. Having to suspend Dale was a hard call to make. I'm always at odds with

Louise. Her going behind my back to curry favor with Fleet is a low point. Then there's Adam Greendeer going along with a sleazy betting pool. You think you know people and they stab you in the back. It's depressing."

"What can I do to help?"

"Stay out of situations that might compromise the investigation."

They reached the flat path on the other side where willow and coast oak were thickest. A snake slithered out from under the sagebrush causing Bandit to rear up, almost tossing Lando onto the ground.

"Whoa there, boy," Lando commanded. "Easy. Easy. It's just a little gopher snake."

"But it's hissing at us," Gemma pointed out, jerking the reins into a halt.

"That's what they do. It's just as scared of us as we are of him or her. Look, it's already moved off into that patch of fountain grass. Nothing to worry about."

"Easy for you to say," Gemma said, patting Gypsy's neck, nudging the horse past Bandit and his skittish behavior.

Lando gave Bandit a little prod, coaxing him into a trot. The horse responded by raising his head and darting past the stretch of path he didn't like.

"You have a way with that horse."

He ran a hand along Bandit's neck. "The more we ride, the more I understand his temperament. Maybe that applies to you, too. The more time we spend together, the better I see why our marriage didn't work out in those early years."

"We hadn't yet begun our journey."

"That's one way of putting it. I prefer to think we had lives to lead, separate from each other, so that when we did come around again, we appreciated things much more than when we were kids."

As they descended out of the canyon, thunder rumbled behind them, a roar so loud it sounded like a sonic boom.

"It seems Aponivi agrees with you."

"If that's his sign of approval I'd hate to be around when he objects to something."

"Me too. Paloma offered me her granddaughter's piano."

"You should take it."

"Do I really have time to learn to play, though? Dale said he'd teach me."

"Then you should make time. Figure out a way to do it. We should both start making more time to do the things we enjoy doing, especially making more time for each other. Both of us have always loved music. It could add another layer to what we already have. And I could still show you how to play guitar."

"I'd like that. Okay. I'll let Paloma know I'll take it."

Before reaching the stables, they watched storm clouds move in from the west. Ominous and dark, the cloudburst seemed to hit just as they reached the barn.

Willow greeted them out of worry. "I was beginning to think I'd have to send out a search party for you guys."

Gemma had to holler over the downpour. "It's like the monsoon came out of nowhere."

Willow dumped grain into a feed bucket and filled up a trough with fresh water. "It does that sometimes. It's almost like the land we live on is smack dab in the middle of a vortex of uncommon weather events, especially during the summer months. In the evening after the chores are all done, we sometimes sit on the porch and watch the sky go from sunny to cloudy in an instant. It isn't the only strange phenomenon either. My grandfather kept track of all the weird weather, even describing strange halos, green fire, or fire in the sky that appeared out of nowhere without warning. My dad still keeps up his writings by adding to it every time there's another unusual occurrence."

Gemma found that fascinating. "I'd love to read about what he wrote sometime. My grandmother kept journals about her life here. It's amazing that generation spent so much more time with books, reading and writing things down, than we do today. Only by delving into the past can you correct the future."

"Who said that?" Lando wanted to know.

"Aponivi," Gemma muttered, without a clue as to how she knew that.

18

A drenching rain made for a cozy night inside Lando's beach house where Gemma and Leia had pooled their talents to fix a scrumptious coconut clam chowder and homemade rolls.

Members of Fortitude sat around the dinner table breaking bread and commiserating. The food was a bonus, served with a fruity but dry vino, and an ambiance that provided their own safe harbor.

"I don't see going back to the Duck & Rum," Radley stated. "But if we want to keep the band together and still play, it seems to be our only option."

Over the course of the evening, Bosco Reynolds had tried defending his boss, only to have the others turn on him. "If it's any consolation, I don't think Adam meant anything by it. Although he has taken in over two thousand dollars."

"It's not a consolation," Lando fired back. "Even if he gives the money back, it's an insult to Gemma and me. I still can't figure out why Harry Ashcomb gives a damn about my love life or Gemma's."

Bosco looked confused. "What does Harry have to do with the betting pool?"

"That's the same thing I wanted to know. Greendeer said it was his idea."

Bosco scratched the side of his jaw, where stubble had grown for several days. "That's odd. I could've sworn it was Sam Wells, playing pool in the back one night with Jeff Tuttle. It was after you and Gemma had that big disagreement over her grandmother. You and Tuttle were in the same camp that thought Marissa's death was an accident. Gemma thought it was murder. And you were upset because Gemma was trying to get Tuttle to change the cause of death. At least that was Tuttle's story. Sam suggested you two would never get along for any length of time. I'm pretty sure betting started that night about when you'd get together and then when you'd split up."

"It's been going on that long?" Gemma asked, astounded. "Don't people have anything better to do than stick their noses into other people's business?"

"What difference does it make?" Lando proffered. "It's still a lousy thing for Greendeer to have done. No one twisted his arm to take the money."

"Does anyone here really think Dale murdered Mallory?" Jimmy said, changing the subject. "That's stupid talk. Dale couldn't hurt a fly. Even when Lando sent us down for training, the guys in L.A. thought Dale wasn't aggressive enough to be a cop."

Dale started to object. "Now wait a minute."

But Lando nodded, glancing over at Dale. "He's right. But aggression isn't exactly a plus to becoming a good cop. You just have to pass the psych tests and have a good head on your shoulders. Dale did both."

Dale sat up a little straighter. "Thanks for that. I wish I'd used the head on my shoulders to keep away from Mallory."

Gemma slapped him on the arm. "So don't make that mistake again. I had this idea. We could put on a concert in the park once a week from now until Labor Day. We have our own equipment and a speaker system."

"Weather permitting," Radley pointed out. "It might work."

"Because of my situation maybe I should drop out," Dale suggested.

"No one's dropping out," Lando stated. "You're our keyboard player no matter what. We play together or not at all. The sooner we find Mallory's killer, the sooner we can get back to normal."

Zeb cleared his throat. "I have some news on that score," he said, eyeing Dale. "It might not be appropriate to go over it now, though."

"I get the message loud and clear," Dale snapped, jumping up from his chair and starting for the door. "I'm leaving. Just let me know if we're still playing Saturday night."

The door slammed, leaving everyone numb.

Bosco got up to follow him out the door. "I'll go buy him a beer. I don't think he should be alone tonight."

Radley got to his feet, too. "You guys carry on. The more support he has, the sooner he'll get back to himself."

"That was awkward," Leia remarked when they'd all three gone. "Poor guy. I've known Dale forever and he's just not capable of cold-blooded murder."

Luke took a pull on his beer. "I hate to see it, but Dale will forever be changed after this. That easy-going guy we know, will disappear. I'm not sure he'll ever get his mojo back the way it was. You can already see the cloud of suspicion taking a toll on him."

Lianne put her hand on Luke's back. "If only we could find something big that would break the case wide open and remove all doubt from Dale."

All eyes turned on Gemma.

Gemma picked up her wine glass. "Don't look at me. Aponivi was no help at all. Even less so than Kamena. There was no real connection between us like I had with her."

"Stands to reason," Lianne began. When she got looks from the others, she went on, "Think about it. Aponivi is a guy. Nothing warm and fuzzy about an ancient shaman who thinks he holds all the answers."

Amused with that description, Gemma took a sip of the Chablis. "Yeah, well, Aponivi said I should right a wrong and then clammed up, did his disappearing act, and left me standing there in the wind wondering what he meant. I don't see how that kind of guidance does anything to help me get better at this. So much for fulfilling a quest. What a crock." She looked over at Zeb and held up her glass. "So if you have answers, Mr. Longhorn, do tell us your news."

Zeb pushed back from the table and stood up. "Lando piqued my interest right from the get-go by hinting that Louise Rawlins didn't exist before she showed up here. I thought he was on to something, so I got a friend of mine in Portland to run facial recognition on Louise's current California driver's license to see if it matched anyone else in the system."

"And by system he means other DMVs going back years," Lando added for clarification.

"The hit that came back looks very similar to a woman by the name of Deborah Borelli out of Tucson, much younger of course. But to verify the direction this was going, I also sent him a photo of

Holly Dowell. Got a hit on Holly as well when she lived in Los Angeles. Same last name matches to Borelli. The sisters grew up in the foster care system in Tucson after their mother abandoned them, left them one afternoon in the care of a neighbor and never came back."

"Then Rawlins must be a married name?" Gemma wanted to know.

"Nope. Neither Louise or rather Deborah has ever been married. Why she became Louise Rawlins is anyone's guess."

"Her fingerprints aren't in the system," Lando added. "So she wasn't picked up on anything illegal as an adult. There's scant details about the kids in Arizona because they were underage and Children's Services frown on divulging much of anything on a juvenile. But something happened around the age of nineteen that prompted Deborah Borelli to become someone else."

Gemma grabbed her laptop. "Something just occurred to me. If Louise got a new identity that year, why not search and see if anything major happened in the news? In this case, it would be news from Arizona or California."

"Throw in Nevada, too," Zeb suggested. "She spent time hanging around Reno before she landed here."

Leia leaned back in her chair. "I find it fascinating that Louise isn't native. I'm almost certain I had a conversation with her last summer where she claimed to be from the same Chippewa tribe as Cheyenne Song."

Lianne had been thumbing through the Internet. "The name Borelli originated in the Tuscany region of Italy. It's definitely not Chippewa."

Lando's cell phone lit up. "Gotta go. SOS from Payce. Seems he has a live one down at Thackery's."

"I'll go," Jimmy offered.

"We'll both go," Lando returned. "Zeb, do me a favor. Hold down the fort here until I see what type of situation Payce has on his hands."

"No problem. Let me know if you need help."

Thackery's Pub was a more fashionable bar than any other in town. It was owned by Peg Thackery, a Brit, who'd moved here after losing her parents in an airplane crash in 1990. Peg offered pricey cocktails, imported cognac, and a list of craft ales as long as your arm.

With a fireplace on one wall and several comfy chairs sitting in front of it, the cozy setting brought people in for its old Victorian charm. It wasn't unusual for customers to spend hours here in one of the big wooden booths, buying rounds of drinks or trading gossip. You could even get your picture taken with a cardboard cut-out of the Queen Mother to use as a Christmas card.

Peg's clientele were loyal return customers who didn't mind warm beer. They came to play darts or cribbage or backgammon. Some even preferred to wait their turn for a crack at the reigning chess champion of the week.

When Lando and Jimmy strolled in, Payce stood in the middle of what seemed like an angry mob. The cop was surrounded by a group of Louise's loyal barflies.

Lando sized up the situation. An inebriated Louise held court, letting her opinion be known about how there was no justice in town.

Louise stood up when she saw Lando enter, swayed on her feet in a grand gesture, and kept preaching her sermon. "Unless you're a personal friend of Chief Bonner's, you're out of luck getting anyone to find a killer around here. Look at that Dale Hooper. He had a fight with my daughter an hour before she died. Is he locked up? Not in Bonner's jail. No one's in Bonner's jail because he's corrupt. One day you'll all figure out what's going on in this town. Bonner's covering up my daughter's murder. The police department is hiding something. They're all in cahoots with the killer. Bonner's inept, in over his head."

Payce spotted the chief. "Glad you're here. Peg called and reported that Louise was drunk. Peg refused to serve her any more drinks. That's when the crowd got rowdy. They took Louise's side. Peg got worried there'd be a riot, so she called it in."

Lando stared at his dispatcher and knew she wasn't drunk at all. She was doing a fine job of acting like she was, though. She wanted him to react, maybe even arrest her for disturbing the peace or drunk and disorderly in front of all of her friends. But Lando refused to take the bait. He looked around at the faces in the throng of customers. Janet Delgado and Claude Mayweather sat a few seats away. He motioned for Janet to follow him into a side corridor that led to the restrooms.

"Get your friend out of here. Take her home and put her to bed."

"I honestly don't know what to think, Chief. I've known Louise for two decades and I've never seen her so…she's all over the place. First, she blames Gemma for killing Mallory. Wants us to follow that way of thinking. Then she mentions that maybe the mayor had something to do with it. Now tonight, she's jumped on Dale's case. Is it the grief making her act this way?"

It didn't appear to be grief to him, Lando decided. But he kept his opinion to himself. "Just get her out of here. Get Claude to help you or anyone else who'll volunteer."

"You aren't arresting her? She said you would."

"Imagine that. Something else Louise is wrong about." He decided to sweeten the pot. "She's probably grief-stricken, like you said, and lashing out at anyone she doesn't like. That's why you should take her home and make her more comfortable. Maybe sit with her and let her cry her eyes out."

"Oh, that's just it, Chief. She only a shed a few tears at the funeral service. I think she must be holding it all in."

"I'm sure that's it," Lando said. "All the more reason, you should look after her."

After leaving Thackery's, Jimmy was all over Lando with questions. "Why didn't you haul her ass in? You had every right to let her cool her heels in jail overnight."

"Because that's what she wanted out of that little performance. Every man and woman in that place would've sworn on a stack of ten Bibles that she was the victim, and beside herself with grief over her daughter's death. That was a no-win situation."

"When I walked in, I didn't see any grieving," Payce added. "She was laughing and having a blast. It was only when she spotted me that she started all that BS about the police department."

"And how corrupt we are," Jimmy snarled. "I'm Jimmy Fox and I haven't once in all my life had to change my name."

Lando whirled around to grab Jimmy. "You can't go saying stuff like that. What you heard back at the house is confidential, a part of the investigation. Got it? You don't go around sharing details like that or spouting off to the wrong people."

"I've got it. Wow, we're all on edge."

"It's only gonna get worse until we figure out what's going on. That's why we keep facts to ourselves." He angled toward Payce. "Try sticking close to Louise's house without anyone picking up the surveillance. If you get caught hanging around her street, just act like you're on regular patrol. I want you to let me know what happens after she gets all tucked in for the night. Understand?"

"You bet. You want me to call you every hour?"

"Make it every two."

"What do you want me to do?" Jimmy asked.

"Keep tabs on our illustrious mayor. And again, keep it very lowkey."

"Sure thing. What are you gonna be doing?"

"Me? I plan to dig deeper into a certain person's background. I want to know why she's so hostile about learning the truth."

It bugged him enough that he spent the next several hours in his office on the computer, combing through state databases hunting for other women named Louise Rawlins. He wasn't so much concerned with Deborah Borelli, but he did want to know how she'd hit upon choosing the name she ended up using her entire adult life. He hit pay dirt in Utah, a state that young Deborah must have passed through on her way to Reno. He set that aside for now and thumbed through Mallory's bank statements for the fourth time.

Around two in the morning, he began to put his theory down on paper.

19

Elnora's house overflowed with Happy Bookers. The librarian took the time to introduce everyone to her new boyfriend, Ansel Conover, who seemed friendly enough carrying around a tray of rolled chicken tacos and dip.

Overall, the turnout was more than Gemma had expected. Just as club members had hoped, there were lots of new faces in the crowd.

Lianne had dragged her reluctant next-door neighbor, Enid Lloyd, to the meeting by promising her food and drink. On the other hand, Gemma had pushed the novel onto Leia hoping the chef would appreciate the depression-era southern recipes. Leia in turn had sweet-talked Rima and Willow into coming.

Gemma joined the others as they took seats in a circle around the living room, determined to fit in with the klatch no matter what.

While Elnora filled their glasses with a nice merlot that went well with the finger food, Gemma decided to bend Ansel's ear on his next trip around the room with the hors d'oeuvres. It didn't take long.

"You have an unusual first name. Anything to do with Ansel Adams, the photographer?"

"My mother was a huge fan. Ansel. Now there's a name that gets you beat up a lot after school. You're from San Francisco, right?"

"Actually I'm from Coyote Wells, born and raised. I spent several years in the Bay Area though until I moved back here a few months ago."

"Weird weather there. Cold in the summer. Is there ever a time when it's warm?"

"Not many know this but the hottest month in San Francisco is actually September."

"Good to know. Maybe I'll surprise Elnora with a trip there in the fall, make the rounds of all the museums. Elnora would love that."

"Didn't you used to teach archaeology at UC Davis?"

"Anthropology," Ansel corrected. "The systematic study of our evolutionary origins. Studying our cultural backgrounds, processing our evolutionary biology, those are some of the most stimulating fields of study. How I do miss the classroom and looking out on the eager faces of my students. They always managed to ask great questions. I had to think on my feet and be prepared for any discussion."

Gemma didn't think she'd ever been that ecstatic about evolutionary origins, but then she'd come a long way since her days as a freshman. "I was wondering. Might you know a good forensic anthropologist, someone who could do a facial reconstruction like I've seen on the Doe Network?"

"What a fascinating question. I believe I could get you in touch with a former colleague of mine who does that sort of thing. Why do you ask?"

She filled him in on the town's Jane Doe. "Her family deserves to know what happened to her. She at least deserves a name."

"That's a noble gesture. Don't leave here without getting Candace Stewart's number. She specializes in facial reconstruction at the Institute of Sciences. She still teaches a class at Cabrillo College."

"Thanks. How much do you think something like that would cost?"

"Don't worry about that yet. Besides, depending on the situation, it might fall under the federal grant Candace obtained. Or, she might get her students to do it gratis as a project. But you do realize the process takes months."

"I just need to get it going. I don't care how long it takes."

"How long what takes?" Leia wanted to know as she elbowed her way into the conversation.

"The Jane Doe project."

"The whole town could take up a collection and pay for it," Leia suggested.

"Now you're talking," Ansel said as he moved on to fulfill his boyfriend duties.

Leia leaned in near Gemma's ear. "When do I get to tell everyone here that those recipes in the book suck?"

"Shh! Don't make waves," Gemma chided. "I don't want to get kicked out my first time here."

"Oh, please. Don't give me that superior attitude. You'd feel differently if it involved chocolate."

"How many recipes did you try anyway? Maybe it was a fluke."

"Mom and I picked ten and split them up between us. Of the five I made, it was that awful breakfast casserole that was the worst. I thought poor Zeb might have to make an appointment to see Luke to get his stomach pumped."

"Oh, come on."

"I'm not kidding. I should've thrown the entire dish down the garbage disposal the first time I sampled it. If the author messed up chocolate truffles the way she screwed up a simple pasta recipe, you'd be livid."

"Well. Yeah. Goes without saying." Gemma looked around the room, her eyes landing on Edna. "Did you know she brings fresh flowers every day out of her garden to half the stores along Water Street, including the shop?"

"Sure. Where do you think the restaurant gets all those hydrangeas we put on the tables? Edna's garden is a showplace."

Elnora called the meeting to order and everyone took their seats. To Gemma's surprise, the book discussion lasted a mere forty-five minutes. All the while she had to keep kicking Leia to prevent her from complaining about the recipes. But in the end Lucinda Fenton was the one who brought it up.

"I think maybe the author left out a few key ingredients. That recipe for homemade dumplings turned out just awful."

That subject had Leia bounding to her feet, thoroughly picking apart each recipe she'd tried and ruined. For the next thirty minutes they discussed flogging the author before the talk turned to more docile gossip. Everyone wandered back over to where the appetizers had been set up to graze and chat about the next book selection.

Getting bored, Rima tapped Gemma on the shoulder. "I thought of something else that happened that summer. It might mean nothing. But then again, it might just help in some way."

"Come with me, let's take this outside so we can hear each other," Gemma said, steering Rima onto a side terrace lined with flowerpots, rows of containers overflowing with every color imaginable of blossoms.

"Geraniums are Elnora's specialty. She grows them from seeds," Rima pointed out.

"So I see. What's up? What did you recall from that summer?"

"Remember how I told you that Lindsay Bishop was the second car accident that summer in August. Well, I forgot one little detail. Lindsay got married that spring, April I believe. She'd only been Aaron Barkley's wife for four months when she had that car wreck. You should check to see if Aaron collected a fat insurance payout afterward. I remember his spending a lot of cash around town after that."

"Why Rima, you think like a super sleuth. I'm proud of you."

"Hey, I watch crime shows. Theo teases me all the time about them. It's sort of a hobby of mine at the end of the day. It's time he respected the importance of murder mysteries."

"I'll say. Any time a spouse ends up dead four months after the wedding is cause for alarm and a reason to ask questions."

"That's just it. I don't think anyone did…ask questions. Do you think the two accidents might be related?"

"You never know. But it's a highly suspicious coincidence. And way past time to start digging for answers."

After she left the meeting, Gemma drove out to that stretch of Lone Coyote Highway where her father had ended up like Hank Montoya and Lindsay Bishop. She got out of the Volvo and walked to the hairpin curve, Dead Man's Curve they called it after all the accidents.

Unlike when her father drove this route, these days this spur was used mainly as a shortcut to connect Coyote Wells to the Interstate, rather than the main thoroughfare it used to be.

Side guardrails, five feet in height and made of steel, had long since been erected by the county so that vehicles would no longer slide off the road and down the steep embankment. Drivers might still lose control on the turn and smash into the guardrail for whatever reason, but they wouldn't end up at the bottom of the ravine, not unless the car went airborne.

Looking out over the route that her father had driven that fateful afternoon from his job at the casino, she realized the narrow shoulder offered no room for error. So how had his car ended up turned in the opposite direction, on the other side of the roadway, heading back toward his workplace?

Standing there in the dark, she willed a vision that might answer her questions. But nothing happened. Distant headlights from an approaching car had her heading back to the Volvo. As she sat behind the wheel, she texted Lando.

I need to see the photos from Michael Coyote's accident.

Should I bring them home or do you want to meet me at the station?

Home.

Mine or yours?

Mine. Need to check on Rufus.

Rufus is with me.

Okay then your house in twenty minutes.

On the commute home, Gemma turned up the volume on the radio. Tonight, the station had dedicated its playlist to 80s rock. She listened to a mix of songs from Prince, Springsteen, and Kenny Loggins, and wondered if she'd ever know anything of value about the man who'd fathered her. What was he really like? And would she be able to accept the truth if it wasn't a rosy, pretty picture?

While Cyndi Lauper's voice crooned from the speakers, the vision came with brutal clarity. The same five men she'd seen before, standing on a concrete roadway, pointing guns. Firing their weapons---rat-a-tat-tat, rat-a-tat-tat, rat-a-tat-tat, rat-a-tat-tat---repeatedly into…a vehicle. Cursing. Screaming. A door on the back of the truck opened. Someone wearing a uniform spilled out of the back, sprawled on the cement. Dead.

There was nowhere for her to pull over, no shoulder to ease off onto, no place to stop except in the middle of the road. She took her foot off the gas and coasted her way down to the bottom of the hill to where a four-way stop, an intersection, offered a place to get out of the traffic lane. Shaken, she gripped the steering wheel with white knuckles, held on like it was her only lifeline.

What was it about these five men that wouldn't leave her alone? And then it hit her. Had Michael Coyote been involved in a robbery, a shootout? She'd been thinking about her father right before the vision. Had he been a party to taking the life of an innocent victim? Had a bullet from Michael's weapon found its mark?

The twenty-minute trip to Lando's took forty minutes longer. When she walked in the door, Lando and Rufus greeted her with the same amount of enthusiasm. But Lando's came with concern. "What took you so long?"

She bent down to rub the dog. "I…I saw something."

"What?"

It all spilled out, everything about the vision came tumbling out in one long barrage of information. "I think maybe Michael Coyote was involved."

"You saw his face?"

She shook her head. "Ski masks, remember?"

"Then how do you know it was him?"

"I don't. But why else would I keep having this same thing pop up on my radar, again and again? My father is the only connection to that part of the highway."

"Not necessarily." He opened a door on the buffet that doubled as a liquor cabinet. "You look like you could use a stiff belt of Jameson's."

"I wouldn't say no." She smiled when she saw that he'd already arranged the file folder and the photos neatly out on the dining room table.

"Have you eaten? I wouldn't want you drinking on an empty stomach."

"Sort of. A bunch of rolled tacos with guac. How about you?"

"Luke and I made Mom feed us---she makes the best chicken fried steak around."

"Now you're just being mean."

"Sorry. But I thought you females would probably pig out at the soiree."

"It wasn't all female. Elnora's boyfriend was there. Ansel Conover." She pulled a business card out of her pocket. "Ansel knows this woman who does facial reconstruction at the Institute of Sciences. Leia suggested we have the town take up a collection for the Jane Doe project. Want me to contact this Dr. Candace Stewart and get the ball rolling? Ansel says it's a long process, very time-consuming. Which means it might take up to six months. But this doctor has students who could help."

He handed her a glass of whiskey. "Sounds like this Ansel guy knows his stuff."

"I had Professor Conover in my freshman year at UC Davis. I wouldn't say it was much of a thrill. I remember his classes were bone dry. Anthropology didn't interest me much. He's a smart guy, though. Elnora actually referred to him as her hunk with spunk. I tried to picture them…you know…doing it…and just couldn't. Thanks for bringing home the file."

"No problem." He flipped open the manila folder. "This is the accident report. Start with that. The rest is…ah…pretty gruesome. Are you sure you want to do this?"

"Why don't you look them over and tell me if you see anything weird or suspicious."

"What am I looking for exactly?" He shuffled through the pictures and stopped at one in particular. "Hold on. Maybe I've just answered my own question."

"How so?"

"Approximately how tall was Michael? Never mind. I'll look it up in the autopsy report."

"What does it say? Van's fairly tall, almost six feet so Michael would probably be near that."

"Yep. Michael was six feet. Look at the driver's seat. It's pulled up all the way for a much shorter person. See. It's locked in the forwardmost position. Someone else other than a tall person was behind the wheel when the vehicle crashed."

"Let me see that." Gemma stared at the image. She rifled through the rest, taking the time to study each frame, wincing at the ones that showed her father's face bloodied and damaged. "Where's the vodka bottle that was supposed to be on the front seat? Whoever took these missed that. It's gotta be here somewhere, right?"

"Take a look at this. The accelerator is jammed. What on earth was Caulfield thinking to let the medical examiner rule this an accident?"

Gemma studied what looked like nothing more than a picture of dirty, metal car parts. "What am I looking at?"

"That's the pedal assembly that shows the throttle. Someone bent the support bracket so that it remained in the forward position. This was no accident, Gemma. Any idiot who knows anything about cars recognizes a stuck gas pedal. I'd bet money that Michael was probably already dead before he went flying into the ravine."

Gemma slid into a chair. "But why?"

"Maybe the answer lies with how Michael's best friend met the same fate eighteen months earlier."

"You might want to add Lindsay Bishop to that. Tonight at the book club, Rima told me Lindsay married Aaron Barkley that spring before she died in August. Four months of wedded bliss is a short time to end up dead in a car accident."

Lando looked surprised. "I had no idea Fleet's father was a widower. The Barkleys were always shoving their wealth in everyone's face, including Fleet's mother, Trina. It never occurred to me that Trina wasn't the first Mrs. Barkley. Do you remember what Fleet got for his sixteenth birthday?"

"A Porsche, and so she wouldn't feel left out, Aaron gave Trina a brand-new Mercedes."

"Back then, I never questioned where they got their money. Is it wrong to do it now?"

"Not if we think Lindsay's death was to collect an insurance payout. Do you have access to her police report? Or Hank Montoya's?"

"I found Michael's file in the basement. I'm sure theirs is in the same file cabinet."

Gemma scooped up the photos and put them back in Michael's file folder. "Then what are we waiting for? Let's go compare car accidents."

At the station, one of Zeb's men was working dispatch, a greenhorn recruit named Cody Chato. Cody greeted them with a cheerful smile as bright as his brand-new badge.

"Only a naïve rookie with an eagerness for the job would still be smiling like that as midnight approached," Lando muttered.

Gemma poked him in the ribs. "Be glad. At least he's willing."

"Zeb didn't give him a choice."

"You guys are out late? Working on a case?" Cody wanted to know.

Lando returned the smile with a little less wattage. "Just doing some research through old files. You working a twelve-hour shift?"

"Yes, sir. Not much happening tonight. But I have coffee to keep me going until Jacob Culross relieves me at four."

"You get sleepy, call someone. That's why we stuck the list of emergency numbers right there on the side panel. Seriously. Twelve hours is a long time to stay in the same spot."

"So far, so good," Cody said, his sunny disposition shining through. "And I'm good with the late hours."

"So nothing's happened at all?"

"Other than Ms. Rawlins calling about an hour ago to report that someone had turned over her trash cans, it's been a fairly quiet night."

"Great. Then we'll be down in the basement if there's anything urgent," Gemma told him as she tugged Lando down the back staircase. "How old would you say Cody is?"

"Twenty-one, right out of basic training."

"He looks more like he's sixteen."

The records room was little more than a corner of the basement. They delved into the file cabinet hunting for what they needed.

While Michael had been driving an older model Camaro he'd restored himself, they discovered Hank had been equally adept at fixing up a vintage SS Chevelle. Lindsay was the only one who'd owned a late model Mazda RX-7.

"Different vehicles, all with defective accelerators," Lando concluded. "I could see the throttle on the older model cars maybe sticking, but the Mazda with less than twelve thousand miles on it? That's a leap. But then again cars do have sensors that sometimes cause the problem. Faulty systems from the factory."

"So you're saying that's how they got away with it, killing three people, making it look like an accident and there's nothing we can do about it because it's perfectly reasonable that cars have sticky throttles?"

"I'm saying one car on the same hairpin turn experiencing the issue might be reasonable. Three is a pattern."

"That means we aren't imagining this? We can prove it, right? Using the photos from the accident scene."

"These photos were taken in the impound lot once they brought the cars up. But it means more than that. We have a killer who knows how a pedal assembly works." Lando's eyes lasered in on Gemma. "I hate to remind you but our suspect, Aaron Barkley, is dead. Besides, Aaron might've sabotaged his first wife's car, but why would he kill Hank first, and then Michael eighteen months later?"

"Maybe Aaron had insurance policies on them."

"Unlikely."

"There's one way to find out. I'm calling Paloma."

"Gemma, it's after midnight. It's waited three decades, it can wait until morning."

"How about we drive by her house and if there's a light on, we stop and ring the doorbell."

Lando shook his head. "And scare her half to death? No one wants to answer the door in the middle of the night."

"We'll play it by ear."

They got into Lando's police cruiser and drove slowly down Dolphin Way to the Mediterranean-style bungalow belonging to Paloma.

When she spotted a light on in the living room, Gemma punched Lando's arm. "Told you she'd be up."

"You're just getting her hopes up. I'm not even sure we should be telling her about this. I'm not even sure we can prove anything."

"Not yet," Gemma countered as she took out her cell phone. "So what if we give her a little slice of hope? What's wrong with hope after all these years of nothing? I'll send her a text. If she replies we'll go in, if not we'll head home."

They waited outside in the car for what seemed like an eternity before the front door opened.

Paloma shouted, "What are you two doing out there lurking around in the dark?"

"I sent you a text to see if you were up."

"I'm up. At my age insomnia is a fact of life. And I don't fiddle with that texting thing."

"We hate to bother you at this late hour, but I have a couple of questions about Michael."

"Michael? You want to talk about Michael at this hour? Come on in. What do you want to know?"

"First, did Michael ever say what he thought happened to Hank Montoya, his best friend?"

"I know who Hank is," Paloma chided as she led them into her brightly lit living room. "Was. Hank's accident put Michael in a dark place. That's when he started fooling around on Katie, acting stupid, doing really crazy things, taking risks."

"Like what?"

Paloma plopped onto the sofa. "I loved my son, but during that time he'd started hanging around with some questionable characters at the casino. I knew he was missing Hank. Mind you, I'm not making excuses for my boy. But for a grown man, he was behaving in a reckless manner. With two little kids and a wife, I tried to knock some sense into his stubborn head. It seemed to me he was bound and determined to get himself into a bad situation."

Lando took a seat across from Paloma. "Did these questionable characters ever come to your house?"

"Not mine. But Katie complained a lot during that time about them hanging around her kids."

"So you have no idea who they were?"

"Not a clue. You could ask Katie, but I doubt she'd be able to give you a single name. You have to understand how busy she was with two little babies. And Michael didn't help her out much."

"Did Michael have a life insurance policy?"

"He did. Katie was the beneficiary. I think it was for a hundred thousand dollars."

"Did anyone else benefit from Michael's death?"

"Not that I know of. I'm pretty sure, no. What's this all about, Gemma? Have you found something?"

Lando cleared his throat. "Let's just say we reopened the case. We're working on a theory."

Paloma began to sob. "I've questioned that car accident ever since Reiner knocked on my door that night and told me Michael lost control of his vehicle. He tried to make me believe it might've been on purpose. He said Michael had been drinking and went over the guardrail at a high rate of speed. I should've done more about it back then."

Gemma wrapped her arms around Paloma's shoulders. "You were in pain and grieving. You couldn't have done a thing to change the outcome. I'm sorry I brought all this hurt back up again."

"Don't be. I need to know the truth. You and Van need to know what happened. Then maybe we can all rest easier about the past."

20

"The past seems to keep haunting everyone around here," Gemma complained the next morning over breakfast.

"If you're still stewing about those car accidents, Lindsay Bishop's is the only one where we might have a motive and a suspect. But since Aaron Barkley is five years in the grave, that won't help us much with the other two or finding the connection."

"Yours is a frustrating way to make a living. I see why solving a cold case is so difficult. It's almost impossible to get at the truth when decades have gone by. Ronald Reagan was president when this happened."

"Contrary to public perception, cold cases are not solved by DNA, but by old witnesses stepping forward. Never underestimate a guilty conscience. That's not to say I wouldn't say no to cracking this case by DNA."

"I doubt you'll discover DNA. In Mallory's maybe. Do you find it odd that murder brings us together so much?"

He laid a hand over hers. "Is it the foundation of our relationship?"

"No, I wouldn't say that."

"There you go."

They cleaned up the dishes together and then went their separate ways.

But halfway to work, Gemma texted Lianne that she'd be a little late, advising her one employee to sell the inventory on hand until she got there.

She swung back to the house to pick up Rufus. The dog would enjoy fresh air and the ride out to the stables. Owning Gypsy gave her a ready-made excuse to go out there any time she felt like it. Today, she used that reason in hopes of persuading Rima to talk about that summer of '84 again.

Willow was happy to see her with Rufus, welcoming them from the bottom step of the front porch. Rufus all but knocked her down.

"Such a beautiful boy," Willow said, giving the pooch a rubdown.

"He's sweet, but he loves it when he's the center of attention. Is your mom in?"

"Sure. How about if I take this sweet guy for a walk around the barn?"

"I'm sure he'd love it. Thanks."

"Go on in, Mom's in the study going over the feed bill. About this time I'm sure she could use a distraction."

Gemma let herself into the house and was admiring the tasteful furnishings when Rima strolled out of the office.

"What brings you out here?"

"I came to see Gypsy. At least that's the excuse I intended to use. I wanted to talk to you again about your brother."

Rima huffed out a sigh. "I was just about to get another cup of coffee. Let's go into the kitchen."

Even though Rima seemed annoyed, Gemma sensed a part of her didn't mind being bothered. "I know you don't like dredging up the past, but you loved your brother. What if I told you that I didn't think his death was alcohol-related at all or that it was even an accident?"

"What? Why would you think that?"

"Did you ever wonder why Michael Coyote ended up the same way?"

Rima lifted a shoulder. "Sure I did. Paloma's son losing his life on that same stretch of road so soon after Hank raised all kinds of red flags. They knew each other, worked at the same casino as blackjack dealers. Why anyone would think the accidents weren't connected is beyond me."

"Exactly. I need to know how deep the connection was between your brother and my…Michael."

"It goes back years to when they were kids. You see, Hank and I came from a large family. Seven kids. Hank was the oldest. After my father died Hank became the head of the family. The pressure was on him to get a good enough job so he could support a bunch of hungry mouths. Times were tough without my dad. But to help out, as soon as I turned thirteen I started trying to find babysitting jobs. At first, I didn't make much money because no one on the reservation had a job. They didn't need a sitter. Then I started looking around in town for couples with kids. I put a card up on the bulletin board at the supermarket. One day, Katie called."

"Is that how you came to know Michael and Katie Coyote?"

"They were my regulars. Katie needed help with Van and Silby, taking care of two little babies so close together was a chore, so I began showing up like a nanny, especially on weekends. Before I go on, let me ask you something. Why do you want to know about Michael and Katie?"

"Not many people know this, but Michael is my biological father. It seems he had an affair with my mother, Genevieve Sarrazin. You probably don't know her. She's been gone from Coyote Wells a long time."

Rima hung her head for a moment before looking up again. "I think I always suspected Michael had someone on the side, several someones. Your mother wasn't the only one he fooled around with. Even a young girl picks up on those kinds of things. There was a great deal of tension in that house between him and Katie. But those are very old memories, Gemma. I'm not sure what exactly you're looking for from me."

"Anything really. I just want to know what you saw when you were there inside the house. Did you ever see people hanging around that looked shady?"

"I don't even know what that means. They had friends who'd drop by now and again. They were really a very typical couple that way. I'm still not sure what you're wanting to know."

Her answer made Gemma smile. "Neither am I. Paloma's been great about trying to tell me little things about Michael. I guess I just wanted to know what you'd witnessed firsthand from him. Was he a good father? A good husband? Or was he the proverbial asshole cheater who was never going to stop fooling around?"

"I see. So Paloma knows we're talking? Is that how you knew I was their babysitter? From Paloma?"

"Paloma knows about me, but it was Van who mentioned it. You see, I'm trying to get to know my brother in all this, too. Although he isn't much help. Van was very small when Michael was alive. A baby. Michael didn't live long enough for any of his children to get to know him, least of all Van or me. And Silby was barely three years older so even if she'd lived I doubt she'd have a good enough memory of him to be worthwhile. The truth is Michael died young, too young."

Rima bit her lip before saying what was on her mind. "I suppose I can admit it now. I had a bit of a crush on him. Michael. He was such a handsome man. He used to stop by the house to see Hank. He and Hank would hang out, do all kinds of things together---shoot hoops, go to the arcade, play video games like a couple of little boys. They even played on the same softball team sponsored by the casino. Hank played shortstop, Michael first base. He could really hit that ball, Michael. But both of them had a wild side we all knew about that started in middle school. They wasted a lot of nights drinking. My mother thought Hank would settle down once he met Donna and started having kids. Mom thought marriage would miraculously keep Hank home at night. And for a while it did. But once the babies came, Hank got bored coming home from work every night to a couple of squalling kids. It wasn't Hank's idea of married life. Then I guess because Hank and Michael worked together and saw each other every day, they kept up their wild ways right up until Hank drove his car into that ravine."

"That's just it. I don't think he did. I don't think Michael's wreck was an accident either. I think it was cleverly staged to look like one. But I think Hank was probably dead before he ever reached that hairpin curve."

"But why? What makes you so sure?"

"Well, I'm not what I'd call sure…yet. But I'm working on that theory and I intend to prove it using Lando's help and Zeb's. That's why I don't want you mentioning this conversation to anyone, Rima. Not a soul can know what we're up to, not even Theo."

"You don't want me to tell Theo? Okay. You can count on me. If, after all this time, I find out Hank died because someone wanted him dead, I want the person responsible to pay."

"Then we have that in common."

She dropped by the station to take Lando to lunch, one of the perks of living in a small town where the nearest restaurant was just around the corner. She picked up Philly cheesesteaks and ice-cold drinks from Captain Jack's.

They made their way along Water Street to the park at the end of Lighthouse Landing. The beautiful summer day had brought out a host of others picnicking near the beach. The benches were all taken, so they detoured around to the pier and found a place to sit near the rocks.

"Remember when we used to dig for clams right down there? We should have a clambake some night before fall gets here."

Lando dug into his sandwich, eating while Gemma told him about what she'd learned from Rima. "Again, I'm not sure you should've given her that kind of hope."

"I knew you'd say that. But you shouldn't ignore the tremendous impact those accidents had on so many people. Aaron Barkley moved on past Lindsay, remarried and had Fleet. Paloma lost her son. Katie lost her husband. Van and Silby lost a father. Toss in the fact that I lost mine as well. And Rima still talks about Hank's death as if it happened yesterday. That's real pain, Lando. Pain that's hung around for three decades. If we're any good at what we do, we have to find out the truth, right the wrong. I think that's what Aponivi is referring to."

"The truth is you don't really know what he's referring to. It could be something that has to do with Mallory, and not Michael Coyote." He finished his food and tossed the wrapper into a nearby trash can. "You remember Mallory, right? The body you found on the beach."

She bumped his shoulder. "No need for sarcasm. I remember it just fine. Did you check out the list I gave you of Mallory's relationships?"

"I put them in alphabetical order."

"You would."

"I'm organized. As of noon today, I'm down to the Os. The woman did have a very active social life. Everyone I've talked to so far has an alibi for Sunday night and they check out with airtight efficiency. Frustration is beginning to set in. Right about now I'd even do a war dance if you came up with a vision that even half explained the motive."

"I'll see what I can conjure up. The problem is, nothing I've seen makes any sense."

"Sometimes murder is like that, no rhyme or reason for it. Maybe Mallory was simply in the wrong place at the wrong time."

"Across the street from your house on a Sunday night? Why was she on that stretch of beach? Who had she gone out there to meet? Or was she just out for a walk and someone attacked her?"

"I still believe her murder has something to do with Louise's secrets, her strange background. It brings around a motive we haven't discovered yet."

"You're the expert. I'm just the amateur sleuth sidekick trying to help out and doing a lousy job of it so far."

21

Fifty-eight-year-old Edna Lloyd delivered her flowers rain or shine, February through November. She could often be seen pulling a red, all-terrain wagon behind her that she used to make her rounds up and down Water Street.

She was particularly fond of hydrangeas, but she also grew gerbera daisies and peonies year-round in the greenhouse she'd built herself. A widow who'd found a way to make a few extra bucks on the side, she didn't sell her flowers, but she wouldn't turn down a donation or two if you wanted to pay her for the lovely bouquets she delivered to the businesses along her route.

Gemma had to admit Edna was a welcome sight. Each morning, Monday through Friday, between eleven o'clock and noon, she could count on Edna showing up with florist-quality buds in hand to brighten up the shop.

This day, Gemma had Edna's favorite chocolate on hand so that when she opened the door, Gemma patted a stool. "Hop up here for a sec and get off your feet. I whipped up a batch of fresh dark chocolate, strawberry crèmes just for you."

"Oh, my. You are too good to me, even better than Marissa."

"How so?"

Edna scooted up to the counter. "Marissa was always a reminder that the both of us had lost so much. My husband died young and left me alone after moving me here. Marissa and I had quite a bit in common. We'd sit for hours reminiscing. I allowed her to talk about Jean-Luc and she had no problem listening to me go on about my

Henry. I'd come in here some days really down, and she never fail to try and cheer me up. But you aren't sad like Marissa. You're so young and vibrant with the rest of your life ahead of you. That Lando Bonner is a mighty handsome catch."

Gemma's lips curved. "He is. Do you often deliver flowers to the police station?"

"I do now that Louise isn't there."

"You didn't like Louise?"

"She didn't like me. Lord, that woman was always screaming, 'No soliciting, no soliciting.' She'd call out from behind that big desk of hers using such obscenities it'd make the hair on your head stand on end. In no time at all she'd be yelling, 'Can't you read the sign on the door you stupid woman?' I'd try to tell her that I wasn't there to solicit anything, but she didn't want to hear it. I hope she's suspended for good."

Lianne laughed from behind the counter. "That seems to be a very popular sentiment."

"I'm trying to talk Lianne into taking her place," Gemma announced.

"You are?" Edna said. "Why?"

"Yeah, why?" Lianne wanted to know. "Are you trying to get rid of me?"

"No way. I just thought you'd be happier. Working for the city, you'd get health benefits."

"I already applied for health insurance after watching that commercial on TV. You know, the one with the catchy jingle. I've been covered for weeks now. Besides, I don't want to work for the police department. I like it here."

"I have that same health plan," Edna replied. "I wouldn't want to work there either, too structured. And I'm not convinced Louise won't be back sitting at that big ol' desk tomorrow when I go by there."

Gemma had that same fear. She glanced over at Lianne. "I just wanted you to have some stability, more than I could give you. I don't want you to leave."

Lianne smiled. "Good thing because I no longer wake up dreading going to work."

"Now see," Edna began. "That's the secret to doing what you love. My Henry didn't make a lot of money, but every morning he got up and went to the Food Mart, where he'd worked hard since he was sixteen. Till the day he died, he loved being assistant manager, a real people person was my Henry."

"How'd Henry die?" Lianne asked.

"Same thing that killed Jean-Luc. Cancer got him."

Gemma wanted to get that sad look off Edna's face and changed the subject. "What do you think happened to Mallory?"

"You ask me, I'd say that girl finally crossed the wrong person and they didn't like it," Edna said, sampling a truffle. "Just like her mother, that one. Always angry, always going on about something or other that wasn't no business of hers."

"You certainly had Mallory pegged."

"I ought to. I knowed that girl since she was no bigger than a sprout. Saw her grow up to be a spoiled brat. But I have to say since she up and got killed, this is the most excitement we've had around here since that armored car heist back in '84. It's the thirty-fourth anniversary, you know. Or maybe it's the thirty-fifth. Heard the reminder on the news a few weeks ago. I forget which station. This isn't the first time Louise has gone into overtime dividing the town." Edna chuckled. "Leave it to that woman to sow bad seeds wherever she goes."

"What did you just say about a heist?" Gemma asked.

"You gettin' hard of hearing, girl? I said, that Wells Fargo armored car got held up in July right out there on the old logging road thirty-four years ago this month. And they never found the people that done it."

Gemma leaned over and gave Edna a huge hug. "Remind me to fix your favorite chocolates more often. In fact, you deserve an entire basket."

"I do?"

Gemma hopped down off the stool. "Lianne, watch the counter for me. I'll be in my office if anything earth-shattering happens. Edna, if what you just told me is half as important as I think it is, I owe you a lot more than a basket of candy."

Gemma closed herself off and for the next hour searched the Internet for any information about the armored car heist. There were varying versions of the daring daylight robbery that went down a few miles outside town before she was ever born.

She shut down her laptop and couldn't get to the police station fast enough. She ran past Payce who was the one on duty sitting behind that big ol' desk.

"You can't go back there," Payce said, blocking her way. "The Chief's got the mayor flipping out, mad as an ornery old hornet."

"Why?"

"'Cause Mayor Barkley wants him to take Louise off suspension. The mayor's not backing him up and last I heard Lando's not backing down."

"Stalemate, huh? We'll see about that. How long has Fleet been in there?"

"Almost thirty whole minutes."

"Payce, don't you have to go to the restroom?" She bobbed her head toward the opposite corridor.

"What?"

"I said, don't you have to go pee or something?"

He grinned, taking the hint. "Okay. Sure. I suppose it won't hurt none if you bust through the door and put an end to the meeting."

Gemma didn't exactly bust through the door, but she did enter without so much as knocking. "Hey, Fleet, long time no see."

Lando sent her a deadly glare and Fleet simply got to his feet. "Gemma, I'm in a closed-door meeting with the mayor. Can't this wait?"

"Ah. Sorry. No one was at the front desk so I just marched on back here. You know me. I didn't think Fleet would mind, seeing as how he may not be in office that much longer."

"What? You can't talk to me like that, Gemma Channing. I'm the mayor."

"Fleet, it's been years since folks around here wondered how your family came into all that money. And you're such a snob who really gets a charge shoving it in everybody else's face."

"What crawled up your britches today, Gemma?" Fleet taunted.

"Your total devotion all of a sudden to Louise Rawlins. It stems from what…exactly?"

Fleet looked confused.

"Too tough a question for you? How about this? Two months ago you were pushing for Lando to can her ass, now you're not. How long had you been sleeping with Mallory when she died? Does your wife know about the affair?"

Fleet dropped back into the chair. "How did you find out?"

"I didn't…not exactly anyway. But I knew Mallory and I know Louise. It doesn't take a rocket scientist to put two and two together. You've got a serious problem…*mayor*. Louise knew about your affair with her daughter. That's what she's holding over your head, isn't it? Using it as leverage, getting you to back off?"

"She threatened to tell Madison about it if I didn't support her and get her back in to the department before the investigation had wrapped up."

Lando aimed his deadly stare onto Fleet. "You've always been a tool, someone without an ounce of integrity. But I had no idea you were such a spineless snake when it comes to doing what's best for Coyote Wells."

"Spineless? It isn't my fault you waited until now to cut her loose. Louise has always been a cancer on this department. She should've been gone months ago when I first suggested it."

"He has a point," Gemma said, taking a seat in one of the empty chairs.

Lando let out a sigh. "Let me ask you something, Mr. Mayor. Did you kill Mallory to keep her quiet about the affair?"

"No way! I'm no killer."

"Then go back to your office, Fleet. We'll figure out a way to keep you out of trouble with Madison. But I won't stand by and watch you give in to Louise now. You're a politician. Figure out how to stall her from going to your wife."

"It isn't just that," Fleet bemoaned. "Louise says she knows other things about my family. Things that will hurt the people I love."

Lando exchanged looks with Gemma. "It's okay. We think we might know what it is. Just give me forty-eight hours to wrap up this investigation and it'll all work out."

"You have a suspect in mind?"

"I do, but I'm not at liberty to risk the case by telling you."

After Fleet left, Gemma cut her eyes to Lando. "You just told him it would all work out. It won't work out for him. Over the next few days it's likely he'll find out some nasty things about his daddy."

"Louise is threatening him anyway so what's the difference? Fleet doesn't need to know his world is about to go topsy-turvy until it goes down. That was a risky thing you did just now, storming in here like that."

"It was. But aren't you glad I got you out of that boring meeting?"

"There is that. What are you doing here anyway?"

"Edna Lloyd pays attention to the news around town better than we do. Were you aware that there was an armored car heist out on the Interstate near the Lone Coyote cutoff thirty-four years ago this month? It's the anniversary of the robbery. Apparently it's been all over the TV. It happened right out there at Dead Man's Curve."

He hooked his thumbs in his jeans. "Wow. With everything else going on, I'd forgotten about that. It's still an open case. Anytime there's another armored car heist anywhere in the US, I still get inquiries about it from the FBI."

"Lando, it happened before any of us were ever born. Remember that suggestion I had about tracking down any major news stories that occurred the year Louise changed her name? This has to be it. They never caught the people responsible. It's my vision. The five men wearing ski masks, shooting down two guards. Right a wrong. This is it."

"Who says they were all men?"

"Exactly. I read on the Internet that the robbers actually managed to hijack the Wells Fargo truck and somehow got it off the Interstate and onto the old logging road itself. Once they had it where they wanted it, two cars cut it off, boxed the truck in where the driver couldn't turn around or back up."

Lando had brought up the information on the computer screen and Gemma leaned over his shoulder to read the official report. "There was no way he could make that ninety-degree turn without going over the edge and taking everyone on board down into the canyon." He turned the screen around so she could see the actual photograph of the crime scene. "The vehicle teetered on the edge for three hours before they towed it to the FBI field office in San Francisco. Two guards dead ended up dead and one wounded."

"Gives me chills," Gemma admitted. "And super weird that it's almost the exact spot where all the car accidents occurred."

"More than weird. Planned out in detail."

"What made you promise Fleet that you could have this wrapped up in two days?"

"Desperation. If we don't have this figured out by then, Louise will go nuclear."

"I only know one way to stop her. Information. That means we go through everything you have on the car accidents and the heist, and find every detail that exists about Deborah Borelli since she popped out of the womb."

They didn't waste time getting started. Gemma let the others know what was happening. "It's all hands on deck," she told Lianne. "It's okay to close up early. We need warm bodies to go through old records, everything in the basement, even if it takes all night."

Luke was willing but couldn't leave the clinic until after five. And Leia was stuck at the restaurant until after the lunch rush. That meant Lianne would be trapped in the windowless basement with Jimmy and Payce, reviewing old files. Zeb would continue with the background audit on Louise while his two recruits, Cody and Jacob, answered calls on patrol.

While the others dug out every tidbit from the past, Lando spent the afternoon on the phone with the FBI, the fax machine humming with documents spitting from its belly.

Gemma headed to the library. Her job was to go through microfiche looking for whatever photographs she could find of Louise and Aaron Barkley when they were younger and then compare them to the facial recognition results from the guy in Portland.

But she knew all the photos in the world wouldn't do much good if there wasn't a solid snapshot that told her who was behind those ski masks. A comparison would only work if she got the vision to last longer, a lot longer, at least a duration that followed the thieves until they removed their masks.

She combed through the library, getting Elnora to assist whenever she couldn't locate what she needed. Without divulging too much to the librarian and raising any suspicions, she was able to find a newspaper clipping with a photo of a young female police officer who'd completed her training at the academy. The article went on to say that Louise was an expert marksman and a role model to the community.

Gemma finished photocopying a few other articles that mentioned Louise's bravery and how she'd won a Citizen of the Year Award after saving a one-year-old child from a burning house.

Which made Gemma wonder, after all the merits Louise had racked up, why had she elected to sit behind a desk?

On the walk back to the station, Gemma ended up dropping in on Alex Kedderson, the town lawyer. A question had been nagging at her for weeks now and he was the only one who could really give her an answer.

Alex's secretary, Helen Chisolm, or maybe she was a paralegal, was packing up for the day. The smartly dressed brunette had already turned off her desktop and was grabbing her purse.

"I need to talk to Mr. Kedderson. It won't take but a few minutes."

"Sure, go on back, Ms. Channing. He's putting the finishing touches on a will."

"Thanks. You have a great evening."

Helen smiled. "You, too. I've been meaning to stop by your chocolate shop. Is it possible to get some of those peanut butter swirls your grandmother used to make?"

"Absolutely. Whatever Gram made, I'm still churning them out."

Kedderson sat behind a massive mahogany workstation with a pile of papers stacked on one side. "Well look who decided to pay me a visit. I thought you were still holding a grudge about your grandmother's will."

"Nah. I finally figured out that you were simply following her instructions to the letter. Something I suppose is a plus for you, sticking to ethics and all that."

"Then what can I do for you this afternoon?"

"In all the years you've been in practice, has Louise Rawlins ever hired you for any reason?"

"Why do you want to know that?"

"Simple curiosity. I mean, Louise's daughter Mallory got into enough trouble over the years that could have kept the right attorney in the lap of luxury twice over."

"It certainly wasn't me."

"So you're saying Louise never hired you to defend Mallory? Not ever?"

"That's right. She took her business out of town to Humboldt."

Gemma took a seat. "Okay. So there's no attorney-client privilege at play here?"

"None whatsoever."

"Then tell me everything you've heard or suspected about those two women that doesn't add up."

They stopped to compare notes at the end of the day sitting around the conference table at the police station. It was a room CWPD used sparingly because they rarely had a reason to hold formal meetings. Business was usually conducted in one of two small interview rooms or lockup, which consisted of two eight by eight jail cells, or Lando's office.

When it came time for food, everyone dived for the burgers and chicken sandwiches Lydia had dropped off for dinner.

Eager to share what she'd discovered, Gemma sat on her news until after everyone had finished eating. "Since Alex Kedderson is the only lawyer in town, I wanted his opinion on how Louise handled Mallory's legal issues. He told me that whenever Mallory got into trouble, which was often, Louise would always hire a lawyer out of town, specifically she'd head to Humboldt to have a guy named Talmadge represent Mallory. Not once did she ever pay Kedderson a retainer fee to do anything for her daughter."

"Which means what?" Lando asked.

"It might mean that there was something Louise didn't want the local attorney to know about, something she wanted to stay in the background and not for local consumption. Kedderson also said Mallory had been in trouble so much that Louise's legal fees had to be in the neighborhood of around $250,000 due to the pricey attorney she hired. According to Alex, Talmadge doesn't come cheap. My point is, where does your dispatcher, who makes no more than fifty-five grand a year, come by that kind of money?"

"Not from the Coyote Wells Police Department," Jimmy grunted.

"Which is my point. Something's not right here, Lando. It's not adding up. Instead of speculating about it, we have confirmation that Louise could afford a quarter of a million dollars in legal fees. Do you know what that kind of legal trouble would do to anyone else in this town? They'd go bankrupt. Does Louise look broke to you?"

Lianne interrupted, "Since her sister and her daughter carry pricey Fendi bags around, it's a valid question. Where did Louise come by that kind of money?"

Gemma went on, "Another question. Why did Louise opt to sit behind a desk instead of continuing her stellar career as a patrol officer?"

"Opt? That's a funny choice of wording. Reiner demoted her three years before I came on board. The story goes that she messed up some arrest and Reiner relegated her to a desk. Instead of it being temporary, he stuck her on dispatch permanently."

Payce seemed to know more. "It was the obvious place to put her. Louise could do less damage working dispatch than any other area in the department."

Lando nodded. "And since I can't locate her personnel file, there's no way of knowing the whole story."

"What not just ask Reiner directly?"

Lando rolled his eyes. "I tried that a week ago when I couldn't find the file. I'm not exactly Reiner's favorite person right now because of the Montalvo case. I *am* still actively trying to nail him for obstructing justice when he let Sandy's murder slide."

Zeb dug into the apple pie Leia had baked that morning. "Need I remind you guys that the clock is ticking. Whatever we do, we need to do it fast. I discovered a contact who knows someone in Children's Services in Arizona. She's looking into putting me in touch with the person in charge of the Borelli kids. If we're lucky maybe we can find a family or two that fostered the girls."

"Well, I've decided to go through Gram's journals and pick up where I left off. I want to see what she has to say about the entire year of 1984 and not what happened during the summer months. Unfortunately, I haven't even finished half of them yet. None are in what I'd call chronological order. It might be time consuming, but I think it's worth a shot, especially if I can find anything in there about the heist. On any given day Gram could be pretty detailed. I could get lucky and she could describe something that didn't appear in the news reports."

"That's not a bad idea," Luke said, eyeing the pie. "Old-timers would be the best source of information during that time."

Lydia playfully swatted the back of her son's head. "Watch who you call an old-timer. What I remember the most about the robbery is how the town swarmed with FBI agents. They hovered around here like sand flies convinced that the guilty parties came from the Rez. Of course, they had no proof of that whatsoever, but it didn't keep them from making silly accusations. After three months not one of them cracked the case. They finally packed up and left sometime in the fall."

"But no matter how the sand flies tried, they couldn't pin it on anyone on the Rez," Leia pointed out. "Major point for us."

Lydia nodded toward her daughter. "It wasn't for lack of tunnel vision. They must've interviewed four hundred people out there, even going so far as roughing some up. It was disappointing that all those federal agents went home without finding a suspect or the money."

"Because they were looking in the wrong place," Gemma offered.

Jimmy picked up his Styrofoam trash and stood up. "All the more reason to think the killers high-tailed it out of town. Think about it. Why would they stick around a place as small as Coyote Wells? Wouldn't they stick out like a sore thumb?"

Gemma's eyes widened as she reached for Lando's hand. "Not if the thieves had established themselves here months before the heist took place."

Lando kicked back in his chair. "Like Louise and Aaron Barkley. Zeb, look up the general time frame when Aaron first made his presence known in town."

Zeb opened his laptop back up and began hitting keys. A few moments went by before he announced, "January 1984 Aaron rents an apartment above the coffee shop on Water Street with Lindsay Bishop on the lease. He turns on utilities that same month in his name and the couple get married three months later."

"And by August she's dead," Luke added. "When exactly does Louise show up?"

Zeb's keystrokes increased as he hit the same websites as before. "Same month. Same year. Different apartment building on Harbor View. She opted for the ocean view."

"That's Dale's complex," Jimmy uttered.

Lando ran a hand through his hair. "The important thing here is Aaron, Lindsay, and Louise all decide to move to Coyote Wells at the same time. They arrive in town and immediately become part of the scene."

"Louise made ends meet by doing odd jobs around town," Lydia provided. "So did Bishop and Barkley."

"You remember that?" Lando asked.

"It was before Louise joined the force. In 1984 Coyote Wells was just a little wide spot in the road with barely a thousand people living here. Newcomers stood out. Same with Lindsay and Aaron Barkley. Rima's the one who jogged my memory. Thirty-four years is a long time. I do recall something odd about Aaron, though. One day he showed up driving a brand-new pickup truck---a shiny red one. For a man who toiled at low-paying jobs since coming here, it was clear he'd come into some money. Rumors said it was due to a win at the casino."

"But you don't think so?" Luke proffered.

"No. At the time they hung out with a lot of shady characters who came in and out of town from Nevada. Their cars had Nevada plates."

Lando and Gemma traded looks. "Maybe that's where we need to start digging deeper and work forward. If Louise spent time in Reno maybe the others did, too."

While the others worked the Reno angle, Gemma headed to Paloma's house where she spent two hours picking her grandmother's brain for anything that happened out of the ordinary during the summer of 1984.

Drinking a cup of hibiscus tea she didn't need or really want, she sat at Paloma's kitchen table prodding and poking her way through the weeks leading up to the heist.

"Oh, I remember the robbery very vividly," Paloma said. "But what hurt the most was how it scarred the community for months afterward. The FBI agents left after a few weeks, but the residents were the ones who suffered. The aftermath was almost as bad as the event itself. Trust became an issue. Neighbors wondered if it was one of our own. Several talked about moving away. That's how scared and mistrusting we were of each other. But the timeframe was more like September rather than the middle of summer. Because in the fall, that's when things started to unravel for real and get even stranger than before."

"Are you sure it wasn't during those final days of August that things got weird?"

"Positive. I was mayor back then and I can tell you for certain Reiner Caulfield had his hands full. It seemed every other week someone died and not in the usual manner. He investigated a string of inexplicable deaths that occurred that fall and into spring."

"And these were in addition to the car accidents over the summer and the death of the young girl found dead on the beach?"

Paloma nodded. "Hank's car accident seemed to set everything in motion. We just didn't know it at the time. But by that fall, Reiner's office was still struggling to keep up. Like the drowning he worked around Labor Day, and the next month, the construction worker who was electrocuted on the job. Then there was a woman down the street killed in a house fire. And then another resident was hit by a train and dragged hundreds of feet to his death. There for a while it got so bad I started to think we were the unluckiest small town in the county. Even Marissa and Jean-Luc started to hint about moving down to L.A. to live near a cousin."

"What stopped them?"

"I imagine it was their stubborn streak. They had one, you know. Those two were determined to stick it out no matter what. And when Michael died a year later, it was your grandmother who got me through those darkest days. So you see, I'm forever grateful she didn't decide to pick up and leave."

Later, Gemma took Paloma's information, her general dates and times of the baffling deaths, and headed back to the library for confirmation. She arrived just as Elnora was about to lock up for the night. Instead of leaving without answers, Gemma decided to test the librarian's memory.

While walking Elnora to her car, Gemma nudged the woman into a conversation about the year of the heist.

"I was glad to put that year behind us," Elnora admitted. "People kept dying. We were all on edge, probably because none of us knew who might be next. Plus, we weren't sure who was responsible for the armored car deaths. Was it our neighbor who shopped at the market with us or was it someone who sat across us in church? You see how easily it was to suspect one another if we let our imaginations run wild with possibilities."

"I do. But was there anything that stood out that made you question anyone specifically?"

"Well, there was that thing that happened out at Shadow Canyon the weekend after the robbery."

"What thing?"

"My first husband, Dan, was quite the ornithologist. That's the study of birds, you know. Anyway, we used to go birdwatching every weekend up on the ridge above Shadow Canyon. You could find red-tailed hawk there, or study the black-headed Grosbeak, or watch California quail in their natural habitat. I loved Dan, I did, but sometimes that man could be such a blowhard when it came to his birds."

To get her back on track, Gemma had to push her to get to the point. "What did you see that caused you to think someone you knew could be involved in the heist?"

"Oh, that. The Saturday after the robbery, we were camping out near that fork in the river. It was our favorite spot. But that morning, through our binoculars, we saw two people, a man and a woman, dragging bags out of the bed of a red pickup truck and hauling them into that nearby cave. You know the one, where all the bats are."

"I'm familiar with it, yes."

"Well, Dan became livid that they were disturbing the entire colony, so much that he wanted to charge down there and confront them. I talked him out of it."

"Did you report what you saw?"

"Of course. We packed up that very morning and drove back into town. We went straight to Reiner Caulfield and told him what we'd seen."

"But nothing happened?"

"He took our report and said he'd check it out. A couple of days later Reiner showed up at the library and told me that the people at the cave had been from the U.S. Forest Service. They were there studying the bats. I told him, then and there, they didn't look like any Forest Service personnel I'd ever seen."

"How did he take that?"

"He assured me I was wrong and told me he had more important things to worry about, so I left it at that."

"Figures," Gemma muttered. "It's a wonder anything ever got done with Caulfield at the helm."

22

"That's the second time someone mentioned a red pickup," Gemma pointed out to Lando as they got ready for bed. "Your mother mentioned Aaron Barkley drove a shiny red one."

But Lando was focused on Reiner's role in not reporting the incident to the federal agents. "I wonder if Reiner got paid off to look the other way? Could I somehow tie him to this whole thing after all? Maybe this is the very thing that could take him down."

"I know you want Reiner, but you're overlooking an important part of what Elnora said. She saw a man and a woman at the cave. What if one of the masked assailants was a female? What if they were not all men?"

They batted that theory around until the wee hours of the night.

Sleep had come in spurts for them both, so Gemma got up as quietly as possible only to look over and see that Lando was wide awake.

"Seriously, you can't sleep either?"

"I keep wondering how they pulled it off without anyone spilling what they knew over the years."

She sat down on his side of the bed. "A million bucks is a lot of incentive for remaining quiet."

"Unless they found that permanent silence was a much better option."

"You think they murdered their co-conspirators?"

"Why not? It would definitely make the most sense. Anyone who might feel guilty down the road would never be able to come clean if they were dead. Where were you going just now?"

"Out to the solarium. I thought I might do a little late-night reading." She scooted closer. "I just want this over with. If it means another sleepless night, then that's what I'll do. Remind me again where everyone slept tonight."

"Jimmy and Payce went home to their respective partners. I believe Zeb and Leia left the station somewhere around eleven to fall into their own beds, followed by Luke and Lianne, who headed to her house where they no doubt fell into bed as exhausted as everyone else."

"Nothing worse than grunt work to beat down your volunteers. So we're probably the only ones wide awake at three in the morning."

"Other than Rufus. The dog seems as restless as we are." He pulled her closer, nibbling her neck. "You know what would get my mind off all this?"

She angled her body closer to give him better access. "I can't imagine."

He ran his hands down her body, beginning to show her, covering her mouth.

"I'm suddenly getting this erotic vision."

"Then I must be doing something right."

"Oh, yeah. Keep that up. Right there. Don't stop."

They didn't stop, and after making love, Lando fell into a deep sleep. But the adrenaline had given her a second wind.

She grabbed a robe and went out to gather up her grandmother's journals.

That's where Lando found her at seven-thirty, slumped in a comfy leather chair, sound asleep. He decided to leave her there. But when he turned around to tiptoe out, the old floor creaked.

Stirring from the sound, she yawned and stretched and lifted her head. "Tiptoeing isn't exactly your strong suit."

"Are you kidding? I'm so light on my feet I could be Fred Astaire."

She yawned again and swung her legs to the floor. "Then I could use some coffee, Fred."

"I was about to let Rufus out and put the coffee on."

She followed him out to the kitchen. "You won't believe what I found. I had to go through a dozen or so of Marissa's journals, mostly skimming for dates, but I found an entry from December 31st, 1984 where she listed all the people in town who'd died that year. She even included the two Wells Fargo guards who were killed in the heist. Two we already knew about, Hank and Lindsay. But two more jumped out at me. One was a Wells Fargo employee named Dave Gilbert, a driver assigned to their armored car division, who *drowned* over Labor Day weekend in a boating accident on Spirit Lake. The other was a man by the name of Arnie Gafford. The week before Christmas Arnie got hit by a train south of town."

Lando stopped his momentum. "That sounds like what Paloma remembers."

"Exactly. But Marissa wrote down details. It's all coming together, Lando. Maybe it's like you said, they got rid of everybody else who was involved so they wouldn't talk."

"Tidy up all the loose lips. This Arnie Gafford, could he be related to Billy?"

"Finding out is your job. But the age is right. If only I could see the rest of that vision, see faces, I could get to the bottom of this really fast."

"That'd be great, but old-time police work is the key here, not waiting around for Aponivi to magically show you what you need to see."

"Maybe not," she muttered. "There might be a shortcut, a way to jumpstart the connection."

Gemma begged off returning to the police station right away with an excuse that she had an errand to run. That little task turned out to be a visit to see Callie Lightfeather. Begging for a little help, a little guidance might be considered the biggest chore of all. That's why Gemma left her pride at the door.

Callie was the expert on so-called tribal legends. Callie knew shamans. Gemma needed whatever expertise the wise old woman was willing to dish. Direction would not only be appreciated, but when shown the path celebrated.

At ninety, the medicine woman seemed to have more energy than a thirty-something on four mocha lattes. Callie stood barely five feet in height, with white hair she wore in a braid down her back that almost reached her ankles. She reminded Gemma of a jovial pixie with a twinkle in her eye who was one step away from sprinkling fairy dust.

Not that Callie would have ever deviated from her Native roots. Of that Gemma was certain. So when she stood in Callie's living room, making her case, she did her best not to melt down and show how desperate she was. Since Callie was her best shot at figuring out psychic stuff, she needed a quick course on remote-controlling her visions.

"I've always been level-headed and practical until Gram died. For the past three months I've been all about trying new things. So I'm really trying hard to understand how I got here. I seem to be at the mercy of three of the most powerful shamans who are confusing the hell out of me."

"You seek answers."

"You don't know the half of it," Gemma admitted, going into detail about the heist that killed two guards. She went on about the predicament she found herself in with little evidence to prove her case. "This has gone on for thirty-four years. It's time the guilty parties are caught."

From this point, Gemma softened her approach. "Callie, you have to help me. I have to *see* beyond the robbery. I have to see who's behind those masks. I need to see it play out. I need to see what they do after they get the money, where they go, what they drive, the make of their cars. It's all essential to tracking all of them down. I need to see who they are with my own eyes."

"You're asking an awful lot of your ability," Callie grumbled. "It's a gift, not an order form."

"But can you help me? Put me in some kind of trance, hypnotize me, or something---I don't care---anything, as long as I can ask Aponivi for help. He said I needed to right a wrong. How can I do that if I don't know the truth? You said Aponivi is the holder of truth. That's what you said. If that's true, then he needs to let me see the truth so I can spread it around."

"You spoke to Aponivi? You had a conversation?"

"Me? Maybe a sentence. At the canyon. It was hard to get my mouth to work. Mostly, it was Aponivi who spoke to me. I heard his voice. It was there one minute and gone the next. I didn't *see* him like I did Kamena. If I could only set eyes on him maybe we could connect, and he'd somehow help me get better at this. This quest to find all three of them was supposed to take my gift to a higher level. It hasn't. Now I know how the tribes felt. I feel like I've been left on my own to figure this out. I feel abandoned."

"That is your weakness. You give up too easily. You're too impatient."

"Do I have to be standing in Shadow Canyon for this to work?"

Callie shook her head. "If you want to connect with Aponivi you don't have to seek him out. With each vision, you've already proven that you don't have to physically stand in Shadow Canyon to learn the truth. You had the first vision at your house, right around the corner from where we are now. The second played out for you near the cave. The third was out on the old logging road. It matters not where you are but how strong your heart is, how willing you are to open your soul to the truth."

"Okay, so what do I do to bring one on and make it last long enough to see the beginning and the end, all the way through?"

"Are you certain you want to see what happened badly enough that you're willing to transcend yourself into the past?"

"Like an out of body experience? Is that the only way?"

"It's a ritual as ancient as the tribes. If you want profound clarity and the ability to see beyond the initial vision, it is the only way."

Gemma swallowed her fear. "Then let's do it."

Callie headed into the kitchen to put on the kettle for tea and Gemma followed, her enthusiasm beginning to wane.

"It would be better if your friends could be here to form a circle."

"If my friends were here they wouldn't let me do this. If anything goes wrong, if I should have a bad reaction or something, could you call Lando's brother Luke for me? He's a doctor. Here's his number," she said, scrawling the information down on a pad on the counter.

After pouring the tea into a pot, Callie lit an altar of aromatic candles, cleansing sage and sweetgrass. She put on music, lilting flutes and gentle drums.

Gemma settled back on the sofa, her stomach beginning to flop before she ever let the tea pass her lips.

Callie handed her a large mug, the eighteen-ounce variety filled with a substance that looked more like rusty water than tea. "Drink it all."

Gemma did as she was told, chugging the bitter, foul-tasting liquid until she could see the bottom of the cup. "What happens now?"

"Shh. Focus. Concentrate. Meditate. Let the spirits know what you want to see. Let Aponivi know."

Gemma heard singing, tribal chanting, and saw dancing around a fire. She smelled the wood burning, flicker orange, and saw the flames reach out toward the sky.

Gemma shifted, barely able to see Callie sitting across the room from her before she floated upward and into the sky. She hovered over the canyon until she ended up in a hut, sitting in a circle with other members of her tribe. The elders were rubbing sage and sweetgrass on their hands and offering the herbs to the fire. It flared and flickered, sending sparks out into the night.

She looked up to see a blast of white light that formed a circle. She called to Aponivi. He came on the silvery wind and lifted her up into the glowing light. He carried her through a rainbow of fiery flames, brilliant colors that popped and whirled around the canyon like a lightning storm.

When she finally got the courage to look down, she saw that she floated over the hairpin curve. The flashes of lightning stopped. The sea of wind ceased its stormy approach. Aponivi turned off a switch and it became summer, a beautiful clear day in July with hardly any clouds in the sky.

She watched the traffic on the Interstate until finally she saw the armored car come into view with the Wells Fargo emblem on the side.

It all happened fast. Two identical red pickups sped into view. At first the drivers of the trucks followed the armored car, and then stepped on the gas to pass. Once in position, both vehicles forced the larger armored car off the Interstate and onto an exit ramp where another red pickup waited.

It was all possible because the driver of the armored car was part of the ruse. He knew what was about to happen and went along with the detour. As soon as the armored car pulled to a stop on the curve, the five men in masks jumped out with guns drawn.

The scene played out in vivid color. Everything was so crystal clear she could stand in awe of the powerful weaponry involved. That is, until the two guards fell out of the back of the truck, bleeding and wounded, the wonder of it all vanished.

She saw every detail. She saw every face. She knew what happened after it was all over.

She couldn't breathe.

When her eyes fluttered open, the first thing she heard was a siren in the distance. Then mutterings from several people all trying to talk at once. The voices blended in her head, indistinct, imperceptible, more like white noise. People moved around her in blue and white blurs.

She was in a hospital, a bed, that much she could tell, lying flat on her back, hooked up to an IV.

Her head felt like someone had crushed her skull with a hammer.

Her eyes finally focused on one face. Lando. He was holding her hand and had tears running down his cheeks. She'd never seen him cry before, not in all the years she'd known him, not even when he fell off his bike.

When she tried to say something, she realized an oxygen mask covered her nose and mouth. Someone took her blood pressure and checked her pulse. A little box with a screen monitored her heart rate.

"Is she gonna be okay?"

"We pumped her stomach, flushed her system, which is probably why she's coming around now. Gemma, can you hear me?"

Gemma moved her head or tried to.

Lando leaned down to whisper in her ear. "You couldn't breathe. The EMTs said you lost consciousness and resorted to intubation to get you to the hospital."

That would explain the raw throat. "How long...have I been here?"

"Six hours. Luke took you off the ventilator a few minutes ago when your lungs checked out and you did just fine."

"Good news." She started to ramble. "I saw everything. The heist...they hid the money in the cave...our cave...at Shadow Canyon just like Elnora reported seeing. I stayed with it until I saw...what happened. I know who pulled it off, every single one of them. I saw them without the masks. I saw...details, the trucks they used, the reason the case...went cold. Now we just have to connect it all with..."

"Shh. Shh. There's plenty of time for that. Rest now. You took an awful risk drinking that stuff. It's a hallucinogenic."

"Whatever it was it worked. Don't blame Callie. She…and Aponivi…showed me the truth. That's why I went there. We'd have never solved it if I hadn't. When do I get to go home? When do we get back to work?"

Lando turned to Luke. "Any chance she'll get out of here today?"

"Are you kidding? We'll see how she feels over the next twelve hours. Right now, she's stuck here until tomorrow morning at least."

"Hear that?" Lando said. "No complaining. Be glad Callie realized you were in trouble and called 911."

She tried to sit up on her elbows but fell back into the fluff and softness of the pillows. "Rufus. Someone needs to look after…"

"I'll take care of the dog. Listen to your doctor."

Luke sent Lando a brotherly look. "I'll try not to make her worse. If only I had some of that prickly pear wonder juice on hand."

"It worked for me," Lando reminded him.

"Figures," Gemma whispered. "Lando here drinks prickly pear juice and rises like Lazarus. I drink weird tasting tea and almost go comatose."

"You drank pure mescaline, a byproduct of peyote," Lando stated.

"Callie's not in trouble, is she?"

"As long as she sticks to her story that you were attending one of her church services, she has nothing to worry about."

"Church service? Sure. It's true. Thanks to Callie, I might've seen the Great Spirit, talked to him, too. After what I saw, we should be on a first name basis."

"What did you see?"

"Grab something to write with and a pad or get a recorder. I'll tell you the best way to track them all down."

23

Nothing like an overnight stay in the hospital to redefine a person's priorities. Luke had let her go home but was adamant she had to stay in bed another day. She didn't try to renegotiate the terms. Instead, she accepted her fate and took it easy. After all, she had her grandmother's journals for reading material and Lando to baby her.

He led her into the bedroom where she got undressed and crawled into her own bed. With Lando standing watch and tucking her in, she felt cared for and loved. He closed the drapes, blocking out the sunlight, and whispered, "Get some rest."

"It's weird wearing my PJs in the middle of the day. I'm sorry I put a dent in your forty-eight-hour window."

He lifted her chin. "I'm sorry you thought you had to resort to drinking mescaline to recreate your vision."

"But it worked."

"Maybe. Zeb and Payce are still checking out everything you saw. It's a slow process. But Zeb is as stoked as I've ever seen him. He's convinced the heist will finally get solved and take the burden off the reservation."

"Lydia mentioned that the feds were sure the perpetrators were from the Rez. They weren't."

"Zeb and the tribal council agree with you. They've always been convinced the killers were outsiders. Now they have a semblance of something to work with, something to back that up."

"You'll see it was for the best." Yawning, she slid under the covers and rolled over, falling into a peaceful slumber.

Hours later, she woke to the sound of Lando's voice, giving commands to Rufus. She got up and wandered out into the kitchen. She couldn't believe what she was seeing. Rufus had gone through the doggie door and back again. Twice.

"How did you get him to do that?" Gemma asked, dropping down on one knee to take the dog's head in her hands. "Aren't you a good boy?"

"I downloaded a series of instructions off the Internet that claimed they were sure fire."

"Your only day off in weeks, and you spend it working with my dog." Her arms went around his waist. "I think I love you. Get him to do it again."

"Come on, Rufus. Go outside. Go on. Show her what a smart boy you are."

Rufus complied by scooting through the opening.

"Amazing. I'd given up."

"Are you hungry? I made you soup."

She glanced at the stove where a pot simmered. "You made soup? Are you sure Leia didn't drop it off and then you dumped it in a pan to warm it up?"

"Nope. It's your favorite. I made it from scratch."

Sniffing the air, she took a guess. "Potato soup with chunks of bacon?"

"Right the first time. You didn't eat much in the hospital."

"Having your stomach pumped tends to put you off food."

"You sit down, and I'll grab a bowl."

The doorbell rang.

"Do you ever get the feeling that we could use some major alone time?" Gemma wondered. "Without people always dropping by."

"Definitely." The ringing became pounding. "Alone by ourselves with no one around to interrupt meals or bedtime sounds too good to be true." Lando threw back the front door. "What?"

The mayor stood there nervous and impatient. "You said forty-eight hours. You gotta keep Louise from telling my wife about Mallory. You gotta do something."

"Shut up, Fleet. Quit your whining. Gemma needs peace and quiet right now. Haven't you heard, she just got out of the hospital."

"Oh. Sorry. But you said…"

"I know what I said. If finding a killer was that easy, you'd be doing it. Now go home and make it up to Madison. You're a politician. Keep stalling Louise and give me time to do my job."

"But you're not even in the office."

"Working from home today, Fleet." With that, Lando shut the door in his face and headed back into the kitchen.

"Lando, your cell phone's ringing. The number comes up as the county medical examiner." She handed him the phone.

"Bonner here. What did you find? Uh-huh. Uh-huh. Uh-huh. Okay. Thanks, Jeff."

"What was that all about?"

"Mallory's lab results. Alcohol content came back to .08. That's legally impaired. Tuttle says she wasn't sexually assaulted after all. But the fact that she was almost drunk could've been the reason she was taken down so easily. Plus, the DNA under her fingernails came back as female."

"Drunk and fighting with another female? That's the Mallory I knew," Gemma declared, sending him a wide smile. "How does it feel to be right?"

"It'll feel even better when I obtain a sample to compare it to." He keyed in a number on his phone. "Judge Hartwell, I hate to interrupt your lunch, but I need a warrant to obtain DNA."

Nothing that came out of his mouth could've surprised her more. "You're sure about this?"

"I've never been surer of anything. I'll be gone a few hours. Eat your soup and get some rest. The next couple of days could be a wild ride. I'll need you at the top of your game."

"I'm not sorry I took that stuff. But I wouldn't do it again." She threw her arms around his neck. "We make a good team."

"Keep that line of thought open until I get back. Should I call Lianne to sit with you?"

"I've already fluffed off enough of the work on Lianne that she can handle. I'll be fine. Go do your job. Don't worry about me."

After he left, she faded in and out, sleepy and tired until she woke hours later to find Lando sitting next to the bed, strumming his guitar. A bubble filled with pure love swelled inside her. "This reminds me of that time I had the flu and you came here to sing to me."

"You were fifteen and sick as a dog, nose as red as Rudolph, barfing up a lung every time you coughed."

"Don't remind me. I thought for sure I'd lose you to Rowena Hartwell, who had the audacity to be as healthy as a horse that day."

"Nah, not me. Zeb was always the one hung up on Rowena."

"Really? Cause I thought you used to follow her around on the playground and push her on the swings."

"I was seven and gullible. Zeb, on the other hand, stalked her plain as day until he was fifteen. Judge Hartwell came close to taking out a restraining order."

"Good to know. How'd collecting the DNA go?"

"Let me tell you, she was not a happy camper. I thought Zeb would have to sit on her while I swabbed her mouth. I dropped the sample directly off at the lab. Tuttle said he'd put a rush on it. We should know if it's a match very soon."

"This town will never be the same again, will it?"

"Maybe it's for the best. With you solving the heist and me finding Mallory's killer, things have to turn around for both of us."

"Public opinion is a fickle creature. When it shifts to our side, I like it. I'm getting my appetite back. How does Chinese sound for dinner? Happy Wok delivers."

"Or we could eat in. I could throw some eggs and bacon together and then put on some music or we could watch a movie."

She tilted her head to study him. "I haven't seen you this domestic in a long time. Bacon and eggs are fine with me. What would we do with an evening at home to ourselves?"

"Nine or ten things come to mind. But you need all your strength back first."

Resigned to no sex, she pulled on a clean T-shirt and a pair of flannel bottoms she usually saved for winter and headed into the kitchen.

"What are you doing?" Lando asked, trailing behind her.

"I'm hungry. I'm scrambling eggs and nuking some bacon."

But before they could get started on making dinner, Lando's cell phone trilled. Payce's number came up on the display. "What's wrong?"

"Chief, you told me to keep an eye on Louise after you took her DNA. I think she might be heading out of town."

"Why?"

"Cause she's packing up her car with luggage. What should I do?"

"Damn it! You can't let her leave. If that's the way she wants it, let's take her down in a very public way, sirens blaring right up to her front door. The neighbors will get an eyeful. If she moves her car an inch, block her in. I'm five minutes out." Even as he ended the call he was moving toward the front door. "Louise isn't staying put. I've gotta stop her."

"Do you have a warrant?"

"Not yet. I was waiting for the DNA results, but now it doesn't matter. I'll arrest her and hold her as a material witness."

24

More warrants took another day. Lando had exceeded his own deadline by an extra seventy-two hours, but the results would be worth the wait. At this point, he didn't much care whether Louise was uncomfortable in her cell or not.

He assembled his staff in the conference room, included Zeb and Jeff Tuttle, along with the mayor and everyone else involved in helping with the case. An unorthodox gathering for sure, but one that deserved to hear the truth as it all played out.

By now, it seemed as if everyone in town had heard the news about Louise's arrest. Many of her supporters jammed the police station lobby, standing alongside reporters from out of town representing all the major networks.

"Are you sure you want to do it this way?" Zeb asked Lando. "It isn't too late to change your mind."

"Hey, Coyote Wells residents deserve to know that no one on the Rez had anything to do with the heist. Once and for all, they deserve to hear the truth about Louise and Mallory's murder, that includes all the dirty details whether they like it or not."

It took another fifteen minutes for Louise to make an appearance, wearing an ugly, orange and white striped jumpsuit. Her hair had been brushed to a shine. She wore makeup that couldn't hide the dark circles under her eyes from lack of sleep.

Lando cleared his throat and looked straight at Louise. "Over the last several weeks, we've built a solid case against you. On so many levels. For starters, you killed your own daughter because she was about to give away the biggest secret of your life to Fleet Barkley. It all started three decades ago when Fleet's father, Aaron, helped you rob the Wells Fargo armored car back in 1984 when you were just nineteen years old. Mallory never knew about your stash of money until just recently. When she discovered the sizeable fortune you kept on hand in one of your accounts, she blackmailed you into giving her four hundred grand, which you apparently didn't miss. But then Mallory couldn't stop wondering where the money came from, and that curiosity set off a chain of events between mother and daughter that led to her demise."

"You don't know what you're talking about," Louise protested.

"Keep telling yourself that, Louise. Over time, Mallory must've suspected you'd done something illegal to come by that much money and it caused her to sit around wondering about it. The more time she spent stewing, the greedier she became. But she had no idea what you'd done. Not until the day she overheard a conversation that took place by chance between Edna Lloyd and Peg Thackery. The two women were standing out on the sidewalk in front of the pub. Edna had stopped with her wagonload of flowers to sell a couple of the bouquets to Peg, who was always willing to take whatever bouquets Edna had on hand to brighten up the bar. The two women had seen the same newscast and were talking about the anniversary of the armored car heist. They mentioned the year it happened. Mallory knew the year you'd arrived in Coyote Wells. She must've known it wasn't a coincidence that you got here six months before the robbery took place. She began to put two and two together. You certainly weren't fessing up to anything, so your daughter decided to take matters into her own hands and try to figure out the details herself, like who your accomplices had been, on her own. With that information in hand, she'd leave you with few options."

Gemma decided to toss in a nugget of her own. "In case you were wondering, that's why Mallory took to sleeping with half the men in town. She was trying to narrow down which ones were the descendants of your partners. The reason? She was pretty sure she could blackmail each of them. She had no idea at the time there were only two surviving sons. And one didn't matter."

Louise looked stricken, like she'd been dealt the death card. "I'd been so careful all these years. I even kept most of the money in a bank in San Francisco so Sam Wells, the bank president here, wouldn't be tempted to run his mouth about how much I had."

"Or none of the other busybodies in town would find out either," Leia added.

"Then what gave it away? What gave me away?"

Lando picked up the thread. "For starters, you always seemed to have enough ready cash on hand whenever Mallory got into trouble through the years, enough to bail her out of jail, enough to hire a lawyer, not just any lawyer, either, but one who charged four hundred dollars an hour. It took some time, but we figured that through the years you must've spent in the neighborhood of two hundred and fifty grand on legal fees. We put our heads together. How could you possibly have that kind of cash on hand on a dispatcher's salary? It didn't make any sense to people who earn what you make. Unless, of course, you'd somehow come into a bunch of money all at once."

Louise looked terrified. "You don't know a thing about me. You have no idea what kind of life I had as a child."

"I think we do, at least we do now. You started life out as Deborah Borelli in Tucson, daughter of a drug-addicted prostitute, who left you and Holly with a neighbor one day when you were very young and never bothered coming back. Flash forward ten years later, when you hit eighteen, you took off for Reno, where you met your den of thieves---Aaron Barkley, Lindsay Bishop, and a man named Arnie Gafford, who as it turns out is the same name listed on Billy Gafford's birth certificate. Arnie was Billy's father. Are you with me so far? Because by this time, you'd changed your name to Louise Rawlins, using a name you got off a headstone in Utah as you made your way from Arizona to Nevada."

Gemma sent Louise a sympathetic look before bringing the hammer down. "You left Tucson looking for excitement, a thrill, some big score to improve your lot in life. Was it your idea or Aaron's to rob an armored car?"

Louise turned a cold stare on Gemma. "I'm not saying another word."

Gemma gave her nemesis a wide smile. "That's okay. Whoever's idea it was, your little gang needed an inside man, someone who had all the routes down perfectly, all the details you'd need to pull off a successful heist and get away with it. You kept your eye out for that person, perusing the casinos along Reno's strip until you found one such guy. It was Arnie who recruited a Wells Fargo driver he'd become friendly with named Dave Gilbert, who surprisingly didn't live long after the robbery. But we'll get to that in a minute."

Gemma took a deep breath before going on. "Initially there were five---Louise, Aaron, Lindsay, Arnie, and the inside man, Dave Gilbert. But you guys were broke. You needed a money man, a backer. For that, you turned to Weldon Callaway, a gun shop owner in Reno who was willing to provide the firepower and the vehicles needed in exchange for a share of the money. Someone decided you needed red pickups to blend in with the red Wells Fargo armored car you had in your sights. Weldon bought three fairly new identical Ford pickups, registering one to Aaron, one to Arnie, and one in his own name. That's why they all had Nevada plates. And in a small town like Coyote Wells, out of state plates stick out, even when we have tourists here, we all look at the different plates from other states. How does the story sound so far, Louise?"

"Like a made-up story. You're so smug, aren't you? The pampered little princess who ran off to the Bay Area and tried to make it in the big city."

"At least I never pulled off a five-million-dollar heist and then turned on my own little band of vultures out of greed. My guess is you probably took care of getting rid of Gilbert yourself. Because that Labor Day weekend there was a boating incident out at Spirit Lake. Gilbert was found floating in the water in what was later determined to be an accidental drowning. Who really knows the truth, though? I think you do, Louise, because you were there. The police report, left over from Caulfield's days---lists you as an eyewitness. You were on the boat that day when Gilbert went into the water."

Louise crossed her arms over her chest in a defiant posture. "Drownings happen all the time."

"Sadly, they do. But it's just another so-called strange death that seems to follow you around. So it isn't too surprising when Weldon, the guy who provided you with the guns and bankrolled your move to Coyote Wells, ends up shot dead in his own store in what was made to look like a robbery a few weeks after it was all over. It appears, you and Aaron are tidying up all the loose ends."

"Like any criminal does who needs to cover up her tracks to keep from getting caught," Zeb said.

It was Lando's turn to stick the knife in and turn the blade. "So let's back up to July 1984. You and your friends had pulled off the biggest armored car heist in California history. You were walking on air. Now you just had to play it safe and smart. The six of you decided you wouldn't split up the loot right away. You couldn't be seen spending any of the five million anywhere just yet. Even though the take was old money---money that had been in circulation for years and there were no pesky sequential numbered bills to worry about, you just had to get through the next few weeks before going after the cold hard cash. But where do you stash that many bags of money? In your case, Aaron had stumbled across a cave one day when he was out hiking. A criminal's dream. Five million in untraceable cash and an out-of-the-way hiding place made for stashing it. At a very young age you were practically millionaires. But you wanted more, Louise. And Aaron wanted more, too. A lot more.

"One by one, your little band started to mysteriously die off. You and Aaron had already gotten rid of Lindsay, Dave Gilbert, and Weldon Callaway. You were down to the next guy on the list. That man had to be Arnie Gafford. So right before Christmas, you arranged for Arnie to get blind, stinking drunk. You provided the booze and took him out to the railroad tracks south of town. You waited for the five a.m. train going southbound to do your dirty work for you. Arnie was hit by that train and dragged to his death. Another death ruled an accident because his blood alcohol level processed out at .30 at autopsy. The coroner decided Arnie simply had too much to drink and passed out on the tracks. The train took care of the rest. You two keep Arnie's share. Instead of a measly million, now there's two and a half million for each of you."

"That's the reason Billy Gafford chose to live here," Lianne pointed out. "It was his father's last known address and the town where he died."

"Exactly. As it turns out, Billy has a sentimental side. He wanted to build a cabin in the general vicinity of where his father spent his last days. But then Louise didn't have to worry about Billy because she already knew he had no idea about the millions taken in the robbery. Billy had been an infant at the time Arnie died, living with his mother down in Los Angeles. Neither you nor Aaron was about to get in touch with Arnie's estranged wife and tell her there was a fortune in stolen money available. You had what you wanted, and Aaron had what he wanted."

"Tell them the rest of it, Lando" Leia prodded.

"Backing up to August, Aaron Barkley had his hands full with a very remorseful wife. You see, Lindsay Bishop had started feeling guilty about what she'd done, especially about killing the two guards. Depression set in. Lindsay started talking about turning herself in and giving the money back. Aaron figured he needed to get rid of her before she went to the police. Although he'd married her a few months before the robbery took place and they were still newlyweds, Aaron wasn't happy with his wife. That summer he'd fallen in love with someone else."

Gemma swung back to Louise. "Take a bow. The two of you were quite the topic of conversation around town during those summer months. I got the down and dirty details from Natalie Henwick and Lucinda Fenton, who had very good memories about seeing the two of you making out all around town. You'd be surprised what we found out when we started asking the right questions. It only took a few to learn how much some of the residents back then remembered your little gang, and how many people recalled so many scintillating details. Even though you did a great job hiding your affair from Lindsay, others in town knew all about it. But by then the affair was the least of your problems. Both of you were starting to get very concerned that Lindsay might be the weakest link. You were afraid she might wake up one day and decide to clear her conscience by going to the authorities and telling them everything she knew about the heist. That would put a great big ding in your plans for the future. Instead of sitting around worrying about it, you guys decided to do away with Lindsay the same way you'd taken care of Hank Montoya back in June."

Rima's hands covered her mouth. "They killed my brother?"

Lando put a hand on Rima's shoulder. "Sorry, Rima, to have to hear it like this but this part came from Donna Montoya, Hank's widow. She told Zeb that Hank must've somehow discovered their plans to hit the armored car. Donna says she thinks he must've overheard them discussing the job out at the casino. But it doesn't really matter how Hank happened on the information because the moment Aaron realized someone else knew, your brother didn't stand a chance of hanging around."

Zeb turned his chair so that he could take his mother by the hand. "That June before the robbery went down, Aaron and his pals figured Hank had to go. They decided the easiest way was by car accident. Louise, who'd worked on cars growing up, knew how to rig an accelerator to stick. As a foster kid back in Tucson, she'd lived with a mechanic and his wife. According to them, she could break down an entire engine and put it back together again like a pro. They said she'd definitely know how to rig a pedal assembly. It explains how Hank's car hit the curve that day and couldn't slow down enough to maneuver the hairpin. It's possible Hank was already dead before he went off into the ravine. We may never know for sure how long Hank lived after overhearing something he shouldn't have. They probably killed him on his way home from the casino. And when it came time to repeat the process for Lindsay's death two months later, Aaron fell back on what had worked before. He sent Louise to fiddle with the pedal assembly on Lindsay's little Mazda RX-7. Later that day, Aaron sent his wife on an errand that made sure she had to take the cutoff onto Lone Coyote Highway. By then, the road had gotten so much negative press, everyone around town knew it was a dangerous section and accepted the accidents as a terrible misfortune. No one will ever know how Louise and Aaron pulled it off exactly, but they got away with it for thirty-four years...that is until Louise decided to kill Mallory. Ironically, her daughter's death prompted a great many questions about Louise's money that just wouldn't go away."

"So why did my son have to die eighteen months later?" Paloma asked.

Gemma circled the conference table and went around to where Paloma sat. "That was pure spite. You see, Aaron and Louise didn't last long after Lindsay's death. Their relationship fizzled out around the time Dave Gilbert drowned over that Labor Day weekend. I suppose you could say the thrill was basically gone. It's a basic question. What's left for two surviving killers to do with each other except to move on past all their misdeeds? Together they were a perfect killing machine, getting rid of anyone who got in their way. But by Thanksgiving, Aaron had met a new woman named Trina who worked at the casino as a cocktail waitress. Trina and Michael were coworkers. And what often happens between coworkers? Trina was one of the women Michael had been seeing. Unfortunately, Trina mentioned their affair to Aaron, who didn't like knowing Michael had slept with his girlfriend. Weeks went by and then months. Aaron couldn't let it go. He approached Louise about working her magic with Michael's car to get him completely out of Trina's life for good. With the old boyfriend out of the way, next thing you know Trina is Mrs. Aaron Barkley, living the good life with the stolen millions."

Horrified by the details, Paloma glared over at Louise. "I hope you rot in prison. I hope all the people you've murdered haunt you every single day of your life until you draw your last breath."

Lydia wrapped her arms around Paloma's shoulders. "She speaks for me, too. You were always a snake among us, spreading your evil everywhere you went. We just didn't know how deep it went."

Gemma cast a pitiful look at Louise. "You really were like a killing machine. Was there ever a day when you thought about any of the people you so callously took away from their families, the kids left behind, the wives you made widows?"

Louise raised her chin. "I'm assuming you can back up all these accusations?"

"We wouldn't be here otherwise," Lando fired back. "Once we received the right tip that pointed us in the direction we needed to go, everything fell into place."

"What about the ten grand Gemma found in Mallory's house?" Leia asked.

Gemma rocked back on her heels. "That part's easy. Louise had to send Lando down a few wrong rabbit holes. That money was part of it, a small token to make Lando think Mallory was into distributing drugs. For planting the money, Louise simply 'borrowed' a bag that belonged to Holly. Whether that was to implicate her own sister, who knows? You just have to remember that Louise had tried pointing the finger at me, using anyone who would listen to put doubt in their minds that I was responsible. But when that didn't work, she tried another tack. Getting Lando to think Mallory's death was drug-related was her next best option. When he didn't fall for that, she set her sights on ruining Dale, making the most out of Denise seeing the two arguing that night in the grocery store parking lot. The scene that night at Thackery's Pub was just to make sure everyone there knew Dale was a suspect and throw doubt on Lando's ability as a cop."

"Explain how Louise actually pulled off Mallory's murder," Lianne prompted. "It's what stumped us all."

Lando nodded. "I admit it gave me more than a few sleepless nights. But in the end, it wasn't as complicated as we thought. That Sunday night after the festival, Dale, Jimmy, and Louise all signed off at the same time. Ten o'clock. While the others went home,

Louise did not. Phone records show Mallory texted her mother at 9:55 that night---five minutes before Louise went off duty. Mallory intended to meet Fleet Barkley on the beach and tell him what she'd found out about the heist. Mallory hoped the mayor would be so afraid for his political career that he'd offer up a sizeable fee to keep quiet."

"In other words, Mallory had found her perfect blackmail mark," Gemma cited.

"That's because there were only two surviving sons of the original gang of thieves---Fleet Barkley and Billy Gafford. But Billy didn't have a political career at stake like Fleet. Plus, he didn't actually have access to a large family fortune from the heist like Fleet. Louise and Aaron had long since taken care of that by getting rid of Arnie, Gilbert, Calloway, and Lindsay, their co-conspirators. That Sunday night, Louise was at her breaking point with Mallory. She couldn't risk anyone else knowing about how she'd gotten all that money, not even her own daughter. Everyone involved in the crime was dead. Aaron had conveniently died of cancer five years earlier, which left Louise the only person alive who knew. That is, until Mallory stuck her nose where it didn't belong. I don't think Louise was completely prepared to deal with the risk of exposure coming from her own daughter. I'm sure that night she tried to reason with Mallory."

Gemma chuckled out loud. "We all know that was almost impossible. Mallory didn't exactly have a habit of listening to reason."

Lando sent her an amused look. "That's true. Anyway, Louise and Mallory got into a heated argument that escalated into a physical altercation. Louise took Mallory down by hitting her over the head with a hefty piece of driftwood. Am I right, Tuttle?"

Jeff stood up and crossed his arms over his chest. "The blow put a four-inch gash on Mallory's scalp. The knock on the head would've been enough to daze her, if not incapacitate her long enough for Louise to get the upper hand and keep it. But it wasn't what killed her."

Lando picked up the narrative again. "While Mallory's on the ground, Louise doesn't waste any time. She jumps on top of the younger woman's chest, wraps a ligature around Mallory's neck--- we think it was the belt she'd worn that night. Louise used the closest item she had on hand, and tightens the noose, strangling

Mallory to death in the process. Louise panicked when she realized what she'd done. She started staging the scene using her police know-how to cover her tracks, most importantly to make sure it looked like a sexual assault."

As if growing bored with Louise, Gemma shifted in her chair. "That's why Louise stripped off all Mallory's clothing. Somewhere along the route home, Louise tossed everything in a dumpster, including the murder weapon. The belt she used is probably under layers of dirt somewhere at the landfill."

"But the icing on the cake is that Mallory fought her attacker," Tuttle stated. "We found DNA under her fingernails that matched back to Louise."

So far Holly Dowell had been silent. But now, from across the room, she shouted, "You took away my daughter! The daughter I gave you to raise. I trusted you. How dare you kill the only thing I ever loved!"

Lando turned to see Holly standing in the doorway holding a Sig Sauer pistol. And it was aimed at Louise's heart.

"She was my baby and you took her from me," Holly screamed. "Why? Why did you have to kill my baby? Mallory was my best friend! You just couldn't stand it because she loved me more than she did you."

Lando took a couple of steps toward the distraught woman, who had tears running down her cheeks. But in her grief, the rage in her eyes told him she could easily pull the trigger. "Put the gun down, Ms. Dowell. Your sister will go to jail and pay for what she did. You have my word on it. Now put the gun down."

"I want her dead!" Holly shouted, her hands beginning to shake, the anger taking over. "She hurts everyone…eventually. Gemma had it right. She's like a killing machine that deserves to die, here, and now."

Lando had moved closer. He put his hands out to take the gun away. "And we'll put her where she belongs. I promise you. Just give me the gun now, Ms. Dowell. You don't want to end up where she's going. Understand? We'll lock her away for what she did to your baby."

Holly sniffed and nodded and then allowed Lando to take the weapon out of her hands. "I hate you!" she roared. "I'll tell them everything I know. Everything you've done over the years. I'll tell them all what a monster you are."

Lando handed the Sig off to Jimmy and then turned to Zeb. "Why don't you take Ms. Dowell home and take her statement. Take one of the federal agents with you just in case what she has to say is significant."

"Will do. Come on, Ms. Dowell, we'll get you home and you can tell me all about your sister."

When they were out of earshot, Lando angled back to the dispatcher. "Still think we don't have much of a case, Louise?"

The color had drained from the woman's face. Louise sat there defeated.

"I'm curious about something," Lydia began. "You said Mallory went out there on the beach to meet the mayor. But what happened to Fleet that night?"

"He happened on the scene after everything had gone down and found the body," Lando provided, looking over at the mayor.

Lydia sent Fleet a look of disgust. "Why didn't he call the police?"

"Because as the cheating husband, he didn't want to get involved. He'd been sleeping with Mallory off and on since May. He saw she was dead and thought his problem was now solved. But he couldn't be the one to find the body and sound the alarm. That would be too risky. Instead her body lies there on the beach until Gemma happens along, taking Rufus for a two o'clock stroll on the beach to let him pee."

"How did you figure all this out?" Lydia wanted to know.

"For several nights in a row, almost everyone in this room volunteered to go through a staggering amount of police reports from 1984. What we discovered was a trail that had been right in front of us the entire time. It was just a matter of taking Caulfield's files and putting the dates and deaths together like a puzzle. And asking the right questions from all the witnesses around town."

Up to now, Fleet had remained silent, but he looked around the room knowing his political career was probably toast. "You have to believe me. I didn't know anything about how my dad got his money."

"That's okay," Lando stated. "The feds are in the other room waiting to explain it to you. They're more than happy to help you understand what's gonna happen next."

After Louise was led out of the room, this time in handcuffs, Lando gave a press conference and a series of interviews with the

FBI at his side. A couple of hours went by before the flurry of activity died down enough that he was ready to head home.

He'd reached the lobby door when Jimmy hurried out into the hallway from the small cell block. "Before you go, Louise is asking for you."

"Me? Why me? Shouldn't she be calling for her attorney?"

"You'd think. But she was very clear. Before the feds take her into custody tomorrow, she says she has one more piece of the puzzle you'll want to hear."

25

Lando brought a chair into the cell block and placed it directly in front of the bars. He faced Louise as she sat on a cot, staring at the woman who looked drained of her arrogance and broken. "Jimmy says you have something to tell me."

"I'll give you the name of the real mastermind if you'll take the death penalty off the table. I realize I'll never be free again, but I'd like to live out my life without having to deal with death row."

"You're saying it wasn't Dave Gilbert?"

Louise's lips curved ever so slightly. "Dave was a driver. His part in the scheme was simple. He let us drive him off the road that day. That's it. Do you honestly believe Dave Gilbert came up with the plan? Someone else on the inside picked the best route that made the most sense, the one that provided the easiest place to take down an armored car, and the one route that would have the most money. He laid out the heist, one detail at a time. He even made us practice. After that, with Dave's cooperation as the driver, it was a piece of cake. It went down exactly as planned."

"You want me to believe there was another inside man?"

"Hey, it would make you look good to the FBI if you could hand them the ringleader after all these years."

"There's just one flaw in your thinking. I don't care about looking good to the FBI."

"Come on, Lando. Think about tying up all the loose ends on your own. You'd be the local hero...again."

"Convince me there's a bigger fish. If I'm leaning that way, I need hard evidence, not just your word. If you can provide that, we have a deal."

"How long have you known me? Do you honestly believe I wouldn't keep an ace in the hole for down the road? He was higher up in the company. He was the one who suggested we approach Dave in the first place. It seemed he already knew Dave had a major gambling problem. That's why Dave had gone to Reno. He arranged for us to bump into Dave at one of the casinos."

"Higher up as in an executive?"

"I'm not saying anything else unless you make me a deal. I want you to contact my lawyer and make the arrangements. Tonight. Tomorrow will be too late."

"Who do you want me to call?"

"Paul Talmadge out of Humboldt." She rattled off the phone number from memory. "I have him on speed dial."

"Okay. But you do realize the money in your account has already been seized by the feds, right? If you were hoping to use it to pay for your high-priced attorney, the money's been frozen. You won't be able to touch it even during the trial."

Her face went gray. Her shoulders drooped. She huffed out a defeated sigh. "Okay. Then work out a deal with the D.A. Tell him the mastermind is someone he knows, someone he has dinner with at least four times a year."

That tidbit got Lando moving.

Hours went by as the D.A. and Louise hammered out an agreement. "You understand this has nothing to do with what the FBI will charge you with, right? Whatever deal you make with them is separate."

"I understand."

"Who was the ringleader?"

"Everyone in this part of the state knows him. No one would ever suspect him of any wrong doing. Not ever. Not after all these years. He left his job at Wells Fargo in 1988, four years after the robbery and went into politics. He was a natural born charmer. His name is state senator Tyson Forsyth. I saved all Tyson's notes from the planning stages and I'm willing to testify against him. I've kept the papers in a safe deposit box at the bank in San Francisco. If I'm going down for something I did thirty-four years ago, I'm taking that sleazebag politician with me."

Hours later, at Gemma's house, Lando stretched out on the sofa with his head in her lap. "What a total mess Louise created. Decades built on lies and deceit."

"The entire thing is so twisted. Do you know how many people got hurt over this? How one event spun out and took so many people down with it? And for what?"

"Last estimate was nine. Louise doesn't seem the least bit bothered by the body count. She's more into making sure we get Tyson Forsyth."

"How hard was it convincing the FBI she was telling the truth, though? A politician involved in stealing from an armored car? What if this is just a ruse?"

"It's not. She offered up conclusive proof. In 1984, it seems Forsyth was facing financial setbacks right and left. He'd made some bad investments, lost close to a million of his own money. He was desperate. He found solace in Reno's gambling scene. It was on one of those trips that he bumped into Aaron, Lindsay, and Louise. They started kicking around a plan and brought in the others as they needed to expand on the plot. We were right about all of it, except for Forsyth. We didn't foresee an even bigger presence as the inside man."

"But it makes perfect sense that Dave Gilbert wouldn't have all the information at his disposal to carry out the entire haul."

"A driver would've been able to change the route, which is what happened. But he wouldn't have been able to divert an extra three million into the van that day. That was one detail the FBI never released to the public."

"So instead of stealing five million it was eight?"

"Big difference, huh?"

"Did the others know?"

"Not according to Louise. She and Aaron were the ones who transported the bags to the cave that night. They had to cut through the Longhorn property to do it without anyone noticing and then wait until daylight to unload the pickup. A month later, they met Forsyth there to divide up the money. Forsyth took his share that August. But the others were instructed to wait so as not to start spending the loot right away and raise suspicions. Once she got her share, Louise very carefully made little deposits into the bank in amounts that were small enough that no one asked questions. She says it took her five years before it was all safely tucked away in the bank. Aaron Barkley apparently did things in a similar manner with his share, choosing to keep a low profile at first and then one day pretending like he'd inherited a fortune from his parents back east. The people around town never suspected a thing. They gave Aaron the benefit of the doubt and assumed he was telling the truth. The same was true for Louise. But she didn't flaunt her money the way Aaron did. Instead, she kept her nose to the grindstone, took a decent-paying job, and hid under the radar in the safest place there was---the Coyote Wells Police Department. No one the wiser. The only time she showed a propensity for extravagance was when Mallory got into trouble."

"And then she whipped out her checkbook, often going overboard with an expensive attorney."

"Parents will do most anything to keep their kids from going to jail. Louise was no exception."

"Why didn't Louise and Aaron ever have a falling out? Why didn't Aaron ever try to kill Louise or vice versa?"

"Good question. I'm thinking they knew too much about each other, shared too many secrets. Although Louise does swear that Aaron had been blackmailing Forsyth for years before his death from cancer."

"Wow. When I wondered what secret Louise was keeping, I never dreamed it would be anything like this."

"Neither did I."

"How sad that she killed the one person she loved most in the world."

"No doubt she loved Mallory, but Louise loved herself more." Lando swung his legs to the floor. "Let's get some sleep. Who knows what tomorrow will bring?"

Just as they headed off to the bedroom, Lando's phone rang. "What now? Bonner here. Uh-huh. Uh-huh. Okay. Thanks for letting me know."

He draped an arm over Gemma's shoulder. "That was the FBI. They arrested Forsyth trying to board a plane in San Francisco bound for São Paulo, Brazil. He's in federal custody."

26

On Saturday night Gemma picked comfort over style for Fortitude's first concert under the stars. Wearing a floral sundress with short cap sleeves and a flowy skirt, she went over the songs before taking the stage, a stage volunteers had helped build and put together in the park over a two-day period. Jimmy's dad had installed lighting and hooked up the sound system. Others had pitched in with paint and added finishing touches that included a fancy velvet curtain sewn together by Lucinda Fenton and Suzanne Swinton. Suzanne had needed to do something to stay busy since Buddy had checked himself into rehab in Crescent City.

The point not lost on anyone was that the open-air concert had gained traction within the community.

All week people had helped get the word out. The Happy Bookers had made posters and put them up all over town. Businesses like Captain Jack's and Babe's had displayed signs at their counters as a reminder. It seemed to pay off. People started showing up at five o'clock in the afternoon to stake out their favorite spots near the lighthouse. They brought their blankets, their coolers and their snacks, spreading out on the green summer grass, ready to put the divisive past few weeks behind them and focus on some tunes.

No one was happier about entertaining the locals than Dale. Back in uniform for several days, he'd taken up his old job with a lot more enthusiasm than he'd had since starting on the force. Even giving Gemma a few lessons on the piano that now adorned her living room had revived his joy in music. If he was being honest, it was a joy he hadn't felt for a long time.

Everything seemed better somehow. Attitudes had changed. For the first time in a long time, the whole town seemed united in camaraderie.

Louise's string of staunch supporters like Claude and Janet were proof that when you got rid of a bad apple, the rot soon disappeared.

"We couldn't believe she had such a murderous past," Claude said when he'd ambled up to Gemma before the show. "We played bridge with that woman. All those years we sat across the table from a murderer. We couldn't believe we'd called her our friend for so many years, couldn't understand how she could do those terrible things."

"Why she's already been sent to a federal lockup near San Francisco awaiting trial," Janet added. "I remember the story on the news about those two guards getting killed. They both left behind small children. What a horrible thing for her to do. And to think she had me believing you're the one who murdered Mallory."

Claude shook his head. "Then she tried to shift the blame to Dale. We should've knowed something was up then. Dale's daddy and me go back forty-five years. I should've knowed that boy couldn't do anything like that."

"Don't worry about it," Gemma crooned.

But Lando wasn't as forgiving. "You should both be ashamed of yourselves. Anyone who treated Gemma like dirt should've known better. She was born here, raised here by grandparents who loved her. Instead of believing Louise's crap, you should be thanking Gemma for going out of her way to get to the bottom of all this, stuff that's been brewing for decades, stuff you rubberstamped as okay. What did you ever do to question Louise about her past? Nothing. Gemma found answers, got to the bottom of all Louise's lies. She's the main reason Louise Rawlins is sitting in jail now."

Gemma smiled and looped her arm through Lando's. "Not quite. Great police work is the real reason Louise finds herself behind bars. And this is the guy you want to have in charge of an investigation. The town's lucky to have Lando Bonner for their police chief. Y'all remember that next time when anyone questions his ethics."

Adam Greendeer pushed his way through the crowd.

Lando glared at the bar owner. "What are you doing here, Greendeer?"

"My place is like a tomb. No one's there." Adam looked around at all the people still making their way into the park. "The whole town's out here tonight. I just wanted you to know that I gave all the money back. Every dime. Whatever I have to do to make it up to you guys, I'll do. Just come back to the Duck & Rum. I'll give you all a nice raise."

"You'll do anything?" Gemma asked.

"Anything. Just name it."

"Hmm. I think I know a way you can make it up to us. Pay for the facial reconstruction for Jane Doe and we'll call it square. That's my vote anyway. I'll have to run it by the other members of the band first."

"Done. What does something like that cost?"

"It's less than you took in for that stupid betting pool. But it if happens to be more, I'll figure out a way to chip in. Agreed?"

"No problem. As long as Fortitude is back next Saturday night, I'm happy."

Fleet stood off to the side in a sulky mood. Things had not been going well for the mayor since Louise's arrest. "Madison's thinking about filing for divorce."

"Thinking isn't so bad," Gemma said cheerily. "Maybe she'll discover she can't live without you."

"Fat chance of that," Fleet muttered. "I'll likely end up broke by the time the feds get finished. And the people around here can't seem to understand that I wasn't the one who robbed that armored car. I wasn't even born yet when my father decided to break the law. I'm a law-abiding citizen, have been my entire life."

Lando put a hand on his shoulder. "You shouldn't be held accountable for the sins of the father. I get it. But people have a strange habit of judging the son. Look, it's concert time. We'll talk about this on Monday."

"I might not be mayor much longer. Harry Ashcomb is getting a petition up for a recall."

"Don't worry about it, Fleet," Lando said with a smile. "You can always go into sales. I hear Natalie Henwick is expanding her real estate office."

Lando grabbed Gemma's hand and they made their way to the back of the stage. Before walking up the steps, she looked over at him. "You were really nice to Fleet just now."

"I was? It's probably because I feel a little sorry for him. It's not his fault his father was a killer and a thief. After all, the feds are coming for the money and anything bought with it. That means Fleet will have to give up his houses, his cars, his furnishings, anything and everything he inherited, everything he owns. And if he doesn't have the cash, they'll seize all his assets until every dollar's been recovered."

"Imagine, growing up your entire life with all those millions at your fingertips and having it all go bye-bye."

"That's probably why Madison looked like she might cry tonight." He held out a set of car keys.

"What are those for?"

"Before we go up on stage, it's a little present. Your new set of wheels. Or advertisement. You pick." He spun her around to see what was parked at the curb on Water Street. "Your grandfather's 1957 panel truck. His pride and joy according to some. The one Jean-Luc drove all over the county. Dale's dad worked on the body, and then found someone who could get it running. Dale recreated the writing on the side or tried to."

Her eyes filled with happy tears. "Where did you find it?"

"Duff had it all this time, rotting away in a mountain of weeds."

"Thank goodness that sweet old man never gets rid of anything." She glanced up on stage at all her friends until she found Dale. "Thank you for this."

Dale gave her a toothy grin. "My pleasure. Thank you for being in my corner when I really needed the support."

She slipped her hand into Lando's. "Your little speech back there to Claude and Janet was great, even sweet. But the truth is I don't really give a hang what Louise's followers think of me or what the town thinks. All I care about is what you think. What about it, Lando Bonner? Are you willing to take one more chance on a girl like me?"

He grinned. "I hear Callie Lightfeather makes a few extra bucks on the side offering wedding ceremonies, peyote-free, of course."

She howled with laughter and looped her arm in his. "Oh, come on, Lando. What would be the fun in that? Go bold. Go wild. Better still, we'll both be ourselves. That way, we can't miss this time around."

Cast of Characters

Gemma Channing – Granddaughter of Marissa and Jean-Luc Sarrazin, now owner of Coyote Chocolate Company, also the daughter of Genevieve Wentworth

Lando Bonner – Coyote Wells police chief, ex-husband of Gemma

Leia Bonner – Daughter of Lydia, sister to Lando and Luke, chef at the family-owned restaurant, Captain Jack's Grill

Dr. Luke Bonner – Doctor on at the reservation clinic, brother to Lando and Leia

Marissa Sarrazin – Gemma's grandmother, Gram who owned Coyote Chocolate Company for forty years.

Jean-Luc Sarrazin – Gemma's grandfather, she calls Poppy

Lydia Bonner – owner of Captain Jack's Grill and mother to triplets Lando, Luke, and Leia

Zebediah Longhorn – Police chief on the reservation

Vince Ballard – Owner of Wind River Vineyard and a real ladies' man

Collette Whittaker – Longtime administrative assistant to Vince Ballard

Lianne Whittaker – Sister of Collette, down from Portland to look for her sister

Marnie Hightower – Eighth grade school teacher at Harbor View Middle School

Daryl Simmons – Former boyfriend of Marnie Hightower, basketball coach at Harbor View Middle School

Paloma Coyote – Her great-grandfather founded the town. Former mayor.

Van Coyote – Paloma's grandson, son of Michael

Michael Coyote – Deceased son of Paloma

Coyote Wells Police Department:

Louise Rawlins – Desk sergeant, mother to Mallory

Payce Davis – Coyote Wells PD

Jimmy Fox – Coyote Wells PD and guitar player for the band Fortitude

Dale Hooper – Coyote Wells PD and keyboard player for the band Fortitude

Mallory Rawlins – Adopted daughter of Louise
Holly Dowell – Sister to Louise, birth mother to Mallory
Elnora Kidman – The town librarian
Adam Greendeer – Owner of Duck & Rum, a bar at the edge of town
Fleet Barkley – Mayor
Reiner Caulfield – Former chief of police
Marshall Montalvo – Real estate developer, wealthiest man in the county
Buddy Swinton – Son of Roland Swinton who owned a pizza parlor in town, now closed
Suzanne Swinton – Buddy's wife, who often calls police on Buddy
Roland Swinton – Owned the pizza parlor next door to the Chocolate Company. Marissa's and Jean-Luc's friend
Genevieve Channing Wentworth – Gemma's estranged mother
Alex Kedderson – Attorney
Duff Northcutt – Friend of Marissa
Billy Gafford – Antisocial guy living on the edge of town near Duff Northcutt
Natalie Henwick – A member of the book club and real estate agent
Lucinda Fenton – Marissa's next-door neighbor
Ginny Sue Maples – Luke's nurse
Radley Fisk – Drummer in the band Fortitude, schoolteacher
Bosco Reynolds – Plays bass guitar for the band Fortitude, bartender at Duck & Rum
Theo Longhorn – Zeb's father
Rima Longhorn – Zeb's mother
Willow Longhorn – Zeb's sister
Cheyenne Song – Veterinarian
Ebbie Lucas – Receptionist for Dr. Song, the veterinarian
Corkie Davenport – Dr. Song's tech nurse
Ansel Conover – Elnora's boyfriend
Enid Lloyd – Lianne's next-door neighbor

Aaron Barkley– Fleet's father
Harry Ashcomb – Pharmacist
Sam Wells – President of the bank and owner of the local radio station

Dear Reader:

If you enjoyed *Shadow Canyon*, please take the time to leave a review.
A review shows others how you feel about my work.
By recommending it to your friends and family, it helps spread the word.
If you have the time, let me know via Facebook or my website.
I'd love to hear from you!

For a complete list of my other books visit my website.
www.vickiemckeehan.com

Want to connect with me to leave a comment?
Go to Facebook
www.facebook.com/VickieMcKeehan

Don't miss these other exciting titles by bestselling author

Vickie McKeehan

The Pelican Pointe Series
PROMISE COVE
HIDDEN MOON BAY
DANCING TIDES
LIGHTHOUSE REEF
STARLIGHT DUNES
LAST CHANCE HARBOR
SEA GLASS COTTAGE
LAVENDER BEACH
SANDCASTLES UNDER THE CHRISTMAS MOON
BENEATH WINTER SAND
KEEPING CAPE SUMMER (2018)

The Evil Secrets Trilogy
JUST EVIL Book One
DEEPER EVIL Book Two
ENDING EVIL Book Three
EVIL SECRETS TRILOGY BOXED SET

The Skye Cree Novels
THE BONES OF OTHERS
THE BONES WILL TELL
THE BOX OF BONES
HIS GARDEN OF BONES
TRUTH IN THE BONES
SEA OF BONES (2018)

The Indigo Brothers Trilogy
INDIGO FIRE
INDIGO HEAT
INDIGO JUSTICE
INDIGO BROTHERS TRILOGY BOXED SET

Coyote Wells Mysteries
MYSTIC FALLS
SHADOW CANYON
SPIRIT LAKE (2018)

ABOUT THE AUTHOR

Shadow Canyon is Vickie McKeehan's twenty-third novel and is the second book in her new Coyote Wells Mystery Series. Vickie's novels have consistently appeared on Amazon's Top 100 lists in Contemporary Romance, Romantic Suspense and Mystery / Thriller. She writes what she loves to read—heartwarming romance laced with suspense, heart-pounding thrillers, and riveting mysteries. Vickie loves to write about compelling and down-to-earth characters in settings that stay with her readers long after they've finished her books. She makes her home in Southern California.

Find Vickie online at
https://www.facebook.com/VickieMcKeehan
http://www.vickiemckeehan.com/
https://vickiemckeehan.wordpress.com

Printed in Great Britain
by Amazon